PRAISE FOR A

Praise for *The Saxon Bride*

"A beautiful first novel to lead off the Norman Conquest series. I'm a big fan of medieval political intrigue, and this novel had plenty. Well done!" — National Best-Selling Author Kathryn Le Veque

"Ashley York's new release, *The Saxon Bride*, is all I had hoped it would be. From the first page to the last, you will become absorbed in Rowena and John's story."

"Ashley York has spun a tale of love, lust and conquering obstacles. The story of John and Rowena will take your breath away."

"I love political intrigue and this story has it in spades. Of course, the love story between John and Rowena doesn't hurt the story either. Enjoy, all you fans of medieval era stories!"

Praise for *The Bruised Thistle*

"Absolutely loved Seumas and Iseabail. This is Ashley York's first book, and I can't wait for the second and third in the series to come out. Keep them coming."

"This was a great story with lots of twists and turns. The character development was artfully woven throughout the entire book."

"Enjoyed this well-written and engaging tale of Iseabail and Seumas, and I am totally looking forward to reading another by Ashley York. Indulge and be delighted!!!"

"*The Bruised Thistle* is a Scottish historical romance with strong characters you can root for, adventure, and a terrific love story...Ashley York brings their world alive with historical details and a feel for the setting, and the characters are endearing in a satisfying love story."

"Powerful, and brilliantly written with engaging and charismatic characters. The storyline is compelling, complex, and intriguing to say the least. A must read and a keeper."

ALSO BY ASHLEY YORK

The Order of The Scottish Thistle series

The Bruised Thistle

The Norman Conquest series

The Saxon Bride

The Saxon Bride

Ashley York

ISBN (print): 0990864022
ISBN-13 (print): 978-0-9908640-2-8
ISBN (ebook): 0990864030
ISBN-13 (ebook): 978-0-9908640-3-5

Publisher's Note: The characters and events portrayed in this book are fictional and or are used fictitiously and solely the product of the author's imagination. Any similarity to real persons, living or dead, places, businesses, events or locales is purely coincidental.

Cover design: Rae Monet, Inc. Design
raemonetinc.com/bookcovers.html

Editing: Scott Moreland

Print Formatting: By Your Side Self-Publishing
www.ByYourSideSelfPub.com

DEDICATION

This book is dedicated to my very first reader, Kathleen. I will never be able to think of this story without remembering our Sunday afternoons at the Brewery with the wonderful sounds of Banish Misfortune surrounding us as we went through every chapter I brought you. What a sweetheart! Your words of encouragement carried me through to the end and your belief in me is more appreciated than you will ever know. Thank you, my dear friend. You are a blessing in my life I never saw coming.

.

ACKNOWLEDGMENTS

I want to thank the HHRW Critters for their immeasurable help in bringing this story to print. You made my story even better. And thank you to my beta readers: Nicole Laverdure, Melba Solis-Zuniga, Deborah Trickey, and Merry Farmer. I also want to thank Rae Monet, Inc. Designs for the beautiful cover.

A very big thank you to my amazing editor Scott Moreland who charged in to save the day. I look forward to many more projects with you.

As always, my most important acknowledgment is to the love of my life, my husband of thirty five years. You are my hero—always.

Prologue

Essex, England 1071

A Norman. I have been given to a Norman to wife.

Rowena Godwinson, daughter of the late Earl of Essex and the last living member of that powerful Saxon family, stood before her reflection in the polished brass. The wedding gown passed down through three generations of Godwin women before her, draped softly across the shoulders, skimming down her waist and falling over the tips of her deerskin slippers. She blinked back with vacant eyes.

Fear tripped up her spine and her stomach clenched. She had lived among the victors for nigh on five years now. Their disdain for her people was quite obvious. Now the man who had usurped her own uncle as rightful king at the Battle of Hastings had ordered her to marry. With both parents dead, she was his ward.

Rowena clenched her teeth and turned to the window. She glimpsed the slate roof of the chapel beyond the trees where the nuptials would take place this very day. Her family's chapel. Countless celebrations with uncles, close friends, and more cousins than she could name, had taken place there. Those were happy years.

"My lady?"

Rowena looked at the drawn face of her handmaiden, Joan. The blonde sheen of her hair, long gone with the stress of the circumstances and occupation they were all forced to live under.

"Yes?"

Joan gulped. "Do you think he will be kind to you? Tonight, I mean?"

Rowena's breath caught in her throat. The marriage bed. How would

1

her husband treat her? With kindness? As her husband, he gained much by this union. A lot of responsibility, yes, but also power. Some men loved power.

She tipped her chin up.

"I believe he will be kind as I will give him no reason not to be."

Joan's eyes rounded. Rowena smiled tightly.

"Fear not, Joan. I will be amicable."

"My lady, would that I could impart upon you my own knowledge, but I have none. Your mother's death before she prepared you leaves you in a bad way."

"Perhaps he will be a gentle man. John." His name was all she knew.

"Yes, my lady. He is one of William's most trusted knights."

"A warrior." Rowena's tone was flat and for an instant she saw again her father. Cold and dead. Blood all around. She forced the memory aside. "Then he will be a good protector."

"Yes, but of whom?"

Norman soldiers had been in the castle and beyond ever since. They had no need for Saxons. If they did have needs, they took what they wanted. When Rowena tried to voice her objections to such ill treatment, it fell on deaf ears.

"I will be by his side now. I will win him over to our cause." Despite her own misgivings, Rowena attempted to reassure her.

Joan sighed her relief. "Then we will pray you please him."

The knock on the door echoed in Rowena's chest. She nodded her consent. Joan opened the door to reveal a burly Norman soldier, his pointed helmet still in place on his head, its shield hiding his face.

"I've come for the Lady Rowena." His voice was muffled but understandable.

He pushed his way past Joan and grabbed Rowena's arm. She jerked away without thinking, and he shoved her back against the wall. Joan's shriek filled the small space. His pungent breath assailed her nostrils as he moved in close.

"Silence!" He threw the command over his shoulder then focused his attention back on Rowena. His helmet dipped as his eyes took in every aspect of her body."I look forward to your joining with Lord John."

Rowena fought to control her outrage. And her fear.

"Do you know what Normans do with their lord's wives?" His voice was quiet, menacing.

She shook her head.

"The lord has first use but then he allows his most loyal soldiers a taste as well."

"What?" Rowena gasped. Why would any man treat his wife so? He

2

must be lying. "What if a child is begotten? How does he know it is his?"

The man threw back his head and laughed. She could see his dark eyes through the slit in the metal when he lowered his head to her. "Don't you know King William is a bastard? He believes it is better to father your heir with your mistress than your wife."

"But...but I heard he loves his Queen."

"Theirs was a marriage of love. Not by proclamation. And not to receive title to the lands."

Without warning, he grabbed her by the arm and dragged her through the doorway. Joan's shrill cries followed her down the hall. Three more soldiers came up alongside of them.

"Did you tell her?" one of them asked.

"She knows the way of it."

Rowena yanked against their firm grasp but they shoved her from behind. Along the road, the onlookers gawked at the treatment of the last Godwinson. She refused to hide her head in shame. In her attempt to keep her dignity, she stopped her struggling and fought to keep up with their long strides. Outside the chapel door, they halted.

"And I look forward," the first guard ran his hand up her side, grabbing her breast as she struggled anew, "my lady, to getting a piece of you for myself."

Rowena spat at him. "Don't touch me!" she screamed. The moisture dripped down his visor.

The man jerked the helmet off, his face a dark scowl. "I'll do even more."

The guards all laughed but when they pushed the door open and she saw the dark-haired man turn towards her, she groaned inwardly. Her new lord and master glowered at her. He had the face of any angel.

Oh, God, what will become of me?

§

The musty smell of incense filled the windowless structure and threatened to suffocate Sir John of Normandy waiting before the altar. Despite his outward appearance of calm, John's insides were tightly wound, his nerves stretched as tight as an archer's bow. Armed guards dragged the struggling woman through the tall wooden doors toward him. John held his breath, his body strained in sympathy with the force of her effort.

"I will never marry that Norman scum!" Rowena screamed, her voice shrieking back in echoes like a curse from the hard stone walls to the small, somber group standing between the unlikely couple. The Norman soldiers gathered as witnesses to the impromptu nuptials shifted uncomfortably. Understandably, they preferred not to look directly at the dark-haired Saxon woman, but toward their leader. John hoped he succeeded at appearing to wait patiently for his bride to be. *Damn.*

Her silver eyes flashed as she jerked against the firm hands. A shiver passed down his spine. She had her father's eyes. Those eyes haunted his dreams. When she spat on the ground, the guard raised his hand to her but John stepped forward, stopping him from slapping her for such a show of disrespect.

"*Enough.*"

The scene did not sit well with him. Her body was small and delicate beside his six-foot frame. She looked much younger than her sixteen years of age. Her attempts at resistance were futile, as had been his own. This marriage would take place. King William himself had ordered it. Her excess of stubbornness was another trait John remembered from her father, Earl Leofwine Godwinson. Common sense seemed a foreign concept to both father and daughter. Rather than accept defeat and come to terms, Leofwine had been determined to fight to the death.

And now five years later, John recognized the same crazed look. Her eyes darting wildly around the tiny church like a trapped animal, desperately searching for escape. The king must be obeyed.

"Please, my lady." John spoke gently as he would to a wild mare. Reaching toward her, he stopped short at the fury in those narrowed eyes. *She will kill me in my sleep.* John could see his death at her delicate hands. His life meant nothing to her. She would prefer him dead. His jaw clenched. There was not a chance in hell he could consummate this marriage.

With a guard on either side forcing her to stand and respond, John of Normandy was wed to Rowena, orphaned daughter of the Saxon Earl of Kent, Essex, Middlesex, Hertford, Surrey and Buckinghamshire and ward of King William. John was now one of the most powerful men in England...and he had no desire for any of it.

After the exchange of vows and the blessing from the French bishop, an awkward silence was mercifully interrupted by the muffled jingling of the hauberks worn by the dust-covered soldiers who entered the chapel.

"Lord John?"

Trying not to notice the woman who trembled beside him with her sobbing, John sighed in relief to see one of William's own messengers rushing toward him.

"Is there a problem?" he asked.

The man handed John a letter. Quickly breaking King William's seal, John read the orders. A new battle had broken out to the north and the king needed reinforcements immediately. Although John's presence was not specifically requested, here was his chance to separate himself from his new bride. Breathing a sigh of relief, there was no reason to delay his departure. Pulling on his leather gloves, he turned away from the brown-haired woman.

"Prepare yourselves. The king needs your assistance," he ordered as he walked away without a word to her. He would live to see another day.

Chapter One

Normandy, 1074

Greetings Lord John,

I bid you come at once to the castle at Montreuil. The King of France wishes to see me well located here for the irritation of my enemies. You and I have much to discuss and plans to make. King Malcolm overwhelms me with skins and vessels of gold and silver, seeking my friendship. He will come to me here. Across the sea, enemies surround me, threatening to undo all I have accomplished. I have shown the utmost care and regard for my subjects but find only deceit and subterfuge.

I have granted you gladly the shires of Essex, Surrey, and Buckingham for your continued loyalty. My hope in giving you the lovely Lady Rowena to wife was only to add to your pleasure as Lord there. I bid you return with me full armed against those who durst move against me. I seek the fealty of your castlemen there by spring next.

William, King of England

Tossing the letter onto the desk, John sighed. The low candle sputtered, spraying small drops of blood-red wax across the parchment. Of course the king wanted their fealty. Nigh on eight years had passed since he'd won the day. Why shouldn't they accept him as their rightful king? And yet they fought...tooth and nail, they resisted.

Having been with the man since the age of eight, John knew William's strengths. Tenacity. Persistence. Mercilessness. Even after being crowned as king, William was met with battle after battle as he made inroads throughout the small island. There needed to be a patient Norman presence in each area if William was to keep England as his own. That was the crux. John was to be that presence.

With a heavy heart, John planned his return to England and to his wife. Lady Rowena. The girl he'd been forced to wed three years earlier wasted away in her bitterness toward everything Norman, no doubt. She'd called him Norman scum. Now John would face her again. What epithet would she throw at him?

He'd tried to convince the king to wed her to another but all he'd wanted to talk about was their great conquest over the Saxons. John's memory of that conquest was of the last man who'd fallen by his sword, the father of the very woman he was forced to marry. The sight of the young Lady Rowena sobbing over her father's body had sent a spear of guilt through his heart. He'd lost many a good night's sleep with those memories.

"Do you yield?" John had shouted the question at him, nigh begged him, for the third time while the rest of the Saxon men were rounded up and disarmed by the Norman soldiers. They had already surrendered. The Earl did not seem to understand his words although John spoke perfect English. Instead, the man turned on him.

"I will never yield to you, Norman scum!" Godwinson ran at John with a crazed look in his silver gray eyes, his heavy battle axe raised at the ready. Trying to avoid him, John had been tripped up in his attempt to side-step the man's attack. The Norman broadsword found its mark in the man's heart, pushed through by Godwinson's own impetus as he fell against John.

John's moan filled his small room, bringing him back to the present. Now, after so much time, what would he find at the castle...the castle that was rightly his? The Saxons had resisted their presence then and they would resist their presence now. The girl's rage was probably doubled. No—she would be a woman now. John hissed through his teeth in irritation. He should have already taken care of this. He just didn't know how to do that short of forcing himself on her. He was not going to accept that role for anyone. Instead he'd kept his distance. He wasn't even sure he remembered what she looked like.

"Do you have to leave now?" So deep in his own thoughts, John hadn't heard Abigail enter the small room. She sauntered toward him, a smile playing on her full, red lips. Always playing the seductress. Did she think she could actually get him to disobey the king's orders? He suppressed a smile at the thought. She thought far too much of herself.

Outside, the sun was already casting dark shadows on the stone floor. *Damn.* He'd meant to be gone by now. No doubt his men waited for him as he sat reminiscing. He snorted and the dark-haired woman frowned in confusion. Without answering, he strode out the door and into the courtyard. Much to his embarrassment, she followed him.

"I'll make it worth your while to stay." Abigail said, grabbing at him when he stopped beside his destrier, causing the animal to pull back. Her ample breasts pressed against him and her green eyes sparkled with lusty promises. His men shifted as they stood around him, avoiding his gaze.

"Abigail." His irritation was rising. He'd explained to her in detail that he had a wife, maybe not a wife of his own choosing, but a wife nonetheless. His own reluctance to go only added to his impatience. A horse whinnied behind him. He would not go against the king. He pulled her away from him, firmly holding her at arm's length.

"Do not make me send you away from here," John directed, his jaw tightened in anger.

Pouting. Ah, yes, her favorite ploy. There had never been any promises between them. He allowed her to play the lady of his manor, and she took charge very well. John was so seldom in residence that it was convenient to have her see to things. Although she enjoyed pretending there was more to the relationship, he'd learned at a young age to live without affection and intimacy. It may be a lonely life to some, but it was the one he desired. He snapped his gloves against his thigh impatiently.

"Go back to your sewing, woman." His voice was menacingly low, but easily heard above the whinnying of the horses that stood saddled and ready, as anxious to be back on the road as his men. "I will have no more of this."

Releasing his arm, she backed away. Her gaze lowered. "I'm sorry, m'lord. Please forgive my insistence at your expense."

He narrowed his eyes and pursed his lips. This shift from aggressor to victim did not sit well with him. She was truly a master at manipulation.

"You leave me no choice. Perhaps some time at the castle in Rouen would be more to your liking?" Her eyes flashed. He'd hit his mark. Court life was not what she desired when she could be free from oversight here. "Tell me your choice."

She huffed. "I will return to my room." John watched her back just long enough to ensure her obedience before pulling on his gloves and facing his men. At attention now, they awaited only a word from him to mount and be off.

"Oh."

Barely able to hide his annoyance at hearing her voice again, John turned slowly toward Abigail.

"What?" He answered her through clenched teeth.

"When will you return?"

"I will not be returning." If she'd hoped for a different answer, she was disappointed yet again.

John mounted his horse. His men followed suit. The large retinue headed out through the gates that protected the only place John called home. He didn't look back at the woman or his manor. Any attachment he had here was tenuous at best as every soldier knew. A fighting man lived from battle to battle, laying his head where his latest conquest was until, God willing, his life ended in honor on the field.

Chapter Two

Rowena stilled her hand, a long length of brown hair looped around it. Seated on the stool beside her small table, she tensed as all the sound around her seemed to stop. Disbelief filled her.

"You did what?" She measured each word as she spoke, her heart sinking in despair.

The younger woman lowered her eyes, cowering in front of her. Her words were barely above a whisper when she answered. "I told them to chop it down."

"Why, Joan?" Releasing her hair, Rowena stood slowly beside her friend. The betrayal strangled her. "Who told you to do such a thing?" Rowena took a steadying breath. "Go tell them you were wrong."

"It's too late, m'lady." The woman virtually shook and yet Rowena had no words of comfort for her.

"No," Rowena whispered as her mind went unbidden to the day her parents had returned from their trip to Jerusalem. They were so young and alive.

"A tree?" Rowena at eight years old had been more than a little disappointed by the present her parents brought her from their faraway travels.

"It was no easy trip either." Her father's voice echoed in her mind as if he were still with her. Tears slid down Rowena's cheeks at the memory. She had nourished that tree alongside her mother until the woman had died two years later.

"Go, Joan." Rowena's voice broke with desperation as she ordered her maidservant to do her bidding. "Let us hope it is not too late." Joan sprinted from the room. Perhaps there was a chance the cypress tree could still be saved.

Alone in her bedchamber, Rowena rubbed the crease between her eyes. None of the treasured items from her parents had survived the Norman invasion. Why would they blatantly cut down the tree her mother had lovingly planted? Maybe for the same reason they tried to wash the only remaining Persian rugs with water or the well-worn silken robes with harsh lye soap, and overwater the fig trees. Where she had once found solace from these little mementos of her life before, their absence now left her with only emptiness.

Gone were the comforting arms of a family that loved her and wanted only the best for her. Gone was her dream of finding a strong Saxon man who would love her and give her children. Gone was the hope for a country at peace. Her uncle was the rightful successor to the throne by King Edward's deathbed decree but the warmongers from across the channel had pushed through their own desires.

Desire! Who needed it? Deep set brown eyes flashed in her mind and she squeezed the brush in her hand until the bristles jabbed into her flesh. *Bastards, all of them.* Those eyes were the eyes that haunted her nights. Too many years ago, the man had taken away her chance for the life she'd dreamt of. Marrying John of Normandy had made everything else impossible. Even the people who knew her best kept their distance from her after that. They knew she was no longer in charge and showed her little respect. No doubt they questioned her loyalties.

The idea of him touching her had repulsed her then…well maybe not repulsed, and yet when he'd left, leaving her a virgin still, she'd realized he'd condemned her to a life of total solitude. With all her family dead, now she didn't even have the chance for her own children.

Forcing her mind to stop obsessing on what she had no control of, Rowena determinedly headed down to the garden. Her small hope was dashed when she saw Joan crying by the garden gate. Her eyes filled and the past eight years of useless existence flashed before her eyes. Running to the felled tree, she paid no heed to the dirt that covered her as she threw herself against the exposed rings, each jagged hewn threatening to pierce her through. Deep inside, the tiny thread that had held her together these long years snapped. Dead, everything that mattered in her life was dead. So why did she have to suffer alone with no hope, no comfort, no one to care about her or love her and never even a chance for happiness?

Gentle arms surrounded her and she yielded to the strength of the red-haired man who came to kneel beside her.

"Shhh, Rowena, shhhh." Arthur's voice was so comforting, her body leaned in toward him and a longing for any connection tightened in her chest. The smell of sweat and leather was strong, but she just wanted to have him comfort her as she knew he longed to. She wanted release from this insane life of total solitude, of people who did her bidding at their own leisure. Her proud Saxon family was gone. Now she was married to a Norman. Where did her loyalty lie?

"Arthur." She sobbed his name. "I can't continue like this." His big hand stroked her hair and held her tighter. "Why am I still alive when all around me are dead?"

"Hush." His overtures were meant to comfort her but his quiet gasp told her she'd wounded him with her words. She didn't want to hurt one of her few remaining allies. He was her only connection to the goings-on of her family property. The only one who patiently answered her endless questions about her property now that she was left uninformed.

Arthur had been ordered to protect the castle by the Normans once he'd sworn his fealty to the king, but she believed Arthur when he told her he truly stayed out of love for her. It was an unrequited love. She was married, after all.

A hysterical laugh made its way up her throat. *The virgin wife.* The irony of having been wed to a man that left her at the first opportunity was too much. William of Normandy had commanded the nuptials for the good of England, so he'd said. He'd professed the desire to have Saxon and Norman blood mixed so that England could live in prosperity and peace. In order for that to happen, her absent husband would have had to show his face and then some.

Arthur tensed as the laugh erupted and echoed against the stone fence that surrounded the garden. The few people that stood around them shifted uneasily at the sound. His arms tightened around her, the laugh muffled against his shoulder as she fought to gain back her control.

"Rowena," he said her name like a caress but his beard scraped against her cheek. "Others are watching. Please keep your dignity."

She knew he was looking out for her, but it felt like a slap in the face. She wanted to pull back and scream at him that she had no dignity left. She'd lost that long ago.

Taking a shaky breath, she pulled herself to standing and looked at the devastation of the tree that had symbolized her last link to who she could have been. If only things had turned out differently. Arthur stood beside her, wearily watching her.

"Burn it." She ordered it with a strong voice while the tears coursed down her face. Holding her head high, she turned back the way she'd come and paid no heed to those who'd witnessed her meltdown and now stepped aside to let the lady of the manor pass.

§

12

John peeled the leather riding gloves from his hand and shifted the stiff chainmail away from his chest, easing its heaviness. A large cypress tree lay on the ground, surrounded by some castle folk when he'd first entered the well-tended garden. There had been the one woman covered with mud and sweat. He thought he'd stumbled upon some ancient pagan ritual with them grouped seemingly in anticipation around the tree. That wouldn't have surprised him. These Saxons were such barbarians.

He'd had to get his ear adjusted to the lilting sound of their English words before he could make out what they were saying. He missed the sweet melodious sound of his own language every time he came back to England but truth to tell, he hadn't been back to *this* place for many years.

The sound of a woman's hysterical laughter had drawn him into the garden. He'd tensed, ready to find perhaps a crazed woman but the lithe body that pushed past him, head held high, did not appear crazed to him. His men-at-arms appeared behind him as she shoved rudely past, but John held his hand up. It didn't matter. This treatment was nothing compared to what he anticipated when he finally found his "wife".

Arthur approached the group of well-armed men. Recognition took a minute.

"My lord." The red head dipped down in respect. "Welcome home. We were not expecting you."

John fought down the urge to laugh. Should he have sent word so the little wife could sharpen her dagger? "Arthur is it?"

"Yes, my lord."

"We have been traveling non-stop and are near overcome with exhaustion. Can you see to the needs of my men? I will also want to meet with those managing my holdings here."

"Certainly, my lord." Arthur signaled to the castle staff whose names John didn't even know before turning back. "Will you be staying long?"

Sensing the desire for a negative answer, John frowned. "This is my home, Arthur. I will be staying indefinitely."

He didn't miss the fleeting expression of anger before the man bowed and walked away.

His men followed Arthur, all but Peter who came to stand beside John. They both watched as Arthur led the group of Norman knights through the garden gate.

"That was strange." The tall, blonde man scratched his nose as he spoke.

"I thought so, too. What does that man care if I stay or go?"

"I'm afraid the answer is plain. Even after all this time and prosperity that the Saxons have experienced under our king, they still resent our

13

being here." John's gut wrenched at the thought. And what would Rowena be like then? Here amongst her own people, festering with continued resentment, she would certainly be a shrew or worse. Wanting to avoid the long-awaited reconciliation, John changed the subject abruptly. "I need a bath." He turned, wrinkled his nose at his companion and added, "And so do you!"

When the two headed back through the gate, they passed a man entering the garden with an axe. John's curiosity got the best of him and he stopped to watch. The man went to the felled tree and started breaking it into smaller chunks.

"That was a beautiful tree," John said under his breath as he approached the man, Peter close behind. "What goes on here?"

John's tone was friendly but the man jumped at the question.

"I am doing as I was ordered." The man's eyes were wide with fear, his bushy gray eyebrows nearly touching his hairline. "I wasn't the one who chopped it down."

John was confused by this reaction. "Was there something wrong with the tree?"

"I don't know." The man stumbled to stand up, his hand shaking as he held the axe. "What would you have me do, my lord?"

"What is your name?"

"Perceval."

John couldn't miss the man's defensiveness. Turning to Peter, he wasn't surprised by his own feelings of unease mirrored there. "Well, Perceval, who ordered the tree chopped down?" The pinched face of his sixteen year old bride flashed in his mind. "Was it Lady Rowena?"

"Oh, no, my lord." The man looked to the left and right, clearly uneasy before he continued, "It was her mother's tree after all." His voice was lowered and John sensed reverence in the use of the title.

"Her mother still lives then?"

"No, my lord." Perceval's mouth slammed shut. His thin lips pressed tightly together as if he had said quite enough.

His continued silence confirmed it. "She's dead then?"

The man nodded.

"But it wasn't Rowena who wanted the tree taken down?"

He shook his head.

"Is Rowena here?"

The man's jaw dropped unexpectedly as if he'd asked if she'd grown a second head. John turned away to hide his smirk at the comical expression.

Peter stepped forward. "Where can we find her then?"

At the sudden tightness in his chest, John's humor fled. He was not ready to confront the woman. He didn't care to know where she was or even what she was doing. Putting his hand on his friend's arm, he answered for himself. "I'm sure she is within and very busy right now. Thank you for your assistance, Perceval."

John turned abruptly, and Peter was left to catch up with John.

"Forgive me if I spoke out of turn. Did you not come to see her?"

"I'm not ready for that battle just yet." John felt like a coward and wanted to redirect his friend before the man asked too many questions. "Check that the horses are taken care of." He didn't turn back to see the look on Peter's face. The man asked too many questions. John didn't need it common knowledge that he had defied the king by not consummating the marriage. That was not the way to go about mixing Saxon and Norman blood.

Heading in through the nearest door of the castle, he found himself in the kitchen. The sweet smell of baking bread and roasting meat beckoned to him. His stomach growled in response. The room was dark except for the firelight and it took a minute for his eyes to adjust. The huge size of the room bespoke of the size of the castle he would now need to call home. The nameless workers scattered within spoke of the challenge he'd face winning them over as the new Norman lord. Winning over his wife would be the biggest challenge, but one he'd prefer to continue to avoid.

Chapter Three

When the Norman knight strode into the kitchen, Rowena's breath caught in her throat. It was her husband. He'd filled out since she'd last seen him. Pain filled her heart. She turned to leave but halted at the sound of his voice.

"You, there." His commanding tone raised her hackles as she turned to face him. She couldn't help but be impressed by his stature and the way he commanded the room when he entered. When she saw he was speaking to the cook, she let out the breath she'd been holding. She continued through the Great Hall that was now full of Norman soldiers, their guttural voices polluting the air with that dreaded language. Her fists clenched at her side, she headed toward the stairs. A burly man stepped in front of her, blocking her way. He was barely out of his youth, still a boy really, and her resentment grew.

"Step aside, sir." She was aghast at his audacity. "You are a guest in my home, and I expect you to behave as such."

He stepped back, his hands raised in surrender. A great roar of laughter erupted around her. Her face flushed.

"Ohhh, excuse me, my lady." She didn't miss the sarcastic tone or the way his eyes assessed her.

"As lady of the manor—" He guffawed to the enjoyment of the men around him. "Can you draw me a bath?"

She knocked his hand away before he was able to grab at her bodice.

"How dare you." Her voice roughened with outrage.

In her own castle, she wasn't even safe. Looking around at the eyes upon her, waiting to see the man's next move, she realized these barbarians were enjoying making a laughing stock out of her. A cry of

16

alarm from the outer bailey had the men scrambling through the door, swords at their side, leaving her alone once again. She didn't hesitate but went directly to the safety of her room. She leaned against the closed door, and her heart pounded through her chest. Her husband had no use for her but apparently didn't feel he needed to restrict his men. *Bastard!*

What was she to do now? Her wayward husband had returned. Why? What did he want? Glancing down at her soiled gown, she was appalled at her appearance. She looked like a peasant. He couldn't find her in this state. After pulling the service dress over her head, she stood in her chemise when a knock sounded on the door.

"Who is it?" Her heart pounded so loudly she had to ask the question again, her hands holding the gown tightly to her chest.

"Joan, my lady."

"Enter." She turned around, throwing the gown to the floor. "Help me find something suitable to wear."

Joan went to the chest in front of the window and pulled out the brown dress. "The man said the tree was diseased."

It took a minute for Rowena to register what Joan was talking about. So much had happened in such a short period of time and the return of her husband had sent her into a maelstrom. She sat on the bed and faced her friend. "Why? Why would they need to chop it down?"

Joan's rounded eyes glistened, the gown crushed against her chest. "They said it was diseased and would kill everything else in the garden. We've had such a rough growing season...the drought." As the tears spilled down her cheek, Rowena was moved by the woman's utter desolation. "I didn't even think about it being from your mother."

Rowena took Joan in her arms as she cried. "Shhh, it's all right." She stroked Joan's long blonde hair. "I forgive you, my dear. It was probably for the best then."

Although her servant, this woman had been a solid friend to Rowena since before the Normans came. Joan had known and loved her parents. Their shared past made a strong bond between them. She hated to see her so upset.

"No." Joan pulled her blotched, red face away from Rowena. "No, my lady, the man lied."

"What do you mean?"

"That tree had nothing wrong with it."

Rowena stood a little taller. Someone had intentionally ripped the last piece of her parents away from her. No, perhaps someone just didn't care for the tree and wanted it removed. "Who was the man?"

"It was a Norman solider."

In her mind's eye she again saw those brown eyes and for the first time they were accompanied by the knowledge of what the man looked like now. Had he ordered the tree removed? She hadn't even known he was here. Clearly he hated her. That wasn't news. When he'd left the same afternoon they were wed, she'd known how much he despised her.

Shame flooded back to her. In this very bed she had waited, covered with nothing but her mother's white robe from her own wedding. Rowena had been ready to receive her husband as was her duty as his wife. All night she waited, with time to think and imagine what it would be like. To be overcome with anxiety. She wanted to be repulsed by him but knew she was luckier than most. He was easy on the eye. Many women met their husbands on their wedding day but they had their wedding night. She did not.

The memory of that total humiliation fueled the rage that shook through her body, the pain as fresh as if it had just happened. Now he's entered her castle and gets to decides what else may live or die? Oh, no, that was not the way of it. Rowena had been playing dead long enough.

"No, Joan, not the brown one. The blue gown."

Surprise widened the woman's eyes. Rowena hadn't worn the blue bliaut in quite a while. It used to be when she heard the king was making his rounds that she would dress according to her station. She'd be beside herself trying to look her best in the hope that her husband would be among his retinue. All her preparations were for naught. The king would politely acknowledge her and take the men aside to discuss business. Her husband was never with them.

Except for his warm brown eyes, she hadn't really remembered what John looked like. When she saw him walk into the kitchen, she was surprised at how it all came back to her. She had been horrified that the king would choose her husband even though she knew it was his right with her father dead. Up until that time, she had been left to her own devices. Although no longer allowed to act as chatelaine, she did what she could to see to the workings within the castle. Arthur had been given the duty that should have been hers. Admittedly, she didn't understand the sudden urgency in seeing her marry and to a Norman no less.

She had acted atrociously, and her cheeks burned at the memory. But John had been so kind to her. He had been patient with her outbursts and even protected her from the man who would have beaten her, the same man who threatened her just prior to entering the chapel. She knew now that the man had been telling her a lie when he said the Normans shared their women. She had certainly overreacted.

No longer. Now she would prepare herself as the noble Saxon woman she was. She came from strong stock, and her husband should see her at her best rather than in turmoil afeared for what evil would befall her. He was blessed not only by the titles bestowed upon him at their joining but also by a generous and loving wife. If given a chance, she would be sure he knew that.

Childish dreams of love and family that she'd shared with her closest friend while snuggled beneath the covers on cold winter nights, no longer brought her to tears. Kate had married a strong, handsome Saxon as they had each expected to. Rowena had not, but if she really needed physical love, Arthur had let her know that she need only say the word. Her strong faith, however, didn't allow for such a thing as adultery. Vows made before God were to be kept.

Naked in the middle of the room, Rowena decided she needed a bath and sent Joan off to accommodate her request. In the small mirror she assessed herself. She didn't look her age, though still a maiden, nineteen was a bit past her prime. Her waist was still small and her breasts were firm. From behind, she saw her derriere was perhaps more womanly. The knock at the door sent her scurrying behind the intricately decorated wooden screen beside the fire.

"Enter."

Joan moved through the door balancing a tub in her arms with a long retinue of strong, young boys carrying steaming buckets in her wake. The moment the door closed behind the last boy, Rowena submerged herself in the lavender scented water. Within a short time she was relaxing, enjoying the feel of Joan's firm fingertips massaging her scalp.

"The place is full of Normans this morning." Joan had much to say.

Rowena just listened.

"They run very big."

Rowena laughed at that.

"Your husband is here also."

Tensing at the statement, she waited but Joan had apparently run out of things to say.

"Did he ask for me?"

Joan sloshed the water over her head before she answered."I didn't hear anything like that."

"But you saw him? With his men?" Rowena spurted the water out of her face as she spoke.

"He was going into the study with Arthur." Joan dowsed her head again.

Sitting up suddenly, Rowena considered whether any good could come out of Arthur spending time with her wayward husband. *No.*

"How did Arthur look?"

"Arthur is a handsome man." Joan scrubbed Rowena's back roughly as she answered. "How do you think he looked?"

Rowena turned slowly to face the irritating woman. She narrowed her eyes to make her point. "I do not believe for one minute that you do not understand exactly what I am asking you."

The blonde's answer was to douse Rowena one more time. Sputtering through her hair now matted to her face, Rowena said, "Oh, you wait, young lady!"

Joan, her eyes twinkling with the mischief she was causing, stood up at the same time as Rowena. Rowena just barely caught the towel thrown at her.

"I will get you back!" Rowena called after her maid who quickly raced away, leaving Rowena to step out of the tub herself.

Joan's laughter resounded down the hall.

Smiling to herself, Rowena was rubbing her body dry when the woman returned.

"Back for more are you?" Rowena's smile quickly evaporated when she found John in the open doorway. Crossing his arms about his chest, his frank appraisal caused her to hold her breath. The towel did very little to shield her nakedness from him as his eyes traveled the length of her, from her bare legs all the way up to her dripping wet hair. Feeling like a horse at auction, she bit her bottom lip while her heart pounded even faster. She glanced up. The appreciation on his face gave her a little thrill.

"But I haven't had any." His eyes turned dark as he walked into the room, closing the door firmly behind him. "You seem to be left without assistance."

"My handmaiden just left." Looking down at her toes, she could feel her body flush from his gaze. "If you would allow me a moment, I co—"

"No, need." His voice was quiet and low. His eyes on her breasts made her more aware that her own breathing had returned as her chest rose and fell. "If I may be so bold...?"

Rowena could not refuse her husband, whatever he intended. "As you wish, my lord."

"Oh, yes, I do wish." He licked his lips as he started toward her, a knowing smile spread across his face.

"It will please me greatly to...assist you." He stepped closer, reaching for the cloth she reluctantly released to him, leaving her completely exposed. "We wouldn't want you to get cold."

She bit her lower lip. He couldn't be expecting her to converse with him while he stood fully clothed and she was completely naked? A glance at his face confirmed his thoughts were not about conversing but of desire. His gaze moved along her body like a caress, no detail of her left untouched.

Rubbing her shoulder with the thick cloth, he leaned in closer, his breath warm against her cheek. Unexpectedly, her senses tuned in to him as if he were the only thing that existed.

When she was just sixteen years old she had stood in the family chapel making vows before the French bishop and God, taking this man as her husband. Despite being forced into the marriage, she had taken those vows to heart. She had waited for this, waited for him to come to her and show her what it was to be a married woman. His consideration despite how she'd acted made her trust he would be gentle. Her stomach fluttered at the thought of finally feeling his touch.

He worked the towel slowly down her arm but his eyes were now on her face, her lips. The heat from his body spoke of his need and she almost welcomed it. As he reached to dry the other arm, his hand grazed her breast. His gaze followed suit. Unwilling to look him directly in the eye, she fixed her eyes on his lips. He rubbed them together as if in anticipation.

My husband desires me.

It sounded sweet in her mind after so many years of his absence. So many years of endless nights. She'd longed to be made into a wife in truth, and this man, her husband, was beyond handsome with his broad expanse of chest, strong arms and firm body. Her breath caught in her throat at the sudden longing that surged through her.

Rowena nearly jumped out of her skin when his rough hand slid down her bare side and pulled her gently against him. A shiver of anticipation ran down her spine and shot through her body like a bolt of lightning. When he finally kissed her, she closed her eyes, convinced she was running out of air.

His mouth was warm and pleasurable, and his tongue insistently coaxed her to open up to its invasion. His caresses were hot on her skin where his hands slipped under her breasts, fondling, then slid around to grasp and lift the same derriere she'd thought just adequate. He seemed to think it was splendid, and molded her tight up against him. Her body melted into him in response. Heat spread up through her core and she moaned. For better or for worse, her husband had come to make good his vows.

§

If he'd had aught to drink, John would have believed he was drunk. The sight of this sensual creature was making a mockery of his tightly held desires. He needed to leave not gawk at this stranger. This was unseemly. But he could not. Not knowing who she was seemed of little importance to his urgent need to have her.

Wetting his lips, he was ready for whatever she offered with her Siren's call. He wanted to take her and bury himself in her till morning. Her skin was slick and soft. Her full breasts begged for his attention, heavy in his hand. He pulled her close. Her taut nipples pressed through his tunic. He coaxed her lips apart, dipping his tongue into the warm recesses of her mouth. He teased her tongue, urging it deeper into his mouth, and at the sound of her moan, his own desire grew, his senses reeling.

"Oh, my lady, you are like a ripe peach ready to be plucked."

Assaulting her with his mouth, he suckled her, grazing her with his teeth. Her quickening breath urged him on. He pressed her firmly against his length, molding her to him, her every curve fitting perfectly. Kissing her deeply, he rubbed her hips against him, conveying his urgency.

"I want to fill you."

Bending slightly, John slid his hand along her satiny thigh and stroked her center lightly at first, then delving deeper and deeper. She was damp with desire, begging him to take her, but her tightness gave him pause. Looking down into her face, her eyes were closed and her lips were slightly parted. She was thoroughly aroused. Slowly he caressed her, mesmerized by the apparent pleasure she was taking from him. His own deep moan surprised him when his passion-numbed mind finally registered the implication of her tightness.

"My love," his voice was horse with the struggle to keep his passion from overwhelming her, "please tell me you are not a virgin."

Her eyes flew open and he was pierced by a pair of silver gray eyes, first confused and then accusing.

"Of course I am a virgin."

His wife! How stupid could he be to not have recognized those eyes?

She shoved him away and ran to the bed. Pulling her gown up to hide her nakedness, she turned on him. "Who did you think that I was?"

John was near to bursting with desire for her, and the reality that this beautiful, passionate woman was his wife cut him to the quick. Her own eyes cried out in pain at his callous advances against her, and he knew it was only a matter of time before the screaming banshee he'd left alone all these years reared her ugly head. But she was his wife. He could have her if he wanted. The fact made him brazen.

"I know you to be my wife."

"You know me not." Her voice was tight.

"I have been remiss." John could afford to apologize, he was desperate to have her. "Let me rectify the situation."

He stepped toward her but stopped short his advance. Her supple lips, sweet as honey but a moment before, were pressed into a hard line. She dragged in a shaky breath. Her hand trembled where she clutched her gown tightly against her breasts.

"Are you such a lecher to come across a naked woman and force yourself on her?"

"Methinks you were not being forced."

"So you seduce naked women you do not even know?"

"No!" He bellowed his answer, dragging his hand through his hair, but his defense would not hold up. He didn't know her as his wife...and he was seducing her. "That is not my way."

"Methinks your way is more than clear."

"No," John's voice was quiet again. How could he convince her he was not like other men? "You called out to me as sure as a Siren's song."

She shook her head, her lips in a tight smile. "So now you are a hero that legends are written of?"

He searched her face before he spoke, "I came across a beautiful woman I would rather die than not have."

Her lips parted with her quiet gasp, her silver eyes rounded with the longing he'd sensed in her response to him.

John stepped toward her and continued, "I was a drowning man and you were refreshing water."

Rowena seemed to lean toward him as well.

A knock at the door startled him, breaking the spell.

"Who is it?" They responded at the same time.

After a long pause, a woman's timid voice answered. "It is Joan."

"Come in." Rowena's voice held a note of desperation.

"Go away!" John commanded.

At the sound of the retreating steps, a crest-fallen look swept across Rowena's face. He had hurt her yet again. But she was not screaming at him or beating his chest. She glanced at the ground.

John fought the need to take her into his arms and finish what he'd started. His hands clenched at his sides to stop from reaching out to her.

Her eyes finally met his, the look of longing replaced by anger. "Why have you come back?"

"I have come to be your husband."

"Why?"

Because the king ordered me here...but now I want you in truth.

"Because we are wed," he said.

He walked toward the bed and tried not to notice her tensing.

"Sit." He settled himself on the bed and indicated the spot beside him. "We have things to discuss."

"Is that why you came in here? To talk?" There was an edge of bitterness in her tone, and she remained where she was. He was immensely glad she didn't know he hadn't been looking for her at all but for her man, Arthur.

"I have wronged you, my lady." He took her hand, and she didn't resist. He pulled her gently toward him, looking up into her eyes. "Verily."

She sat beside him finally, a bit farther away than he would have liked. He glanced at her hand, caressing it as he spoke, her skin so soft beneath his calloused fingers. "Would you always have been willing as my wife?"

She gasped at his hard words but he needed to know. There was a long wait for her answer. "I take my vows to heart." Her voice sounded small. "As my husband, you have rights."

His gut wrenched at her admission. He had been a coward, but no more. He looked her squarely in the eyes. "I have rights as your husband...but I would prefer that you would give willingly."

"My lord, I believe I have been exceedingly willing with you. Speak plain. What is it you want from me really?"

He traced his fingers lightly up her arm to her shoulder, her silky skin responding with tiny goose bumps. Slowly, he urged her closer, pushing his advance. She stiffened in response, but he chiseled away at her resistance with gentle kisses, along her cheek, her jaw, willing her closer to him.

"Please." Her voice was quiet.

He pulled back reluctantly, tamping down his desire. "Shall we talk first?"

The knock at the door startled them both.

"Who is it?" John's voice was harsh.

"Arthur."

Color spread across her face.

"Not now, Arthur." John's voice brooked no discussion and yet the man's footsteps did not retreat and a few seconds later there was another knock.

"My lady?" Arthur's voice sounded concerned and gentle.

John watched Rowena's color deepen when she opened her mouth to answer. He was filled with some heretofore unknown emotion. He interrupted whatever she might have said with his command. "Go away, Arthur."

This time footsteps led away from the door. They were alone again.

"You have grown into a beautiful woman." His finger traced her cheek as he spoke quietly, her high color receding. With his lips close to her ear, he whispered, "I find you much to my liking." He put his lips against her cheek, and his hand slid up the gown she still gripped.

She released the garment.

His body responded with anticipation. With the tip of his tongue, he traced her luscious red lips. So sweet. Her breath fell soft against his mouth. He opened his eyes slightly and was surprised to find her watching him. "Let me love you *now*, Rowena."

"How do I know you speak the truth? How do I know you do not often sneak into women's chambers?"

"Because I am here, not somewhere else. My desire is for you and you alone." He spoke the truth but could not prove it was so.

"Not so on our wedding night."

"I was Norman scum to you." Her jaw dropped, clearly mortified at the reminder of her own words, true though they were. "I thought you might kill me in my sleep."

"I had just been told that I would be shared by your men."

John pulled back, distressed at the obvious lie. "Who told you such a thing?"

The only reason for the lie would have been to frighten her. It had worked.

"The guard who brought me into the church, John."

It was the first time she'd said his name, and it brought him pleasure to hear it from her lips.

"I beg your forgiveness." She stared blankly back at him as he spoke. "I had no idea you were being so cruelly treated. It was not our intent."

"Your intent was only to force my marrying you so that you could leave me here to rot away of old age?"

That hadn't been his intent but rather his reaction to her crazed behavior. Her point was well taken. If he had known of her mistreatment, things would have progressed quite differently.

"Clearly we have both wronged you—William in his choice of husband for you and myself in abandoning you."

He wanted to take her and show her how repentant he really was, but her eyes flashed a warning. He had missed his golden opportunity. She was now wiser and it would be an uphill battle for him to gain her acquiescence again.

"I believe William knew what he wanted when he forced this marriage upon us. You on the other hand, I have no sympathy for."

In all her bare splendor she stood beside him.

His breath caught in his throat. She was perfection in every sense, and he was a very blessed man. His hand itched to pull her back to him, but she continued behind the wooden screen.

"You may leave now and please send Joan to me," she said.

Duly chastised, he grinned at her commanding tone. The screen, however, did nothing to suppress his knowledge of every detail of the beauty that stood on the other side and the longing it enflamed. John tamped down his desire. For now.

"I will get Joan for you, my lady, and thereafter you will attend me at supper."

§

When the door closed behind her husband, Rowena slid to the small stool, still shaking at her bold behavior. He had allowed her to walk away from him when she had feared he would pull her back to him. She knew it and he knew it. That he would be returning for her said it all. He would return for her and...expect what? Was he going to stay and be her husband in every way? Was he going to expect her to share her bed with him? After all this time, she wasn't sure what she wanted. He had walked away from her and left her alone. Not just alone but untouchable as his wife.

"Humph." She had crumbled under his attention after determining to be strong and show him she had no need for him. Did she need him after all?

Rubbing her arms, she could still feel the heat from his body and her own response to it. That had taken her aback. She had been treating this as a child's game. If he did not want her, then she wanted him even less. But in his arms she had come alive, feeling things she'd never imagined. She wanted more.

She smiled. It appeared the attraction was mutual.

"My lady, what has happened here?"

Rowena stood behind the screen, startled from her thoughts by Joan's entrance.

"Are you well? Arthur was beside himself. Please come out and show me you are well."

"Calm yourself. I am not clothed and wish to dress for dinner. Will you assist me?"

Joan's look of worry quickly turned to a knowing smile when she came around the screen to help her with the gown. Her presumptuous expression made Rowena bite her lip to keep from smiling. Yes, her husband found her pleasing. There. It was out and even Joan knew it. How much Joan knew would be left up to her imagination. That was until Rowena saw the mark that held Joan's attention. A love bite. Proof of what had transpired or almost transpired.

"You can stop smiling." Rowena tightened her lips to convey her disapproval. "I am a virgin still."

Joan's crestfallen face was almost comical except that it really wasn't.

The whole situation was intolerable. Well, Rowena would find out this night if the man who was her husband was worthy of the title. If he was, she would commence with the bedding and that would be the end of that. The massive jolt of heated desire that shot up through her body made her catch her breath. Well, she would just have to ignore that for now. She just wasn't sure if she could.

Chapter Four

John's patience was growing thin. As Peter had been chatting on about horses and soldiers for nigh an hour, his desire for his wife did not diminish. Where was Rowena?

"You can just tell me to shut up," Peter raised one eyebrow as he spoke.

John had no time to placate the man. "Continue," he ordered as he took another swallow of the local mead. Its bitterness reminded him of sweeter nectar he would prefer to taste. What was taking her so long? He'd gone to escort her down and been told she was not ready. The audacious way the servant spoke to him had left him with much to say in response and yet when he'd opened his mouth to speak his mind, he recalled of the wrong done Rowena and chose to walk away. Now he was left waiting for her.

"You're as antsy as a bridegroom."

If only you knew, my friend. John scowled in response.

Peter finally gave up and walked away which left John to pace in front of the roaring fire, his patience lessening by the minute. He was relieved that the large group of people milling around the Great Hall did not approach him to welcome the long awaited Norman lord. He wanted to be left alone...preferably with his wife. The mead he'd been drinking was affecting his composure. Thoughts of her flying through the window, rushing out the garden door, and hiding away in the night had him ready to crack. What could possibly take her this long?

The memory of a much younger Rowena hanging on to her father's body flashed in his mind. Every detail, the smell of the dying, the sound of the horses whining to avoid the carnage, the call of the soldiers as they dragged the few survivors back to camp, it all came to life again. He did not deserve to be with this woman. If she ever learned of his part in her father's death, she would never forgive him.

The sight of the woman adorned in a gown of blue velvet drove all concerns out of his mind and took his breath away. She was beautiful, truly beautiful. Her dark hair spread about her shoulders was encircled by a thin silver wreath around her head. His gaze worked its way down her elegant neck to a tightly fitted bodice adorning those lovely breasts to a narrowed waist and the sweep of a skirt that hid her other treasures he could still feel the touch of. A tightening in his breeches had him clearing his throat as he quickly crossed the distance to take her hand. Arthur was already beside her but withdrew when John offered her his arm and escorted her to the head table, his gaze holding hers.

"My lady, you look beautiful." Leaning closer to her ear, he whispered, "Like a ripe peach." Her smell was intoxicating and his desire for her easily outweighed his hunger. This would be a long meal.

§

John's breath against Rowena's neck sent a shiver down her spine. Knowing now how easily she could be distracted, she fought to keep her head. Those who'd been waiting for the new lord of the manor acknowledged him with some excitement when he entered, Rowena at his side. John accepted their respectful greetings as if he'd always been such a high ranking lord yet Joan had said he was only a knight.

"My lord," a burly man with a ruddy complexion bowed overly long before them, causing his face to turn even redder. "Accept the greetings of a distant friend. I am Mort of Bedgrove near Aylesbury, at your service."

"And what would that service be?" John paused beside the extravagantly dressed man. It was not a man Rowena had ever seen before. John's mouth twitched with humor as he seemed to take in all the fine silk, silver bells and feather adornments in one glance.

The man bowed again before answering. "My lord..." Stepping closer, the man was a head shorter than John but he managed to look him directly in the face when he answered. "Whatever service that you might need."

John's humor fled. Rowena sensed a sudden tension between the two men. Their eyes were locked as if sizing each other up. His arm finally relaxed where her fingers lay lightly atop it. Smiling, he tipped his head in acknowledgment and continued on.

Finally reaching the far center wall, John and Rowena took their seats at the long table. It was covered with a clean cloth and adorned with small bunches of the last flowers from the garden. The scene was festive and Rowena's own spirits seemed to lift as well. It was a time to celebrate. The long awaited lord had finally returned. There would be time later to find out what that would mean to her. For her people, it was time for celebration. A time for peace.

Once everyone settled, three young girls came out of the kitchen with the first removes. The red-haired one, Ruth, made a beeline for their table and Rowena clenched her jaw. John was served first. Rowena did not miss the provocative way the cook's daughter looked at him, or her saucy smile when she filled his cup of mead. Dipping her shoulder so her tunic fell open, she gave him an eyeful.

"Ruth." Finally getting her attention, Rowena shot the serving girl a look of disapproval. "I think you are needed in the kitchen. Send someone else to see to our needs."

Ruth tossed her red hair over her shoulder in a huff as she sashayed away. Rowena would need to address this behavior. It was unbecoming. If it meant replacing Ruth entirely, so be it. She'd have to find work elsewhere. Having already found her once in a compromising situation was bad enough. Rowena should have gotten rid of her then. She'd only kept her on at her mother's appeal.

The memory of Ruth up against the wall, her skirts bunched up at her waist, and the grunting soldier having at her, flashed in Rowena's mind. She'd wondered at Ruth's expression. Her eyes had been closed and she appeared to be quite enjoying herself. Yet it looked so brutish. Heat spread quickly up Rowena's face as she remembered her own response to her husband's intimate touch. Would it be like that for her? Would she enjoy her husband like Ruth seemed to enjoy every man?

Glancing at John, Rowena was relieved to see he paid no heed to the girl's behavior. He did not watch her as she walked away, and he didn't seem to notice her blatant invitation. Yes, Ruth definitely had to go.

The meal was eaten with the new apple wine Rowena had chosen. The assortment of breads, meats and pies was plentiful. The mead and cider flowed without restraint. All seemed relaxed, happy even. At the tables grouped with eight and ten people each, there was an easy exchange as they talked amongst themselves and the noise level rose as the amount of drink increased. The Normans, however, sat off by themselves and spoke more quietly. They were soldiers after all. Rowena tried to squelch her uneasiness at this realization.

Wondering if John noticed the subdued behavior of his men, she was startled to find his gaze running over her body. Her own breath quickened. It felt as if he were actually touching her. The memory of his touch had left a lasting impression. He wet his lips before taking his goblet to his mouth, opening it right before the cold metal touched his lips. The movement along his throat as he drank mesmerized her. She found herself wanting to put her lips there, to taste him. She looked away. She could never be so bold.

Her response to his looks was quite disconcerting. She cleared her throat."How do you find your manor after your long absence, my lord?"

John eyebrows shot up. She hadn't meant to find fault...or maybe she did.

"I was taken aback to find you do not care for the stores and such. Is there a reason you refuse to act as is your right as my wife?"

Her mouth opened slightly at the lie. "My lord, I have been given no such leave. Your king replaced me as chatelaine on his first visit here."

John searched her face before correcting her. "Our king."

"Yes." Rowena dropped her gaze. A slip of the tongue.

"You would accept this position then?"

She looked up but hesitated, not wanting to overstep her bounds. "It would give me great pleasure to be in charge of the running of the castle."

"Then run it you shall."

Rowena nibbled at her lip to hide her smile. Since the Normans had come, no one obeyed her unless they wanted to. The king had never come to meet with her but instead with those he had put in charge of her. Now John was giving her back her rightful place. Things were progressing better than she had hoped.

The young girl, Sarah, had replaced Ruth and was in front of the table offering a basket of almond-stuffed dates dripping with honey. Rowena returned her genuine smile. She was a lovely child. Serving the lord and lady was a big responsibility.

Offering the sweets to the new lord, Sarah's face fell as he declined with a shake of his hand.

"Oh, yes, please." Rowena hurriedly accepted the sweet. Sarah beamed in appreciation and moved on to the next table.

Rowena put the treat to her mouth and took a small bite. The honey smeared her lips. Quickly, John was leaning toward her, pulling her close. He licked her lips before kissing her. He was so tender that she was moved by the gesture and leaned into him, wanting the kiss to continue.

The burst of applause from those present in the hall surprised Rowena. She smiled in answer when they separated at last. Not all present looked happy with their display of affection. Noticing John had not yet moved away, she realized he was waiting for another kiss. She kissed him chastely. He frowned but pulled back.

The young man on her left caught her eye. He sat against the wall, his clay whistle on his lap. He had a small smile and looked at her expectantly. It was Cedric, the performer. Too shy to come to the table himself, he was apparently hoping Rowena would intervene on his behalf. She did not disappoint. Trying not to smile at his bashfulness, she turned back toward John.

"My lord..." Catching him unguarded, she was taken aback by the look of sadness she saw there. It passed so quickly, she wondered if she had imagined it.

"My lady?"

A ripple of delight washed over her at the title. She glanced away to hide her pleasure.

"Our performer tonight is a bit shy and hoping you would enjoy hearing his songs," she said. "He is very good. Will you address him?"

She tipped her head slightly indicating the man.

"Please." John smiled warmly at the performer and stood, facing those in hall. "Friends and visitors, let us rejoice in the blessing of music that God has given us by listening to..." realizing he didn't know the man's name, his composure fell slightly and he looked to Rowena to complete the introduction. "Rowena?"

"Cedric."

"Cedric." John lifted his cup.

Applause broke out with murmurs of excitement as the man stepped into the middle of the hall. A sudden hush fell like a blanket over the hall in anticipation of the entertainment as Cedric produced one long note from his whistle then cleared his throat. No longer the shy young man, he took over the music with confidence, having nothing more than his voice and a whistle.

Lifting his strong, clear voice, he told the story of the fallen soldier. He had been killed by an arrow and left to die alone by his companions. While he suffered the inevitable, it was a fallow deer that came to be with him. The story was enchanting and one of Rowena's favorites. She brushed away a tear and clapped enthusiastically. Cedric blushed as he bowed low. Next taking up his whistle, the pleasant music increased the peaceful mood that fell over the hushed crowd.

John wiped at her cheek, his touch light. "That song brought tears?"

Rowena dipped her head, shrugging a shoulder. "I think it is a lovely story. 'Tis all."

"Ah, my wife has great sentiment." He took her hand in his. "I will remember that."

The way he held her hand was comforting. She felt suddenly less alone.

"What was the commotion in the yard earlier?" she asked John in a hushed tone without looking directly at him. The quiet sound of the whistle filled the cavernous space.

"Your men are not accustomed to the size of our war horses. They were frightened." Even with his soft tone his disdain was apparent.

She stilled and considered why his words sounded insulting. Glancing at the soldiers' table again, she saw the man who had accosted her in the hall. He was not looking at her now. In fact, he looked as if he were being ostracized by the other men.

"Who is that man sitting by himself?" Her eyes stayed on him while John looked to see who she meant.

"He is a new man. I believe his name is Stephen. He is from the king's family."

Her eyes narrowed as she spoke, "He forced his attention on me in the hall this morning."

"What? You must be wrong!" John stood before she realized his intent. "Stephen. Come here." His voice was suddenly that of the lord of the manor. Cedric ceased his playing. Unsure what had happened, he looked at the others around the hall. They were watching the new lord to see what the commotion was.

Stephen's behavior said it all. The reluctant way he rose. His downcast eyes. The way he didn't acknowledge the others at his own table. This was a guilty man.

"My lord." Stephen bowed stiffly before John and Rowena.

"I understand you have met my wife? The Lady Rowena?"

The man had the decency to look chagrinned but avoided her gaze. "My lord, I am afraid I have offended your lady. I was very forward with her earlier thinking she was a peasant woman. I would ask that you forgive me for this show of disrespect."

Rowena was taken aback by the sudden show of respect given her, by a Norman no less. Or was it just while she was actually with him? In truth, the man should not have been harassing any of her women, peasant or not. She took a sip of wine and waited for her husband's response.

"I don't know how you deal with woman in Blois, Stephen, but we are not forward with women… any women. It is much more rewarding to have a willing woman than one who disdains your advances. Do you understand?"

"Yes, my lord, I beg your forgiveness."

John spoke louder to include his men seated at the table to his right when he answered. "Peter, Ronald and Louis shall have a reprieve from their nightly guard duties since I believe Stephen here would like to assist them. Am I correct?"

Stephen of Blois bowed deeply. "You are correct."

The man walked stiffly away and Rowena wondered about any repercussions from this show in her defense. Her experience was that the Normans had a deep dislike for the Saxons. None of her women ever ventured out alone. An empty alley could easily turn into the perfect place for an attack. It seemed a very ungracious way for the victors to behave. Would not protecting their new conquests have been more chivalrous?

Raising his hand for Cedric to continue, John's reassuring smile seemed to cause a collective sigh of relief. No trouble here. He sat down and continued to keep an eye on his men.

Stephen was quickly included back but no one spoke directly to him. The other soldiers handed him the meat and wine. His conscience clear, he was now able to eat.

Rowena felt a glow of pride in her husband. He had not been accepting of the behavior she had been treated to. He was showing himself to be a fair man, a good leader.

The long note signaled the end of the piece and Cedric's performance was met with sincere appreciation. The crowd clapped and lifted their mugs to him. He lifted his whistle and bowed in acknowledgement. Addressing the lord and lady, he bowed formally before leaving the hall.

"Would you have been so quick to my defense on our wedding night had you known that the king's guard had fondled me and promised to make use of me when you were done?"

She wanted to know but regretted the question as soon as it was spoken.

John choked on his wine, Peter quickly walked over to pat his liege lord on the back. "What ails you?"

John shook his head as he struggled to stop the spasms down his throat. "Enough, Peter. Sit."

Peter's eyes on Rowena were surprisingly untrusting. She glanced down at her cup.

Wiping his face, John turned toward her. "You must have misunderstood. You were distraught."

She tightened her jaw and faced him. He did seem sincere in what he was suggesting.

"I promise you, I understood. His filthy hands on my breasts did much to make me understand."

"No," John shook his head vehemently. "This would be reprehensible. It cannot be true."

Rowena felt her face turn red in anger. She rose from the bench.

"I do not appreciate being called a liar by anyone, my lord."

Her head held high, she made her way across the hall. His accusation felt like a knife to her heart. She would never lie about such a thing as that, and she was mistaken to believe he was chivalrous. She needed to get away from him so that she could think. She just hoped her thoughts would not be about him.

Chapter Five

John knew his words offended Rowena, but he could not believe what she said. To make such an accusation against William's man was outrageous. He watched as she stiffly crossed the hall to the stairs, the slight sway of her hips a reminder of how he hoped the meal would end. Instead she was angry with him again.

John planned to win Rowena with his charming ways, but instead she'd earned his regard by showing herself to be a gently raised woman with compassion for even younglings. The look of disappoint that swept across the face of the young serving girl made him regret his unkind dismissal. But before he'd been able to remedy the situation, Rowena's enthusiasm had brought a smile back to the child's face. His urge to kiss his thoughtful wife had been more than a lustful show of ownership. He'd been overwhelmed by her consideration for those beneath her station. The bard was the same.

When she dismissed the lusty kitchen servant, he liked that she was staking a claim on him. It gave him hope. Now this.

Closing his eyes in frustration, he fought to control his own ardor at the mere thought of her. She required his patience. He could win her over. The knowledge that the king required consummation, and John now whole-heartedly agreed, made biding his time a tactic he'd prefer not to use.

Across the dimly lit hall, he saw a man quickly follow up the stairs Rowena had just ascended. Her man-at-arms? Arthur? Unaware that he had risen from the table until Peter stood at his side, John's disbelief quickly turned into an even stronger emotion. Betrayal.

"John, what is amiss?" Tracking his gaze, Peter reacted as any friend would. "That man is certainly always underfoot isn't he?"

"Isn't he, though?" John's tossed his cup down and stalked across the hall. Silence fell over the room but John could not think clearly. What was Arthur doing following his wife? Why would the king's guard molest her? None of this made sense but if Arthur was who John was beginning to believe him to be, there would be bloodshed this very night.

Peter stood at John's elbow before he reached the stairs. "Please, calm yourself before you go up there."

His voice landed on John's ears as if through a fog. He would not wait. "Step aside. You do not understand."

"Perhaps I do." Peter dragged at his arm, his voice quiet. "I have kept your secret about Rowena."

John glanced up the stairs, but shook his head hoping to clear it. He reluctantly tried to make sense out of what his friend said. "What secret?"

"Had William known you left Rowena intact, he would have been furious. He desires Norman-Saxon children to solidify his claim. You choosing not to do your duty could be considered treason."

Peter spoke the truth. William was like a father to him but, as his leader, John obeyed his orders. William had all but commanded John to get his wife with child, yet he left her untouched.

"Did you see how crazed she behaved that day? She would have cut my throat had I stayed here. I would not have gotten within an arm's length of her without a guard on either side. Or should I have sought their assistance in the bedding of my wife?"

John defended his actions but now knew that his concerns had been unfounded. She would have accepted him as her husband, and he wouldn't now be panting at her heels. A flash of Rowena's writhing body sent a shiver of desire coursing through his body. Was Arthur now getting what she had refused him earlier?

Peter dragged John deeper into the darkened stairs and looked to see that no one else could hear them. "You don't recognize Stephen, do you?" It sounded like an accusation, and John shook his head. "He is Adele's affianced."

Adele was one of William's children, his only daughter. "Are you certain?"

"William sent him to train with you so he could learn how to be a better man. William sees he leaves much to be desired as a son-in-law but Adele will not hear of marrying anyone else. She has her eyes set on Stephen. William's only hope is that he can learn from you."

John knew that Rowena's story had been true about the man making moves against her in her own castle. Now the realization that he was the king's future son-in-law put a new light on things. Perhaps she told the truth about William's guard.

"Do you remember the ceremony?"

"I left with William before you took your vows. He sent me back to retrieve the sheets which were nowhere to be found."

Sheets with his virgin wife's blood could not be found when there had been no consummation of the vows. "William suspected?"

"He had his doubts about you wanting to bed the lady. I brought him the proof he sought."

John blanched. "I did not know. I give you my thanks. If I had known my wife's nature, I would not have left her." He heard the desire in his voice and was not surprised to see his friend's raised eyebrows. "It's true. She is a contradiction to the barbaric surroundings of this place."

Remembering Arthur, he pulled his arm away and started again up the stairs.

"Wait, John, wait." Peter followed him. Arthur stood outside Rowena's door as John and Peter both came to a stop in the hall. The click of the latch on the door reverberated through the silent hall. John's blood boiled. He strode toward the man.

"Arthur, may I assist you?"

"No, my lord." Arthur lowered his eyes respectfully. John hadn't missed the smirk he now hid.

"Then why are you outside my wife's door?" His voice sounded menacing even to his own ears. The blood coursing through his veins throbbed in his ears, his fists clenched at his side, at the thought of any man touching Rowena.

"I was concerned for her when she left the hall."

John stepped closer, grasping the front of Arthur's tunic as he spoke in hushed tones, "Why would *my* wife be of any concern to *you*?"

They were nose to nose, but Arthur refused to take a defensive stance.

"My apologies, my lord, I have clearly overstepped my bounds." He avoided eye contact as well.

John was disappointed that the man gave him no excuse to pulverize him, but he slowly released his tunic and took a step back.

"I believe you now understand your place?"

Arthur stared back at him, tipping his head in acknowledgement. "Aye. That I do."

John had no actual proof that Arthur lied about why he was in Rowena's chamber.

Forcing his breathing to a normal rhythm, he backed away from Arthur with a flourish down the hall. The red-haired man took the escape without a moment's hesitation. Peter and John watched him until he was gone.

38

John's hand was on the latch when Peter grabbed it.

"John, don't see her like this."

John could not actually see anything. Did his wife entertain the man in her bedchamber? Had a guard manhandled her before escorting her to him all those years ago?

"Remove your hand from me." John's gaze held his friend's until Peter released his hand. "Go below. I will be down anon."

Peter seemed to sigh in relief and followed where Arthur had gone.

John did hesitate before he opened Rowena's door. What was the proper course of action? If it were a battle, John would know just what to do but this involved a woman's feelings, totally unexplored ground. His throbbing increased. He pushed the door open in time to hear her gasp and watch her turn away. He had seen the tears and felt chagrined.

"My apologies for not knocking." What a fake. He had no remorse for not knocking. He'd wanted to catch her in her lies.

Her long hair cascaded down her stiff back, curling at her hips. He remembered the softness of that lovely derriere. He paused. He needed to get his wits about him. Shifting toward the fire, he felt very much like the flames that licked hungrily at the logs. He was being eaten up with desire for this woman.

He cleared his throat. "Can you tell me why Arthur thinks he needs to be concerned about you?"

"Arthur is my friend." Her quiet voice sounded sad. John took a step toward her then stopped himself. He picked up the brush from her table. The smell of her hair wafted up to him.

"Does he normally come to your bedchamber?"

Her back stiffened even more. He pulled a long strand of brown hair from the brush.

"Sometimes."

John firmly placed the brush back on the table. He closed his eyes and took a deep breath. His fists balled at his side. A knock on the door sent him lurching toward the door. He jerked it open. A surprised blonde woman took a step back at the sight of him.

"Oh, my lord," she bowed. "Forgive my intrusion." She glanced over his shoulder. "I've come to assist Lady Rowena with her gown."

The woman was making it up as she went he'd wager, but he didn't care. "She no longer requires your assistance." The thick-skulled woman looked perplexed, so he explained himself. "*I* will assist my wife."

"Yes, my lord." She backed away from the door as he all but slammed it in her face. He dragged his hand through his hair. His torment at the situation deepened.

"I must allow you to touch me, then?" Rowena's voice cut to the quick as he turned to face her.

Her passionate response to his touch earlier came quickly to his mind. *Allowing* him to touch her? He repulsed her so? He had to stop himself from closing the distance between them and demonstrating the truth to her. He licked his dry lips before he continued.

"I would not have us interrupted at this time." Her shoulders seemed to slouch. In relief? She may think she didn't want him but she was still his wife. "We have much to say to each other."

The silence grew. On the one hand he was beside himself that anyone had so violated her before their wedding. When he thought of her fear it all made sense now. He should have protected her even then, and his own excoriation made it worse. Of course she hated him. She knew nothing about Normans. She had been threatened by one of the king's own guards.

Had she been here with her lover, Arthur? Is that who comforted her? John knew there were ways to be intimate without losing one's virginity. Those ways were still punishable offenses. So did he comfort her for her abuses or punish her for adultery? He rubbed his throbbing head and dropped to sit on the stool beside the fire.

§

Rowena could not miss the anger in his face when he had burst into the room. When she had been assessing his worth, she was finding there was much to praise him for. Intelligent, well-spoken, gracious, considerate. Every woman, Norman or Saxon, had been treated respectfully. The rumors had flown when William of Normandy had been crowned. The Normans raped women in packs, murdered small children by throwing them into the river, and tore down churches and burned Saxon priests at the stake. Her treatment prior to wedding John seemed to support what she'd heard. Rowena had seen no such thing since.

"As my wife, Rowena..."

Her eyes narrowed at use of the title.

"...you will not allow men into your bedchamber. Other than me, that is."

A little shiver passed through her at the idea of him coming to her in the middle of the night. She could again feel his fingers caressing her. Perhaps he had indeed returned to be her husband in truth. The possibility excited her.

Arthur had followed her and even taken her in his arms to comfort her. In the past she had welcomed the feel of his arms around her, seldom as that happened, but she was already different. His arms no longer felt right around her. She had tried to tell him he could not be in her room, it wasn't seemly. He had looked so hurt.

"Do you not understand me, wife?"

The title bristled her. "Yes, husband, I understand you fine."

The use of titles did not make it any more true. Men always thought it did. They were wrong. Turning to him, she felt her cheeks grow hot as he caressed her ever so slowly with his eyes, finally resting on her face before he spoke again.

"Husband I will be soon enough."

His answer told her he didn't miss her meaning. He stood suddenly, and the fire silhouetting his large frame caused her breath to catch at his imposing size. From his powerful legs, slightly parted and ready for attack, to his solid torso, ready to receive the assault, to his burly arms more than willing to instigate the encounter. This was certainly no complacent lord of the manor; this was a well-honed fighting machine. Rowena was confused when she realized her own longing to touch him. His brown hair looked soft and the shadow of a beard around his chin caused her hand to itch for the touch of both.

"Know this, Rowena..."

Her breath quickened when he stepped toward her, his eyes piercing her own.

"...there will be no one but me."

He stopped just short of touching her but that now familiar heat reached out to her.

"You are mine and only mine."

His voice was quiet as he spoke the ominous words. Tipping his head slightly, John raised his eyebrows as if to ask if she needed any clarification. She did not. His meaning was quite clear. With tender fingers he stroked her chin and gently pulled her face closer. He lightly touched his lips to hers. "Good night, then."

Rowena watched him leave. She finally let go of the breath she'd been holding forever and collapsed on the bed. Deep gulps of air did nothing to settle her chaotic emotions. She rolled onto her side and tried to erase the feel of his hands on her, his lips on her. But a stronger desire burned even hotter to try and remember every detail, every sensation, to relive it exactly as it had been. Her restlessness only increased.

The fire burned brightly in the room and the candle beside the window gave off a soft glow. Her room, which had always seemed so peaceful, suddenly felt empty and cold. She stood to leave and realized she wasn't safe to wonder the halls. Norman scum.

Chapter Six

It had taken every ounce of strength for John to simply kiss Rowena and walk away when all he wanted to do was make her his in truth.

Peter was leaning against the wall beside the stairs when John came back to the hall. John rolled his eyes.

"Lying in wait, are you?" Glancing around the hall and not finding Arthur, John headed to the stable.

Peter tagged along. "How did it go?"

John pretended not to hear.

"The time with your wife?" Peter continued. "You don't appear any more relaxed."

John clenched his fist and turned to his friend. "It may be a good idea to keep out of my concerns."

Peter laughed quietly.

John's blood boiled. "Where is Arthur?"

"He did not stay here. He simply passed through the hall to the outside."

In the inner bailey, the stars twinkled overhead. John paused to take in the fresh scent of hay from the barn and the smoke from fires burning beyond in the village. It was a peaceful setting and did nothing to lessen the tension gripping his body. Rowena's dark hair sweeping down her gently heaving chest and her soft lips trembling in her upset called out to him that he needed to be with her right now. That was where his peace would be found.

"You seem more like a strained rope about to break."

"Peter," John turned on his friend. "If you are unable to stay out of what doesn't concern you, at least stop…talking so much." He scratched at his head before looking around. All that he saw was his but he knew it not at all. Very much like his wife. He finally located the stables and quickly closed the distance.

"Why did you not just bed her and be done with it?" Peter moved quickly to keep up with him.

John's jaw clenched. "I see you know nothing about women. That would explain your unmarried status."

"No. I choose the life of a soldier over a coddled man." Peter paused in the doorway of the barn. "Although coddling does have its advantages."

"Jeanette would say that it does." John thought of Peter's petite, red-haired mistress and added in irritation, "She would also say you agreed but not to the word coddling." John came out of the last stall and paused in the darkened aisle. "Damn."

"Did you actually think you would find Arthur hiding in one of the stalls?"

John paused long enough to glare at the man. "Perhaps."

"Get ahold of yourself."

Exhaling sharply, John felt as if he would explode. Where was Arthur? He would like to throttle the man. No, what he wanted was to throttle his wife. Well, maybe not actually throttle.

"My wife does not seem happy with me."

"I wonder why. Did you actually accuse her of entertaining a lover?"

"Not in so many words. I think she has to be made to understand."

"Certainly." Peter leaned against the low wooden stall. "I actually enjoy making Jeanette 'understand'. She does, too."

"Is that all you ever think about?"

"Yes... I would have to say, yes."

John settled down on the bale of hay at the end of the aisle. Leaning his head back against the wall, he closed his eyes and sighed wearily."You are exasperating."

"Are you sure it's me who is exasperating you?"

Opening one eye, he did his best to shoot daggers at his friend. "Why are you still here?"

"I want to know what happened when you spoke with the lovely Rowena."

Picking up the thick rope that lay discarded across the bale, John flicked the darkened ends aimlessly, contemplating his answer. "Nothing happened."

"Did you try to make anything happen?"

Irritated, John looked up at Peter. "Just to cover what is none of your concern, I felt since I had called her both a liar and an adulteress within a very short amount of time, I probably should not be forcing myself on her."

Peter's jaw dropped, adding to John's misery. "Tell me you did not."

"Oh, yes, I did."

"So you changed your mind about wanting to bed her? About consummating the marriage?"

The rope end disintegrated between his fingers as he rubbed the twines apart. "No, Peter, I did not change my mind. I am just failing miserably at the task at hand."

He pulled the remainder of the long rope loose from behind the hay and held the end closer to his nose. He sniffed.

"What is that?" Peter asked.

"I'd say this rope has been tampered with and yet..." holding it stretched so his friend could see that the rope had been knotted into a horse's lead..."it was made to look as if it was sound. Tell me what happened earlier with the horses."

"I did not arrive until the beasts had been settled. Apparently, Mark's horse had broken loose and was causing havoc. A young boy had been trampled but he is expected to live."

The silence in the stall was interrupted by cows munching and the occasional braying of the donkey. John rubbed the blackened ash from the rope between his fingers.

"It was deliberate," Peter finally said.

"So it would appear, but why?" John's body was exhausted but his mind raced.

"To increase the resentment toward us?"

"At the very least to make us appear shallow and uncaring. Where is the boy who was injured?"

"He is one of the stable hands here. His father is the village cooper."

"Did anyone visit the lad?"

Peter nodded, searching his memory. "Mark went to see the boy. He brought him food."

"I will see him myself on the morrow. If our horse has injured him, we will make amends. If, however, someone intentionally caused the incident, we will find the guilty party."

King William had given John until the spring to win over the loyalty of the villagers. Incidents like these only made his task that much more difficult. He needed to show that he had the Saxon's best interest at heart, and that the Normans and Saxons could live in peace together. Convincing Rowena of this would be a step in the right direction. How could he win her? Admittedly, he wanted her to be his wife in truth.

"Have you the names of the local men?" John asked.

"Word has been sent, and they are expecting your arrival."

"Perhaps it would be worth my time to see to my work before my pleasure."

"Would we be leaving tomorrow then?"

"It would probably be best if we did."

Peter stood a little straighter, all duty. "I will see that the men are ready, my lord."

Alone in the barn, John realized what a mess he had made of everything. Raised by a cruel peasant couple, he never did anything right according to them. A smack upside the head was his reward for even trying. In his sixth year, he was shipped off to the monastery at Mont Saint-Michel in Normandy where he studied with the monks. Who would have thought a skinny little good for nothing would take to his lessons so well?

The one man did. Duke William. John liked the big man who smelled of horses and leather with the kind blue eyes.

"You speak Latin very well, son. What is your name?"

"I am called John."

"Well, John, I am called William."

John pretended William was his father. He was a bastard, too, but he knew who his father was. What had the king been about? Why did he find any interest in a scrawny little boy? How did he know what John could become?

Now of all the knights under his command, King William weds the Saxon princess to John. Yet another test and he falls short again. Damn. Rowena was correct to scoff at his interest. He was nothing but a nameless bastard.

John pushed himself off the bale, brushed at his seat. The close confines of an unknown castle were not what he needed right now. He headed toward the only lit building visible from where he stood. The sign of "Owl and Thistle" swung noiselessly above the door of the two-story tavern. John did not doubt he would be welcomed as Lord of the manor. Perhaps he would find a soft place to lie after all.

Chapter Seven

When John arrived at the Owl and Thistle, the taverners could barely contain their enthusiasm at having the new Lord himself stay with them. They ran around seeing about improving his accommodations. His presence caused quite a bit of commotion.

With much on his mind, he sat in the quiet hall on the long wooden bench.

The tinkle of a bell sounded nearby. John turned toward the front entrance, unsure if he'd heard anything. He listened. It stopped. Crossing his legs at the ankles, he began to get comfortable and heard it again.

John stood abruptly and went back the way he'd come in. A strangely dressed man bent at the waist, peered out the door.

"Do you look for something in particular?" John asked.

The man jumped and turned. His face was inscrutable until he smiled broadly. "Ah, my lord." He opened his arms as if in welcome to a close friend. "How wonderful that you grace my presence again."

John pressed his lips together. It was the man he'd met earlier at the feast. The strange declaration made him think twice about this being a coincidence. "And what say you, Mort of Bedgrove near Aylesbury was it?"

Mort nodded and closed the distance. He wrapped a beefy arm around John's shoulder to steer him back to the bench he'd vacated. "Ah, my lord, I have many duties that take me to strange places."

The man stopped and motioned to the bench. John remained standing.

Mort raised his brows in a questioning way, his hand at his chest. "May I?"

John dipped his head and Mort settled himself upon the seat. "This inn is the one closest to the goings-on. As I said, I am at your service which requires my being nearby."

John drew his brows together in a thoughtful way. "And what was the service again?"

Mort's eyes locked with his. "Whatever is required of me."

John did not flinch but inside he fumed. What game was William playing at, sending one of his spies? To do what? Keep an eye on him?

"And you do this why?"

Mort finally looked down at his hands, the bells on his arms sounding with the movement. "Methinks you are not as in the dark as you would have me believe."

"So tell me why the king sent you here?"

Mort smiled at him. "I knew you were a wise one. The king always checks on what is his. He does not like to be uninformed."

"So there is nothing I need to know about?"

Mort searched his face. John wanted the man to share what he knew, regardless of his orders from the king. If there was trouble about, John needed to know so he could be prepared.

"I like you, Sir John. I believe you have a good heart. How you have stayed that way with all that is going on around you is a mystery to me." His fat hand patted John's arm as he stood before him. "If you need me, you know where I will be."

Mort glanced up and down the hall as if to get his bearings, then headed back out the door.

John closed his eyes and shook his head. William was so predictable. He gives John orders then sends his lackey to ensure those orders are followed. Trust was a word the king used only with his wife and family. Even though John would pretend William was his father, he never measured up.

The day William brought the sword to him at the monastery was such a day.

"Take it." William shoved the long sword at him, hilt first."See how it feels to hold it."

John shook his head despite how much he wanted to please the man. The monks did not abide violence.

William gave the sword back to the little blonde squire, Peter, and walked back into the monastery.

"What's wrong with you that you don't want to touch the Duke's sword?" Peter's face twisted in disapproval. "He brought it just for you."

And now Rowena.

John had much to think about and returned to his chamber. He settled down on the only stool in the room while it was swept, washed, and aired out. Sleep would help him decide what to do.

A raven-haired woman who wore her clothing tight and revealing came in to change the bed—housekeeping was plainly not her primary occupation. After making a clean bed for him, which involved overlong stretches with tantalizing glimpses of her well-rounded bottom, a little girl came in to remove the dirty sheets and handed him a rose.

John smiled at the little girl. "Thank you. And what is your name?"

"I am called Matilda, my lord. Very nice to make your acquaintance."

"Out." The woman hurried the small child out, closing the door behind the child. "And I am called Felicity," she said then stretched across the freshly made bed, giving him a more intimate view of her wares.

He had not come to the inn for carnal satisfaction but a place separate from Rowena, a place to get away from the turmoil she created in him. This woman's blatant attempts at seduction were very entertaining. He decided to play along.

"Interested, my lord?" She'd purred like a cat.

"What, specifically, would you be offering?"

Felicity frowned, clearly confused. He kept a straight face, as best as he could with her squishing her face up, clearly perplexed.

"A romp?" she finally answered him, posing it as a question.

He sat on the bed beside her. Immediately, she straddled his lap, her skirts hiked up around her. Her aim was particularly good and John felt an immediate rush of blood in response. She arched back, guiding his mouth toward her partially exposed breast.

He turned his head away. This needed to end.

"Umm."

She started grinding against him, guiding his hands between her thighs.

"I don't think…"

She knew her trade. She moaned with satisfaction—

His eyes flew open at the sound and he grabbed his hands away from her flesh and out of her reach.

"Cease this, woman. I am not interested."

She rubbed along his tight crotch and smiled. "I say you are."

"Enough." He shoved her off his lap and stood beside the bed. Sitting on her haunches, she watched him curiously. He scratched his scalp in irritation and saw her smile at his obvious interest, protruding as it was. "Well, I am not interested despite what it may look like."

She dropped to her knees on the floor in front of him and grabbed at the ties at his waist. "I will make you feel better."

"No," he said, twisting away from her.

The door burst open, and they both turned toward the sound.

"I came to see if you needed anything else, my lord." The woman's face burst into a toothless smile. The innkeeper's wife looked to be already counting the money she anticipated for this little "extra" service. "I see you are already being taken care of. Very good. Pardon me."

John looked down to find Felicity smiling up at him, her thick tongue slowly making its way around her lips.

"I am not interested," John stated again. Well, his body may be interested but not with this woman. Felicity's moan had yanked him back to reality. It had been wrong to his ears. It was not Rowena—his wife.

He groaned in frustration knowing all he had to do was go back to Rowena, walk into her room and take her. That was the release he needed. All this frustration building up inside, all this pent up desire. She was his wife. He had every right to do just that, and yet he didn't want it to be like that. He wanted her to be like she had been earlier, full of desire and passion for him.

Felicity plopped down on the stool beside the fire. "So you're pining after someone in particular?"

John laughed out loud at the absurdity of his answer. "Yes. My wife." Her shocked expression said it all. "It is a private matter."

"The Lady Rowena, is she sick then? She cannot see to your needs?"

"No. Not sick. We're just…not able to be together right now."

"Is she big with child?" Felicity paused, scrunching her face as if trying to figure out whether the lady of the manor could be pregnant.

"No. Stop prying and cover yourself. I will not be tempted."

Felicity smiled and stood up then.

"You know where to find me," she said.

Her sashaying hips held his attention as she walked out of the room.

Chapter Eight

John arose early to the sound of rattling pots and pans from the kitchen and the shouts of a bossy woman. The innkeeper's wife's voice was not the most pleasant to hear. He stretched in his bed before rising, fully clothed. Splashing cold water on his face from the pitcher beside the bed, he shivered and realized there was no towel for drying. A quiet knock on his door was answered with a grumpier response than he had intended.

"Excuse me, my lord," the plump redhead's smile vanished when she saw him standing there fully clothed. Her jaw dropped. "You slept alone?"

"Of course. Have you a towel?"

"Oh." Sticking her head into the hall, she bellowed the order and quickly handed him a towel. Her smile was sickly sweet. "Were your accommodations lacking then?"

Sitting on the side of the bed, John began pulling on stockings and boots before he answered. "The accommodations were fine."

When he stood to attach his scabbard, she grew agitated, speaking too quickly to be immediately understood. "My lord, we are getting breakfast for you."

John responded when he was finally able to decipher her words. "I am fine," he insisted.

When he reached for the door, she turned a pouting smile at him. Her grip was tight on his arm, stopping him from leaving. "Will you be staying here again, my lord?"

The sparse furnishings were adequate; a bed, a washstand, a sizeable fire. The alternative arrangements would be awhile in working out. Rowena's smiling face had him grinning to himself. He scratched at his whiskers. Still, better to be prepared. "Yes. Keep the room for me."

The sun was just rising above the horizon and the day's concerns were closing in. In the Great Hall at the castle, John found his men breaking their fast. Mark sat next to Peter at the table.

"Mark." John straightened his sword as he stood beside them. "How is the boy who was trampled?"

The dark-haired man shoved the honey covered biscuit into his mouth before he answered. "He is mending." Crumbled bits of biscuit flew out with his words.

"Good. We will see him before we leave this morning." John glanced around the Hall, empty except for his own men. "Has anyone seen Arthur?"

Peter's attention was now fixed on John. "What do you need to see Arthur for?"

The man's suspicious tone couldn't be missed. John lifted one eyebrow in answer and pursed his lips. "The condition of the village, Peter."

"Mayhap we can meet him with you?" Peter patted Mark's back and nodded enthusiastically. Mark frowned. He obviously did not understand the strange suggestion.

John shook his head. "I told him we would speak today."

"That was before you wanted to cut his head off his shoulders." Peter glanced around as he spoke.

Mark shoved another biscuit into his mouth. Shaking his head as he chewed, he finally answered. "Is there fomefing amiff?" Taking a generous gulp of the cider, he burped loudly.

John snorted again. "No. Mayhap I can see him later."

"It hasn't concerned you overmuch to this point," Peter reprimanded him with his tone.

"You have made your point. Mark, have you adequately stuffed yourself?"

Standing only as high as John's chin, Mark nodded, patting his stomach. "I have, my lord. I will take you to the boy."

The lanes were still empty at this early hour, and John was glad to have a moment to consider how he should approach this attempted sabotage. Certainly the lad should not suffer because of it. He wasn't the culprit. John could make financial reparations and possibly give him a different job at the castle if he was maimed beyond hope. John preferred to have people working rather than living on handouts. The whole incident did not make a very good first impression of him or his soldiers.

They needed to win the family over.

A man with long, scraggly hair was at the front door of a clean little cottage, dipping his wooden ladle into the rain barrel. Mark tipped his head toward the man and spoke in quiet tones. "That's the boy's father. Anton." John turned a questioning eye to Mark who shrugged his shoulder. It was an odd name.

"Hail, sir," John called out as they approached the man. He immediately bowed to his lord and master. "How fares your son this day?"

"My lord, he has slept through the night. I thank you for your concern. Your man here brought a generous helping from the castle to fill his stomach last night. Thank you again, Sir Mark."

Mark smiled. John appreciated Mark's gesture. Normans really were not monsters. He just needed to make sure these people realized that.

"Yes, we are all very sorry that your son was injured."

"Oh, my lord, it was an accident is all. The boy knows that."

Mark and Anton exchanged glances, and John could see that already a friendship, or at the very least mutual respect, was growing between these two. Good. One less thing for John to worry about.

"If you want for anything, please come to me."

Gesturing to the darkened doorway behind him, the man said, "Would you care to come see him?"

"Is he awake then?"

"Well, no, but he could be awakened for you, my lord."

John smiled warmly at the man's genuine gesture of hospitality. "No, let your son sleep for now. I will come again." He grasped the man's hand as he spoke. "Speedy recovery to him."

"Yes, my lord."

The burden seemed lighter on John's shoulders as he passed back along the lane, stopping just inside the barn. "Mayhap this will not be so bad."

Peter came out leading John's horse. "It went well then?"

"It did. The boy's father seems to be a good man. He does not seem to harbor any undue hostility toward us."

Mark answered after retrieving his own mount. "It was the damndest thing." He rubbed his horses flank as he spoke. "My leather halter had been replaced by one made of rope and I'm not sure why."

"That is strange." Peter did not elaborate but met John's eyes. John knew that until he decided to say something himself, Peter would never mention anything they suspected. Not even to Mark.

Leading the horses into the outer bailey, John passed by the man from the garden the day before. "Good morrow," John said.

Perceval dipped his head in respect. "My lord. How fare ye this day?"

"I am well," John answered, continuing on with Peter and Mark on either side.

"Pray you stay that way." It took John a moment to realize what the man had said. Peter and Mark showed no indication that they'd heard him at all. Stopping his horse, John turned to see the man just standing in the road. He was looking down, kicking a small stone back and forth.

"Go on ahead." John handed off his horse to Mark. "I will come to you anon," John said and headed back to the man.

"Did I hear you right?"

"Mayhap you did." Perceval turned half toward John as he spoke.

"Have you something to say to me? Please say it directly."

Perceval looked around the area as if searching for something. He spit on the ground, wiped his nose and finally faced John. "Did you find the Lady Rowena?"

"I did." John knew now why the man had reacted as if he'd had two heads when he asked about his wife. "You could have mentioned that she was the young lady who'd just left."

"You don't recognize your own wife?" John detected a Scottish lilt to his voice.

"It had been awhile."

Perceval looked down at the stone, shaking his head in bewilderment. After a moment's pause he spoke again. "Perhaps it's been too long, my lord."

"You have my ear."

"Some here have made their own plans while the Lady Rowena waited for you."

The man's obtuseness was beginning to get irritating. "Some have, have they?"

Judging by the lopsided grin on Perceval's face, he didn't miss John's sarcasm. "Aye."

"Care to share?"

Perceval looked around again and moved closer to John. "It's not a laughing matter, my lord. I heard say that your days as lord here are numbered."

"Are you threatening me?" John pulled back, a little unsure of this man and his point.

"Not me. And it's not you I worry about. 'Tis the Lady Rowena. She's not been safe while you were gone."

Immediately alert, John considered how she could have been threatened. She was here unprotected without him. Had there been visitors that were a threat? Had people made threats against her directly?

Thoroughly frustrated at his lack of information, John gave vent to his irritation. "Speak plain, man! I would not have Lady Rowena hurt in any way. Where does the threat come from?"

"From within the castle."

They heard the footsteps from down the lane before Arthur emerged into the open. Perceval quickly passed on as if he and John had not been speaking at all. John schooled his features to cover his worry before Arthur could see it.

"Good day, my lord." Arthur spoke as he passed John, his head held high.

"Arthur," John called to the man effectively stopping him. "Have you a moment?" He fought to hide his irritation with this man. He resented having to bring his concerns to Arthur but there was no one else he could ask.

"Certainly, my lord." Arthur seemed reluctant as he walked slowly back to stand beside John.

Good. John felt the same way.

"Is it the maps you'd like to see?"

"No, I'm leaving with my men and want to make sure the castle is well guarded."

Arthur stood taller as if he had been insulted. "Guarded against what in particular?"

"Anyone who would make trouble for us here."

Arthur frowned before he answered him. "Yes, my lord."

"My thanks. Oh, and you will no longer need to see to the accounts."

Arthur frowned. "My lord?"

"Lady Rowena will take her rightful place as my wife and see to the stores and all that entails."

"Yes, my lord."

John watched the man swagger away. How could William have placed such a pompous ass in charge of the area? Certainly there was more to the situation than John knew about. There had to be. He would find out soon enough. Searching the area, there was no sign of Perceval so John went on to join his men.

Chapter Nine

After having to *ask* for the key to the stores for the past eight years, Rowena was a woman with a mission searching out the long-nosed steward that Arthur had appointed under direct orders from the king.

The man was quickly located lounging on the bench in the Hall and in the way of the servants who needed to put the room back in order. His eyes were assessing each of the women as they crossed before him. Her irritation sparked, and she walked right up to him.

"Joshua, there you are." *In the way again I see.*

He stood up. "Aye, my lady."

Eye level with Rowena, she couldn't be sure if the action was meant to be respectful or intimidate. A Norman placed in authority over her usually held a definite air of smugness and superiority. Today she had recourse. She squared her shoulders.

"My lord has decided I may be the keeper of my own keys."

His face flushed as he mumbled over the objection. "But...I don't know...I need to..."

She narrowed her eyes, her jaw tight. "I said my lord has ordered it."

Despite her determined stance, past instances such as these had hurriedly erupted into major confrontations. Without knowing John's exact whereabouts, Rowena felt her confidence dissipating.

"Be quick about it, man." Peter came up from behind Rowena, presumably from the kitchen area and stood beside her. His tone brooked no questions.

Rowena breathed a sigh of relief when the steward fumbled for the keys tied around his waist, unable to get the things removed quickly enough.

The steward tried to hand the keys first to Peter but he shook his head, arms crossed about his chest. With great reluctance he placed them in Rowena's waiting palm. She tipped her head dismissively and the man departed. She glanced at Peter, a smile on her lips but found him frowning down at her. She swallowed before she spoke.

"I thank you for your assistance."

"It is the least John would expect of me."

"And yet I sense reluctance from you."

Peter bowed his head. "My apologies, my lady. That you should sense my reluctance speaks of my own shortcomings. Certainly not a reflection of how you deserve to be treated."

Something about the way he said the words gave her pause. John had told him of her encounters with the guards before their wedding. Did the man doubt her as well?

"Did you have something you wished to ask me?" she asked.

A slight curl to his lips made him look much younger. "My apologies again, my lady. I have...had questions about the situation here. However, I do not believe our lord would appreciate me broaching the subject with you."

Her ire raised, she fought down the urge to defend herself. She had just won a huge battle and this was a moot point. She knew what happened. Whether or not they chose to believe her was irrelevant and not worth the struggle. She began to move but his gentle hand on her arm stopped her.

"I would like you to know that my lord does not deal idly with any threat to what is his."

Here we go again. Yes, he owned her.

"He would give his dying breath to defend you. Do not doubt it."

Peter turned toward the gate and continued out toward the stables.

Her breath caught in her throat. John would defend her with his life? Perhaps her husband was not her owner but her protective knight. Saxon or Norman, the difference had yet to be determined.

Rowena continued on to the closets and outbuilding that held an abundance of supplies. Along with the inventory of the stores and cleaning out what had been left to rot, she found all well-kept under lock and key. It was clear, however, that Arthur's interest was not in keeping up with the tally and even the armory was ill-kept.

Too proud to ask directly the whereabouts of her husband, it wasn't until before the evening meal two days later, exhausted but happy that the Great Hall again smelled of clean rushes and fall lavender, that Rowena learned her husband had left the castle proper. Retreating to the privacy of her bedchamber rather than dine alone again, she felt the loss of knowing that her anticipation of the last few days had been for naught. He would not be surprising her, finding her setting his castle to rights because he was not here. The despair overcame her when she realized she missed his company. Had she once again been abandoned?

"No, my lady, it is not the same. Your husband is seeing to the villagers. He is fulfilling the requirements of his station. That is all." Joan tried to reassure her.

Rowena pouted at the table in her room. "He didn't even say goodbye."

"Are you sure he was not trying to say goodbye the last time you saw him?"

Rowena raised an indignant brow at Joan. "I know exactly what he was trying to do."

Joan looked down at her sewing before she finally spoke again. "Did you not want to?" Her voice was quiet in the room. The burning logs hissed as if in answer to such an absurd question.

"I do not know," Rowena answered just as quietly, her own emotions still in turmoil. What *did* she want? She needed rest.

"You knew well enough when he wasn't here."

Rowena had often gone on little rants when she felt particularly lonely and put upon. Not allowed to act as lady of the manor left her with too much time on her hands. During her bouts of selfishness, she spoke of her abandonment by a husband who had total say over her but didn't even show his face. What Joan didn't know was that Rowena had come close to asking Arthur to be her lover, desperate to overcome her loneliness. She had spent the next two weeks in the chapel, three times a day, asking for forgiveness for her transgression.

"Now that he is here, though..." Rowena stopped midsentence.

"It is just shyness, my lady. He is your husband." Joan took her hands in a motherly gesture. Her voice was quietly reassuring. "You do not need to be afraid of him. He is ordered by God to love you and care for you, as his own body even."

Rowena snorted at the suggestion. "Where has he been then? Do you know he questioned me about Arthur?"

Joan's tone quickly changed to disapproval. "Arthur is too protective of you."

"Someone has had to be." Rowena knew her defense was weak. True, she had been left unprotected but surrounded by Norman wolves since the death of her father. Her only memory of that day was crying over his blood-soaked body. These wolves would as soon devour her as look at her. Remembering the cypress tree, Rowena was almost afraid to ask but knew she had to. "Was it John who told you my mother's tree was diseased?"

"Oh, no, my lady!" Joan was quite adamant. "I am sure the man had lighter hair."

"You are sure?"

"Well, I am almost sure. I do not really remember. What reason would he have?"

"Because he hates all things Saxon?"

Joan frowned as she considered this. She began to slowly shake her head as she spoke. "No, your husband does not seem to harbor any malice against the Saxons.   Why the rest of the Normans amongst us do seems strange to me."

Rowena blew a puff of air in exasperation. She knew nothing about her husband. Joan was correct in her assessment of John's apparent fairness to the Saxons. Word of his visit to the injured boy had come to her. She'd swelled with pride that her husband would care for her people so.

"I do not want to turn Arthur completely away from me. I need him as an ally in case John does not stay." Rowena struggled with how she felt about the man who had been so very protective of her.

"I would not suggest you count him as an ally against your husband and his people. If he is inappropriately attentive, he may find himself at odds with his lordship."

"What would make you think his lordship would care?"

"Do you not understand that is why he questioned you about Arthur?"

"I thought it was more that he owned me and no one else could have me. Even if that meant that no one had me." Rowena pushed herself away from the table, her agitation getting the better of her. If what Peter had told her was true, and she had no reason to doubt his sincerity, John would defend her always.

Pacing the small area like a confined animal, she finally paused to look out the window. The dreary day reflected her feelings, rain threatening at any moment. "Do you know when my husband will be returning?"

"I am back now."

John stood in the doorway handsomely dressed as befit the new Lord of Essex. Rowena's breath caught in her throat. She looked away before the immense pleasure she felt at his return showed on her face.

Joan quickly gathered her sewing and removed herself from the room, closing the door behind her.

"Will you attend me, my lady?"

Rowena went to him and helped him remove his surcoat before seeing to the heavier chainmail. He smelled like horses and leather. Manly. Rowena tried not to close her eyes as she drank in the intoxicating smell of him. Why would a dirty, sweaty man make her feel so light headed? She stepped away when she realized why, the chainmail slipping forward off his arms. His hooded eyes told her that he knew what she was feeling.

"Is there a problem?" His deep voice seemed to reverberate through her body.

Quickly putting the heavy material down, she headed to the door. "I will order a bath for you."

"Wait."

Rowena froze with her hand on the latch and heard him coming closer to her. He stood close behind her, his breath soft against her cheek.

"Yes?" *Be done with this*. Her body yearned for his arms to pull her against him, to feel his kiss again. She licked her lips.

"Why are you leaving in such a hurry?" His hand lightly touched the side of her head as he spoke, pushing her hair away from her face. He leaned in closer to her exposed ear. A responding shiver ran down her body. "Are you afraid of me?"

She backed up to the door with a thud and faced him. Her pulse was racing as she lied. "No, my lord. Methinks you have a rather strong odor about you and I would have you take a bath before the evening meal."

John backed away quickly, his eyes flying open. "I am sorry if I offend you. Please see to the bath."

Rowena felt only slightly guilty when he turned away from her, standing like a lost little boy in the middle of the room.

§

John rubbed his scalp with his hand then realized that too was dirty. He'd been offending her with his smell? He could have sworn there was desire in her eyes. Damn. Would he get nowhere with this woman?

Dropping down on the stool in disgust, he grabbed at the mud covered boot. Another reason to see him as dirty. He flung it across the room. It hit the wall with a satisfactory thud and the second one followed suit. Standing up to remove his breeches, he pulled at the belt viciously. Perhaps he was just wrong about her. Maybe there was no deep-seated passion for him. Perhaps she's already had many lovers and doesn't want to be saddled with a husband. This was just insane. His breeches fell to his feet and he heard the gasp behind him.

Turning toward the sound, Rowena's eyes seemed glued to his nakedness. Her gaze traveled the length of his legs and stopped a bit short of his navel. Perhaps being near him had done nothing for her, but he was clearly aroused. She appeared to be in shock at the sight. Not exactly what he would have expected from a tried woman.

For a split second, John had thought of covering himself to ease her consternation then thought better of it. Slowly, he pulled his feet from the cloth puddled around his legs. His gaze stayed on Rowena's face as she stared at him. He stood akimbo. It was time she face his desire for her.

"Rowena?"

She dragged her eyes up to his face and he saw her embarrassment in the crimson red of her cheeks.

"Is there something else you needed?" The color suffused her face as she mutely shook her head and started to back away. "No. Wait."

John got to the door just short of grabbing her and she was gone. The women in the hall giggled at his nakedness when he stopped in the doorway. He pushed the door shut and sat again on the stool. Damn. She looked so frightened. Why did he have to embarrass her? Shoving his legs back into his pants, he grabbed the rest of his clothes and huffed out of the door, slamming it behind him.

Chapter Ten

Rowena tossed and turned through the night. Just as she dozed off, virile men would prance through her exhausted mind, all looking like John. Finally throwing back the covers, she sat up and stared at the metal tub that still sat in front of the fire, its water cold.

Where had John gone when he left the room? She had acted like an idiot. She'd never seen a man so...aroused before. She could not help her reaction. It was menacing to say the least.

She wrapped herself in her woolen blanket and hobbled to the window. The cloudy night gave off no light at all and even the normal sound of crickets and frogs was missing.

Leaning her forehead against the cold stone wall, she closed her eyes. When she was a girl, things had always seemed so simple. Her parents loved her and protected her. Her large family of uncles and cousins gathered often at this very place. All gone now. Dead. She was unsure about her cousins but she assumed they, too, had died in the fighting.

It was not enough that the Normans came with their huge horses and trampled the people, they kept coming back to quell any resistance. Who would resist? They were the victors. It would be foolish to believe the Saxons could ever win against their superior forces. She was tired of all the loneliness. The idea that John would be her defender had sparked something deep inside her. So why would she think John could be that to her? Because he desired her? That didn't mean he cared, just that he could rut like an animal.

The heat rushed into her face at the memory. She tried to erase the image of him as he stood naked in the middle of this very room. She desired him, too.

Now even Arthur could not give her solace. If John did not choose to stay, she would be even more alone than she had imagined before his return. She hunkered down beside the dying embers and poked them with the iron stick until a flame burst through the log. Sitting on the stool, she stared into the red, blue flames and tried to think of a way to live the rest of her life with no one to love her.

No. She didn't want to do it. It was wrong for her to think of Arthur as a way out of her loneliness but it was also wrong for her husband to not see to her needs. Not just physical but companionship, safety...all the things she needed. Could she really take him to her bed? It was acceptable, was it not, when one's husband refused to do his duty?

Or was she being like the serpent in the garden asking "are you sure God said you could not eat the fruit of this tree"?

She paced the length of the room. She stopped when she noticed the light coming through the window. Sunrise at last. The footfall in the hall gave her pause. She opened her door as quietly as possible, and she saw Arthur's back as he was passing by her door. He turned at the movement and their eyes met.

"Were you at my door, Arthur?"

"I was, my lady. I worry about you." He took the step that closed the distance between them. She could see the desire in his eyes. Her lungs expanded with a deep breath of resignation.

Someone wants my company.

Stepping back, she opened the door to him.

§

John's hand gripped the dagger at his waist. His blood frozen in his veins as he watched Rowena's door slowly shut. He would have sworn he was wrong about her. Torn between the desire to rip the door from its hinges and tear her lover apart with his bare hands as she watched or flinging her own worthless body from the window, John just stood, rooted to the darkened stairs where he watched.

Should he wait and see how long the man remained with his wife? Should he confront them with the proof having seen her welcome him into her bedchamber. His head hurt. This was not going as he had planned. He had come back from another night at the Owl and Thistle with the hope of spending intimate time with his wife. He had thought of the stories he would tell her to make her laugh. He wanted her to see him as he really was.

What wasted ideas.

Who was he? An orphan boy raised by a bastard king.

John turned back the way he had come. He entered the Great Hall to find Peter already preparing for the day's journey to visit the other villages.

"Good night?" Peter smiled as he rolled the blanket tightly around his belongings.

John grunted as he continued past his friend.

"John?" Peter followed him into the kitchen but stilled when he saw the look of murderous rage. "What is amiss?"

"I was wrong in trusting my wife. She has just now taken her lover into her bedchamber." Pouring a cup of aged cider from the pitcher, John dropped to the hard wooden bench beside the cooking fire. "She is a whore."

Peter looked around before he spoke in hushed tones. "John, have a care. This is Rowena's land. These are her people. *You* are the Norman."

Noticing the servants for the first time at the work table a short distance away, John struggled to keep his feelings in check. He swallowed down his irritation with the cider before he spoke.

"I would have a hard time forgetting that fact." The cider sloshed down his chin.

"It did not go that badly yesterday." Peter's eyes remained on John. "The villagers could have been much more unreceptive."

"Much more unreceptive? Is that a polite way of saying they could have just killed me on the spot? Would that have been 'more unreceptive'?"

John went to stand beside the fire with his back to the room. He watched the flames greedily licking at the dry wood. The scent of honey bread and fresh cream permeated the space. All he could see was Rowena's upturned face in the throes of passion. Smashing his fist into the iron rack beside him, the rack flew back against the wall. Crocks of butter crashed onto the floor.

"Who do these people think that I am? Their lackey?" John faced Peter who quickly backed out of harm's way. The workers at the table did the same. "Do they think they can just violate my property?"

Peter took a step toward his friend, "John, perhaps..."

"No." John stepped away, his arms pulled from Peter's reach. "This is enough. Gather the men. We will put to rest any idea that I may be ousted and that William will not remain the rightful king once and for all."

"Perhaps..." Peter paused.

John glared at him, waiting for his answer.

"...you should just see Rowena before we leave? Confirm that what you believe is the truth?"

John glanced toward the ceiling wondering if she was indeed just over his head at that very moment moaning for Arthur. The man would be dead if he went there now.

He considered Peter's suggestion. Was not knowing even worse than murder? It would be better to know. And the man deserved to be killed. John headed back to the stairs taking them two at a time.

Rowena's door stood open as he slowly approached it. He was too late to catch them in the act. She was still wearing her bed clothes. Her maid rummaged noisily through her chest of clothes when John stalked into the room.

"Leave us."

Joan jumped at his voice and cowered as she passed by him.

Rowena turned to look at him. He searched her face. There were no visible signs of the encounter. Her lips were not red or puffy from passionate kisses. There were no marks that he could see on her face or hands. Perhaps beneath her bed gown there would be visible signs. Dare he order her to strip? Even in his rage he knew that would not be proper. He did not want to humiliate her. Why did he care for her feelings when she was playing him for the fool? The answer startled him. Because she was his.

"You return," Rowena spoke firmly to him, raising his ire at her audacity. Not the response he would have expected from an adulteress with much to hide.

"So it seems." When she would have turned away from him, he grabbed her arm to still her movement. "How did you sleep?"

Her silver eyes showed confusion at the question. "Well enough." Dark circles showed she was lying.

"I see." He was uncertain whether he wanted to pull her up against him and taste her lips once more or shove her cruelly away from him. He let go of her arm. She remained where she was.

"Will you be breaking your fast with me then?" Her eyes looked almost hopeful. Was the puffiness from lack of sleep or crying?

"I am leaving." He was sure he saw disappointment this time.

"When?" She looked down at the ground. Afraid of the answer?

"Immediately." He needed to know if he was right with what he thought she was feeling. He had been so wrong about her passions the night before. He was probably wrong now. "Do you wish me to stay?"

Her head snapped up and she seemed to be searching his face. What was she looking for? "Your choice, my lord. Whatever you desire." She blanched and he supposed it was her choice of words when she turned her reddening face away in embarrassment.

"You are what I desire." John wished he could take those words back. He did not want her to know how she made him feel, how deeply she affected him.

"You have me." Her words sounded breathy, her hands gripped tightly at her side.

"It would appear I do not." He watched for any shift, any acknowledgment that she feared being discovered but he saw none.

"It would appear then that you do not desire me." She lifted her nose slightly. Defiance.

"I say it was quite apparent that I do, but then you rushed out of the room last night."

Her eyes rounded as if with pain at the statement.

He did not want to hurt her but he could not say why not. It was certainly what she deserved.

"I was..." She glanced again at the ground. "...shocked at the sight."

"At my arousal?"

She nodded slightly but did not look at him.

He moved in closer, gently grasping her chin, tipping her head so he could see into her eyes. "You have never seen a man's arousal before?"

Tears trembled in her lashes and his heart went out to her. She shook her head slowly, a single tear falling down each cheek."I have not." Her voice was quiet.

"Then I apologize at offending you with my desire." He actually believed she was telling him the truth. Then why did she open the door for Arthur so easily? His confusion was complete. He dropped his hand from her face and turned away.

"At the king's order, I am to survey my lands and make my presence known. I will return when I have completed my duty."

He slammed the door behind him.

He did not look back.

Chapter Eleven

As had become her morning habit, Rowena visited the chapel to ask forgiveness for her transgressions and to pray for a peaceful existence with her husband. She did not ask for forgiveness for the deep desire and longing she had for her husband. That was acceptable. God had created her to have those feelings for him. She asked for forgiveness in thinking she had any desire for Arthur. Uncovering her head as she exited the stone building, Rowena was impatient to be on her way and left Joan to catch up with her.

She ambled down the worn path. Three men ahead of her caught her eye. They were shabbily dressed, nearly blocking the road. With sudden alarm she glanced around the area and realized how unwise she had been to go out without a guard. The area was completely secluded. Joan had accompanied her to the chapel but they both knew she was not an adequate defense against the rougher elements. In the past, it had been Arthur who had been their protection. It was so awkward between them now that she preferred to go alone. One man stepped toward her and the others seemed to keep watch up the alley. Covered with a dark hood, the man was not anyone Rowena recognized. Her heart beat loudly in fear.

"Rowena." His raspy voice whispered her name. There was something familiar about it.

Torn between running away to safety and confronting the hooded man, Rowena chose the latter. She squared her shoulders and spoke with authority. "What is it you want?"

"Do you not recognize your own kin?" He pulled back the hood enough to show his face.

"Cousin!" Her fear was replaced with relief then delight at seeing one of her own family. She embraced him, holding him tight. His strong arms about her seemed to speak of family loyalty and protection, both which were no longer a part of her life.

"I feared all were dead." Her voice was muffled against his firm shoulder as tears ran unchecked. She released him with great reluctance.

"All but me." He took her by her fingertips, stretching out her arms. "Our little Rowena has blossomed into a beautiful woman."

He gently kissed her cheek and embraced her again. She closed her eyes and allowed herself to feel again the protection of family love and acceptance, fleeting as it was.

"Where have you been?" she asked. He settled her hand in the crook of his arm and led her toward the alley where the other two men waited.

He surprised her when he put his finger to his lip. She obeyed.

"Malcolm," he addressed the taller of the two men, "what say you find us something to eat?" Turning to include the smaller man, a swarthy blonde with a thick white scar down his cheek, he asked. "Roland?"

The two men exchanged glances then accepted the coin Leofrid held up to them. Once they were out of earshot, Rowena repeated her question.

"I have been hiding. There is a price for my capture."

"I do not believe they think you are still alive."

He raised one slender brow. "Oh, they know I'm alive. They hunt me like a dog." He shook his head as if to clear his mind of some unpleasantness. She could only guess at his hardships. Leofrid's mouth tightened into a grim smile. He tipped his head to one side. "How fare ye?"

He glanced around, assessing the area as his eyes took in everything around him. His wariness sent a chill up her spine. Rowena hesitated, unsure how to answer him but his suddenly probing glance caused her to blush. "I fare well enough."

"You've been bedding the Norman, haven't you!?" It was more an accusation than a question, and he did seem to find humor in it.

Rowena gasped. "Of course not!"

His eyes widened in surprise.

"Are you not wed to one?"

Her embarrassment deepened when she realized he had been teasing her.

"He has not bedded you yet? Is there something wrong with the man?"

"I cannot say." Rowena was mortified at discussing these intimate details of her married life with her cousin, no matter how close they had been as children. Leofrid's instant defensiveness on her behalf warmed her heart.

"Ah, then why would he not gladly and thankfully accept the wonderful gift he received from his king?"

She seriously doubted that John thought of her as any kind of prize and she frowned at him. "I cannot say."

Leofrid had always been very considerate of her and she could see it now in the way he looked at her. He took her hand and kissed it lightly. "You are a gift, Cousin, and he is very blessed to have you to wife."

She did not feel wanted when her husband left her untouched but she thought it best not to mention that detail.

"You are very kind." Smiling, she could almost believe her whole family was alive and well and just waiting around the corner. "I have missed you!"

"And I you."

Rowena glanced down the alley where the other two men had disappeared. She was concerned for Leofrid as well. "Are those two friends of yours?"

He shook his head, a disgusted look on his face. "A wanted man has no friends. I am thankful I have found men to join forces with so that I am able to survive."

"It is that bad?"

He raised his eyebrows as if to ask if she was really that naive.

"Is there any way I can be of assistance to you?"

He smirked at her in response. "Not yet but I wanted to talk to you, to see if you were well. And I do see you are well, if a little sad."

Was she so transparent? Maybe just to her cousin.

"I must be off. I do not want my 'friends' to see you with me again. They are ruthless and have been known to take noblewomen in exchange for ransom. I would not want to see that happen to you." He patted her hand reassuringly. "I am afraid ransom is not all they take from the women. I cannot really control them. They don't know who I am, and I want to keep it that way. Take care, Rowena. I do not want to see you traveling unaccompanied again."

He sounded so like her own father, a lump grew in her throat.

Kissing her lightly on each cheek, he smiled, his green eyes sparkling. "Goodbye for now."

"Goodbye for now." He headed in the same direction the other two had gone.

She fought back the sadness that threatened to engulf her. Alone again. She quickly went out to where more people milled around, then took the road leading up to the castle. Her cousin looked terrible. She prayed he was not ill. Her heart swelled with the satisfaction of knowing she was not the sole survivor of the Godwin family.

The days dragged by. With each group of men entering through the town gate, she would stand at the window in her room and search for any sign of John. When the Norman men came into the Great Hall, she would stand close by, listening for any word of him as they talked amongst themselves. She could understand their language better than she could speak it, but much of what they said never made sense. She listened just for his name. There was nothing. She was convinced he would not return.

Alone in the garden, the bright sun bleached the scene into colorless drabness. Butterflies flitted by, creating dark shadows against the bushes. Where she had once seen only the peace and beauty of the surrounding, she now saw a vast space of emptiness.

"My lady?"

She startled at the sound, turned and found Arthur standing where the cypress had once been, the dirt around him raw and exposed. With his head uncovered, his thick red hair resting on his shoulder, he looked hopeful. Rowena wondered what news could leave such a happy countenance on the man. The last time she had seen him, she had been contemplating turning against her vows and accepting a long overdue overture of love. She took a deep breath and steeled herself for whatever he was about to say.

"Yes, Arthur?"

"I have come to bid you goodbye."

Tipping her head, she considered why he would appear so happy about leaving her if he truly was in love with her. Waiting, he offered no additional explanation. She finally broke the heavy silence. "I do not understand."

"I have orders to head north at once."

"These orders are from my husband, then?" She didn't miss his disappointment at her question. He knew how she felt about her husband. Arthur had tried long and hard to distract her from him.

When she let him into her room that morning, she went willingly into his arms and found them lacking. She felt nothing, no passion, no desire. Her desire was for her husband alone, which was shocking to her as well.

The memory of his soft hand caressing her and his lips against her own brought to her again the repulsion she had experienced at Arthur's touch. He had seen it, too. His face had distorted into a mask of rage when he left her that morning. She had never even seen him angry before that.

"No, my lady." He spoke through clenched teeth. "They are the king's orders."

69

"I see." She cast her eyes down to spare him her own feelings of disappointment. Word, any word, from her husband would have been welcome at this time.

"I leave immediately." He held his head proudly, and Rowena felt great sympathy for him. She had hurt him so badly but had not meant to. She took a step toward him and made to reach out to him, but when he stiffened, she dropped her hand to her side. No, he did not want her touch now. "I am sorry, Arthur."

He closed his eyes in distress, struggling with himself. His emotions in check, he finally met her gaze. "I came only to bid you goodbye, my lady."

He turned away from her, strode to the garden gate and was gone.

"Good bye, my friend." She said the words on a whisper, and the bushes rustled with the breeze in answer.

The sweet smell of the late summer flowers wafted up to her. She took a deep breath, wrapping her arms around herself. Despite attempts to keep busy with the garden, helping in the kitchen, maintaining the stores, and keeping an inventory of her holdings, she knew the loneliness would not be filled. Wallowing would help nothing. If she was to be alone, she needed to be strong. She just did not want to be alone.

To add to her loneliness, the Lady Katherine came to call not long after John's departure. Her childhood friend came yearly for a visit. She brought news to Rowena of all her womanly accomplishments from her betrothal to one of the only remaining Saxons to the intimate details of married life.

Giles had somehow found favor with the new king and been allowed to keep his titles and his lands. He was a powerful Saxon accepted into the Norman nobility. He also doted on his wife. With each visit Rowena was reminded of how much her life had changed and how many of her dreams would never see fulfillment.

Rowena had hesitated a hair's breadth at the sight of her extremely pregnant friend before she embraced her. Her voice sounded stilted when she spoke.

"It is so good to see you, my dear. Look at you so big with child." Rowena's hand hovered over the belly, wanting to feel for the child that lay hidden inside but afraid she would burst out with the tears that threatened to engulf her.

Katey appeared to notice nothing and placed Rowena's hand against her side just as the babe gave a powerful lurch. "My sweet that was a kick. He will be strong."

"He? You believe you carry a son?" How wonderful to have a son. Rowena choked back a cry, determined not to let her dear friend see her own distress. "How happy you must be."

"I believe it is a boy. Giles believes it also. Oh," she quickly reached for Rowena's hand again, "that was an elbow, methinks." Katey smiled and Rowena tried to be happy at her friend's total contentment.

The two sat side by side at Katey's insistence, settling in front of the fire. She held both of Rowena's hands and spoke as if their lives were so similar.

"We are verily blessed. Giles is just the Saxon I had dreamed of and he is a good—" Katey winked at Rowena, "strong man."

Katey loved to speak of her husband's prowess as a lover. The talk made Rowena uncomfortable. She did not want her virgin state to be known. It demonstrated her unwanted status.

Rowena smiled and accepted the wine and cheese brought in by the young kitchen girl, Lydia. She was a favorite helper of Rowena's, always listening attentively to her stories. Rowena enjoyed telling stories from her childhood as she worked. They were the Saxon stories that had been passed down for hundreds of years. Some were true, some not so true. But the child was a delightful listener, and it helped Rowena pass the time.

"Thank you, Lydia."

Offering the repast to her friend, Rowena tried to change the subject. "I am glad you are happy. You verily glow."

Katey's flawless skin looked like it had been kissed by the sun with the slightest blush at her cheeks. Her thick brown hair was wavier than usual and it shone with health and vitality. Giles entered the Hall and even when he was speaking to some of the Norman men, his eyes scanned the room, resting finally on his wife. He quickly finished with the men and all but bounded toward them. Katey heard him, and when their eyes met, their happiness in each other was apparent. Rowena's heart lurched at her own desire for such total contentment.

"Greetings, Lady Rowena. How fare ye?" Finally tearing his gaze from his wife, Giles placed a wet kiss on the back of Rowena's hand.

"I am well, sir. I see you have much to celebrate." Rowena wiped the wetness from her hand when Giles moved to sit beside his wife, kissing her cheek.

"That we do." He was beaming as his hand went protectively to the large swell of his wife's belly. "My wife holds up very well, much to my liking."

When his hand slipped lower, Rowena looked away in embarrassment. Like many men she saw, Giles was not afraid of crude, familial gestures with his wife in front of others. Their bawdiness did not show a care for the privacy of the intimacies they shared.

"What of you?"

Rowena's head snapped up at the question. She could not help that her eyes were wide with shock. Was he actually asking if she was to John's liking?

Giles and Katey burst into laughter, and her face turned hot with embarrassment.

"Be off with you, Giles, stop torturing our host." Katey pushed her husband affectionately, and he stood beside her at the bench.

"Will your husband be returning anon?" he asked.

Rowena struggled for composure when all she wanted to do was scream at this man. What right did he have to question her about the intimacy of her marriage? Or was he simply asking how she was? Heat flooded her face again, and she stumbled over her answer, "Sir, I am... I am not sure when my husband will complete his duties. I have not... I have not heard."

Giles and Katey exchanged quick glances.

"I am sorry I will not be here for his return." Giles kissed his wife. "I beg your leave, my lady. I need to see to the horses and gather the supplies I have brought for your husband. The grape yield this fall was especially good."

Giles winked at his wife and removed himself. Although disappointed at having missed John, Giles seemed contented just to see the smile on his wife's face.

"He does love me so." Katey leaned in closer and added, "He does not seem to be able to get enough of me."

Rowena's jaw dropped at the admission. "Even in your condition? Is that safe?"

Katey tilted her head and frowned, all but scolding her. She was going to make an excellent mother. "I will not disappoint my husband, Rowena. I will not have my husband seeking another for his pleasure."

Duly chastised, Rowena said, "Of course not, Katey."

The firm set of her lips was unmistakable. Katey was determined to not lose her husband's attention merely because she was with child. A change of subject was in order.

"Will you be staying for supper then? And overnight perhaps? Can I see to your rooms?"

"That would be lovely. I was so looking forward to meeting your Norman. Will he be back soon?"

Over the years, Rowena had needed to make up stories to explain her missing husband. She did not want it known that he had abandoned her.

The implication of ownership and desire in Katey's question caused a catch in Rowena's throat. "I am not privy to that information. He has a lot of land to cover."

Katey frowned before she answered. "That's true. The Godwinson's legacy is not easily managed. We will stay just the one night, I am sorry to say. Giles prefers his own home and does not travel well. To me," Katey smiled warmly, "this is just like home with all the time I spent here as a child."

"I treasure the memories, Katey. Things were much simpler then."

Giles returned to the Hall and begged leave for him and his wife to both rest after their long travels and to prepare for the evening meal. Rowena suspected from their giggling that there was a double meaning to his request for privacy. The whisper into his wife's ear and the possessive way he wrapped his arm about her waist as the two ascended the stairs seemed to confirm her suspicions. It had been a very trying visit.

With nowhere else to go, Rowena now sat in front of the fire. She glanced at her hand, still able to feel the little foot as it had kicked out from within its mother's womb. She placed her hand on her own middle and rubbed slightly. At least one of them had the life they'd dreamed of.

Chapter Twelve

John brushed the dirt from his knees as he stood beside the decapitated body. On the hill, his men searched amongst the rest of the fallen villagers for any sign of survivors. There did not appear to be any. The houses stood in dark silhouette against the setting sun, the burned out shells still smoking as the last of the fire died out.

Peter shook his head, his voice raw with emotion. "We will be blamed for this as well."

"I believe that is the point." John wiped the soot and sweat from his face. The smoke burned his nostrils. "They were thorough. Not one survivor."

"So they murder their own? That is insane."

"This certainly justifies the villager's total distrust of us."

For weeks now John and his men had traveled hundreds of miles from village to village with nothing to show for it. The overseers were polite enough, always offering him meat and wine for his men, and fodder for the horses, but the people did not trust them. Instead of engaging with the new lord, the tenants shied away from him, averting their gaze, and only answering questions reluctantly. He soon found out why.

On the road to Buckinghamshire, John and his retinue had stopped at an inn to rest but found it filled with angry men. He'd slipped in unseen. In short order John learned what had the villagers so upset. They believed that at the king's bidding, the Normans were laying waste the land, murdering the people, burning their villages, and driving off their livestock. When they spotted John, they stopped talking.

Within a few days John had arrived at one of the devastated villages to see the destruction first hand. It was a village north of the castle. And there were more spread far across his lands, but John always arrived too late, never discovered any sign of who they were, and always found total destruction. To a man, the other villagers blamed the Normans.

John did not appreciate being wrongly accused. Nothing he said could convince them, and he needed to find who was doing this. His frustration with their lack of progress grew. How could he win people over that believed him capable of these things? He wanted the situation settled; he wanted to be home. If his travels brought him nearer to the castle, he wanted nothing more than to go to his wife but he knew the destruction needed to be seen to first.

It was all new to him, this idea of home. To be able to sleep protected from the elements; out of the cold, the rain, the wind, these basic desires satisfied a soldier. John now had unsettling dreams of a soft place to sleep, warm meals, comfortable surroundings and well kept grounds. He also had dreams of the feel of Rowena's hands on him, of her soft voice whispering words of pleasure at his company, and the desire to bear his children. Every morning he awoke with feelings of desolation and longing. He was miserable.

"Here." The shout came from the far end of the field. A soldier struggled with moving one of the bodies. The Normans all ran toward him.

"He is alive?" Peter's voice sounded hopeful, but John tried to keep his own emotions in check. They had been wrong before.

"The buggar was buried under tha' rottin' carcass." All looked to see the maggot covered torso of a man. "Heard him moanin', I did. Gaw, that is disgustin'." The scraggly-haired man with only one front tooth frantically brushed the squirming vermin off his mud encrusted sleeve.

Peter brought the water skin to the lips of the boy he'd uncovered. He looked to be eleven or twelve. His eyes were wide, hauntingly staring at nothing. "Here, son, have some water."

Greedily sucking on the skin, the boy's eyes never focused on them.

"Is he mad?" John whispered to Peter who shrugged uncertainly.

The boy began to shake and the soldiers backed away in fear.

"Remove the bodies," John ordered, worried the closeness of his dead companions may be affecting the boy's state of mind. The soldiers set about lifting and dragging away the victims of the brutal attack. The boy's eyes closed and John reacted with a start, afraid he'd lost his only witness to the atrocities around him.

"I will stay with him," Peter offered.

Sighing, John walked to where a makeshift grave had been dug, the pile of carcasses accumulating at the bottom of the hole. Senseless death. The smoldering buildings were a good sign. It meant they were getting closer to whoever was doing this. They were perhaps two days too late. At the last decimated village, the vultures were already well into their work.

By moonrise, the boy had taken some broth and seemed to be getting better. His fingers had been chopped clean off but Peter had bandaged his hand as best he could. The boy had not said a word. Camped a short distance from the burned out village, the men were hidden just beyond the tree line in case anyone returned to the area.

John sat propped against a log at the edge of the clearing. It was his watch and he was glad for it. His dreams of Rowena were keeping him from getting a good night's rest. The stars twinkled in a clear sky and an owl could be heard close by. The night passed peacefully, but John's mind would not settle.

Seeing Arthur go into her room in the wee hours of the morning could not be explained any other way. John knew that. Yet he struggled to come up with a different explanation. She was a contradiction; one moment the passionate lover and the next the untried virgin. They could not both be true. If she had taken a lover, he would not feel the need to continue as her husband, consummated or not. He could actually be done with her and rightfully take the land that was now his by marriage. The very idea sparked his pulse. He did not want to be separated from her. He wanted her to be his.

Peter joined him, a mug of warm cider in his hand. "Nice night."

John grunted in response.

"Thinking of her again?"

John turned to his friend. He thought he had been so circumspect. Apparently not so much. "How is the boy?"

"He is sleeping."

"Has he said aught?"

"He did wake up and asked me who I was."

A small man came from the woods behind them. "My lord?"

"Yes, Sean?"

"The boy has awakened. He is sitting up and asking questions."

Peter and John followed the man back toward where the small fire still burned. The drawn faces of the soldiers reflected the eerie firelight, their fear of the boy apparent. Perhaps a soldier's worst nightmare was to be left for dead on the battlefield. That this boy had survived such an event awed them and frightened them at the same time.

The boy's eyes went immediately to Peter who smiled at him. John sat beside him. "How fare ye?"

"I am alive. No one will answer me, sir. Are you Normans?"

John met Peter's level gaze before he answered. "We are. Is there aught you require?" An empty bowl sat in his lap and the boy appeared to understand him.

"Normans are not as bad as they say, methinks."

John smiled at his frankness. "What is your name?"

"I am called Aldred."

"Aldred. Do you remember what happened in your village?"

The boy's pained look said he did. John's heart quickened in anticipation of finally getting some answers.

"Aye." The boy looked at the men watching him. "The men...they dressed the same but they didn't sound like you."

They were dressed as Normans. It was intentional, then, they were in disguise hoping to have people believe they were indeed Normans. "Do you remember aught else?"

"Yes. They went into the priest's house first. I heard screaming from Father Anselm and ran to me mum." Aldred's eyes overflowed with tears. "They did terrible things to her. They cut my fingers clear off me hand when I came at them." The boy's mangled hand waived in the air, he seemed mesmerized by the sight of it.

"I'm sorry about your mum." John tried to be patient with the boy. He had been through a lot, but John desperately needed answers.

"One man, he had bright red hair, had these blue eyes that pierced right through me." The boy shivered as if the memory could hurt him. "He looked like a crazed one. He cut the head off of the butcher, he did."

The headless body must have been the butcher. Perhaps a closer look might give them a better idea what he used to do the deed. He had not seen many red-haired men in the area. One sniffing after his wife was enough.

"Do you remember aught else?"

"They sounded like we do."

"You think they were from around here?"

"You are not, right?"

John nodded.

"Then I would say they were."

If this was all the boy knew, then they only had confirmation that their suspicions were correct. They weren't any closer to finding them, though. One of them had red hair. Taking a chance, John smiled at the boy reassuringly.

"It cannot have been easy to wait them out."

"No. The sweat poured off me. The butcher is very heavy. When I awoke to them standing over me, I tried not to move. They thought me dead."

So he had been close enough to hear them talking. He might have heard something that could help them but John did not want to cause him undue pain.

"Were they laughing?"

"Oh no. They were angry. The one man— the red-haired man— yelled at them. He told them they were wretched men and if Leofrid knew they wanted to plunder, he would have their heads."

John patted the boy's shoulder and stood up. Peter put his arm around the boy and told him he was a good help. Leofrid. Was it Godwinson? Weren't they all killed years ago? He ran his hand through his hair. When Peter stood beside him, he saw that he, too, had recognized the name.

"But it cannot be him. He was killed."

"You are right. It cannot be. If he had lived," John measured his words carefully, "would he really stay around? I know Harold is dead, as are his brothers."

"Then where would Leofrid's allegiance lie?" Peter completed his thought. The two turned toward each other. There was only one man who still lived and still desired to be King of England. Canute. He would take great pleasure, no doubt, in daily annoying the current king.

"I must get word to William."

"I will go, John. Mayhap you should return to Rowena. The king will receive me. I will leave without delay."

The thought of Rowena brought turmoil and desire. He couldn't leave the villages unprotected from men who would kill their own just to lay the blame at his feet. "No. I must see to my people. They are under my protection."

"As is Rowena. Philip can see to the villagers. Philip." Peter did not wait for confirmation and John did not gainsay him.

John gave the order. "Break camp at daybreak and see that the villages are protected. Peter travels to the king posthaste."

"I will send reinforcements for you to have a well-protected area around my lands," John added, already gathering his few belongings. "Since I don't know where the local men's loyalty lies, I will send only our men. Do you understand?"

"Yes, my lord."

"The king is two day's ride from here and he will want to see more men added as well. How will we know who to trust?" Peter's question held validity.

"Trust only the ones we have known. No one else."

Chapter Thirteen

As John approached the castle, a group of children played beside the water surrounding the stone edifice. A circle of five little girls and one little red-haired boy walked around in a circle as they sang.

"Ring around, ring around." The little blonde girl sang her heart out, her head tipped back, her mouth gaping open. "Alive-ee live oh."

An auburn-haired child with a smattering of freckles across the bridge of her nose broke away from her friends to stand beside the road as he passed. She smiled.

"Good day, my lord."

He smiled back and tipped his head. He remembered the girl from the first night he had stayed at the Owl and Thistle. She'd left a rose on his pillow before Felicity had hurried her off.

"Thank you again for the rose, Matilda."

The little blonde girl's jaw dropped. She said in a loud whisper, "His lordship knows your name?'

John laughed. He was someone of importance now.

John dismounted and called together the men still remaining at the castle to keep them abreast of what was happening. They needed to be forewarned of the trouble they were facing.

"The attacks are laid at our feet, even if we had nothing to do with them." He looked into each man's eyes, loyalty and honor etched on their heart. "We need to convince the Saxons we are on their side. And that we don't condone this type of treatment."

"My lord, how can we prove it is not us?"

"There is only one way. By looking out for their interests above our own."

The men's gazes did not waiver. They understood what he was asking.

"I need twelve men dispatched immediately. Philip will apprise you of what is needed when you arrive at the camp."

In short order, the men were divided. The remaining thirteen were to remain diligent and especially attentive to any talk around them in case something could be discovered about the attacks.

Entering the Great Hall, John sought out his wife and found her in front of the fire with her head bent over an embroidery frame. As he approached, her quiet humming drifted to him. Stopping a few feet away, he decided to watch her. Her delicate hands nimbly pierced the needlework of green and red vines, carefully working the piece that would one day grace the walls.

Around the hall, on all sides, were similar tapestries, intricately created. He had noticed them before. The skill of the needlepoint was unquestionable. He swelled with pride that his wife was so talented. Her humming stopped abruptly when she tangled her thread, her face becoming intensely focused as she tried to dislodge the knot.

"Damn." She pierced herself with the needle. Putting her index finger to her mouth, he knew the exact moment she caught sight of him. She seemed to freeze. He willed her to keep her eyes on him as he slowly closed the distance between them. He sat on the bench across from her, choosing to continue his observations of her.

"You look well," he said.

"I have been better." She indicated her bleeding finger.

He took her hand. She tensed, yet her face showed no emotion. Blood gathered at the top of her finger, and he put it into his own mouth. Her chest rose as she gasped, her eyes trained on his mouth. He sucked lightly. Her head rose, and her eyes narrowed ever so slightly as if she were resisting what she felt. When he took her finger out of his mouth, her glazed eyes seemed to clear and she stared back at him. Recognizing her desire, he fought the smile tugging at his lips. Undeniable. Her breathing ragged, she started to pull her hand back, but he resisted and turned his focus again to her injury.

Holding the finger at eye level between them, he watched her face from the corner of his eye. The blood again pooled and he looked past it to see her face as he again sucked the blood from her finger. Her chest swelled with her deep, slow breath. He licked the digit in his mouth. Her breathing became more shallow and she fought to keep her eyes focused.

Absolutely indisputable.

Like a bolt of lightning, the reality struck him. He had not been wrong about her. She did desire him. She had lied about finding his odor offensive and him needing a bath. The smile came, and he could not help the satisfaction he felt. She had hidden her desire all along. She saw his smile, and her face scrunched up in confusion. He withdrew her finger slightly.

"I'm afraid you may bleed to death," he stated simply.

"So you smile?" She sounded more sarcastic than upset. Her eyes darkened.

"That is not why I smile."

"Then, pray tell, what do you find so enjoyable?"

Debating the best course of action, he glanced around the hall with the many people milling about and realized it was not the best time or place to force his advantage. He could afford to be patient now that he knew her true feelings. He suffered from the same ailment. They could help each other, but not now. Now there was too much between them to be settled. He could afford to wait.

"To be this close to you makes me smile. Is that so bad a thing?" He could see her withdrawal even though she did not move. "There." He turned her finger toward her, showing the blood had stopped. "I never questioned your ability to survive."

He pulled her chin to him and kissed her lightly on the lips. He pulled back slightly and looked deeper into her eyes. Slowly closing the distance between them, he held her gaze until his lips moved more forcibly against her own. He tried to convey the hint of passion they would share, to try and wipe away any memories that were not of him, and to imbue it with the promise of what their married life would soon consist of.

He finally drew away. Her lashes fluttered open, silver eyes turned to smoky gray. He smiled again and left the hall. He could certainly wait now that he knew there would be a satisfactory ending to his abstinence. Mayhap this very night.

In the kitchen, he glanced around at the many people working in preparation for the evening meal. It took a minute to find the gray-haired woman he knew to be the cook.

"Ah, Ada, there you are."

"Yes, my lord? Did you need something?"

"I need information. You know the whereabouts of most of the inhabitants you cook for?"

"I do, my lord. I have to make enough food."

"Arthur? Can you tell me his whereabouts?"

"He is gone, sir."

John frowned. Left the castle? "How long has he been gone?"

"He left shortly after you did. Said he had king's business."

John knew the king was just returning from Normandy and could not have sent word to Arthur except through him. Arthur had given his allegiance to William right after his crowning. He'd been part of a mass dedication ceremony where even the Scottish King Malcolm, came to swear his fealty. That was when Arthur had been given the commission to look after the territory until William decided to give it to John. Arthur had been here with no one to oversee him.

When John took Rowena to wife, he had given no thought to any change in men. He stayed with the men William put in place. John wasn't sure what the king saw in the man, if he had done anything to gain his trust. He imagined regular reports were sent to the king since they had not been sent to him.

He wondered how Rowena felt about Arthur's absence. Turning back toward the door he had just entered, he considered the wisdom of approaching his wife on the subject. Better not to stir up that hornet's nest right now.

"Thank you for your help, Ada."

"My pleasure, my lord. Oh—"

John turned toward the woman.

"Felicity was asking for you."

Perplexed at the name, hearing it out of context, it took him a minute to remember the woman from the inn. "Yes?"

Ada stepped closer and lowered her voice, her eyes intent upon him. "She just sends her greetings."

He watched the gray-haired woman waddle back to the fire at the far end of the kitchen. John had not the slightest clue as to why Felicity would send a message to him. He snorted at the absurdity of women and continued back into the Great Hall. Rowena's seat was now empty. He knew she had probably retired to her chamber. His lip curled slightly when he remembered the look of longing in her eyes after his kiss. His conquest gave him great satisfaction until he felt again that raw craving surge through him. It had been a very long time. He hoped he would be able to win her over before he burst with his own desire.

Chapter Fourteen

Safe in the privacy of her bedchamber and out of sight of curious eyes, Rowena gave in to her desire to moan as she closed her eyes and felt again the touch of her husband's lips on her own. Firm and demanding with a hint of something she longed for but could not name. She ran her tongue over her dry lips. What should she do? She knew what her body wanted and those longings came to life every night as she slept alone.

In her dreams, John came to her as naked and stunning as he had looked beside the tub. She was no longer afraid but desperate to have him press himself against her, touch her. Despite the satisfaction she felt in his arms, she would awaken with her body on fire, aching with desire. How could she have these feelings for a man she barely knew? Did he have the same feelings for her?

The clash of swords drew her to the window. In the practice area below, her husband ran through his daily regimen. A disciplined soldier, every plane on his body was rock hard as he slashed at the straw stuffed body hanging from an iron hook. He removed his sweat covered tunic. Her mouth went dry. She leaned her forehead against the cold stone wall, her breath coming quicker as his movements got more forceful. People were gathering in the area to watch the lord of the castle as he practiced with such intensity but Rowena gave them little attention. Her gaze focused on her husband. He lunged and stretched, his muscles glistening with sheer power, bulging with each thrust to the headless sack.

Even from this distance, Rowena could see that John was breathing heavily when he stepped away from the practice dummy. John smiled as a man covered with hay and leather approached him, his sword drawn.

Rowena could not hear the words but the crowd that had gathered laughed at John's comment which caused his opponent to tip down the visor on his heavy helmet. She saw her own Saxon warriors gathering around, admiring John's ability as well.

John was relentless in his attack. His sparring partner thrust and deflected as sword then bare hands were used against him. Her men were silent, intent on watching the fight. Bulging muscles engulfed the man before being able to free himself from John's attack. Splaying her fingers around the window sill, she leaned closer. The sweat poured from John's body causing his skin to glisten in the setting sun. With closed eyes, she would swear she could actually smell him.

She opened her eyes in time to see one last shove, and John had the man beneath him, his arm pressed against the man's neck. The other man raised his hands in surrender. The crowd cheered at their lord's prowess. Her own men raised their voices in a heartfelt "Hizzah!"

Rowena took a shaky breath and started to pull back but John turned unexpectedly toward her window. His eyes locked onto hers and she could not move. Time seemed to stand still as she watched his lean body shake with the intensity of his work out. His breathing labored. She could almost feel his breath against her skin.

"My lady?" Rowena jumped and pulled away from the window at the sound of Joan coming through her door. The woman looked taken aback to find her mistress almost hanging out the window and breathing heavily.

Trying to appear nonchalant, Rowena walked unsteadily toward Joan. "Yes?"

"What is amiss?"

"Naught—there is naught amiss." Rowena responded with irritation. She pushed the hair away from her face and felt the dampness against her neck.

Shaking her head slightly, Joan continued. "I have news for you, my lady."

"News?" Rowena tried again to focus. "I have a great thirst. Could you see to that first?"

Joan dipped her head in acknowledgement and headed back out the door. Sitting on her bed, Rowena closed her eyes to relive the look on her husband's face. Desire. She would have been a virgin no more if she had been any closer to him. She knew it in his look. He wanted her right then and there. A ripple of anticipation shot up her body.

By the time Joan returned, Rowena had composed herself adequately. Taking a long draw of the cider, Rowena raised her eyebrows expectantly at her friend. "Yes, Joan? What news have you?"

"It is your husband."

Rowena's brows quickly came together at that answer. "What of him?"

"Well, he has a room at the Owl and Thistle."

Feeling like the air had been knocked out of her, Rowena asked, "Why does he have a room at the inn?"

Joan looked around uncomfortably before she finally met her eyes. "Perhaps he does not feel welcome here?"

Rowena considered what welcome meant and what her friend tried not to say. When she understood her meaning, she felt her own cheeks grow hot. "You mean he has been going there for womanly companionship?"

"It would appear so."

"You believe he would break his vows so easily?"

Joan's expression said it all. She not only believed it but expected it. Rowena turned from her friend before the tears filled her eyes. How naïve. To think that the wedding vows they had made would keep him from seeking another's company. She was probably the only one in the castle who didn't know of his liaisons. No doubt he'd had many bed partners over the years. He was a virile man with physical needs. It was not unheard of for a man to seek his release outside of his marriage. It was just embarrassing to have him do it with her own people. She believed him to be more caring than that.

"My lady?" Joan laid her hand gently on Rowena's rounded shoulder. Her compassion made her desolation seem so much worse.

"Leave me." There was a catch in her throat.

Joan did not question it. "Yes, my lady." Joan paused at the open door. "I thought you would want to know."

Rowena kept her back to her friend but nodded. The sob caught in her throat and when she heard the door close, she threw herself on her bed. How could she believe he would not take another to bed? He certainly did not come to her. Desire had clearly been on his face. Yet he was not here.

Rowena sat up on her bed, filling with rage at the injustice. She looked around. "No, he is not here. Then where is he?" She shouted her question to the empty room. Covering her face with her hands, Rowena wept bitterly. First he left her physically alone with the distance of an ocean between them and now he leaves her to find anyone else he can.

Lying on her back, she remembered how he had looked at her when he saw to her pricked finger. His eyes had spoken volumes about his desire. Then why did he not take her? He was seeing to his needs with another.

Chapter Fifteen

John rubbed the towel against his sweaty neck and chest as Mark repeated what he had heard. The harsh reality of his world had come tumbling down when he had been interrupted from his determined trek to his wife's chamber by the man before him now. John knew the exact minute that Rowena had started watching him. He had actually felt her eyes on him. He had been determined to beat his desire for her out of him by sheer exhaustion but when his eyes had locked onto her, he had known he'd lost this most important of battles. He *needed* to have his wife beneath him, receiving his need or he would die.

"The men had been bribed, two and three shillings apiece for each village. The victims were not known to the men. Their leader made sure of that."

"And their leader? Was there a name?"

"Only the description of a tall, red-haired man. I do not believe they knew his name. The men had been selected because of their family size and need. These men did the job so they could provide for their families. It was that simple."

"That is not simple."

"No, my lord." Mark lowered his eyes. "It is cruel to keep men starving and reward them for doing murder for you.

"But where did he get the money?"

Mark looked John in the face. "I have also heard a Godwinson has returned from Ireland."

John saw again the silver eyes of Rowena's father. "Ireland? How can that be? They were all killed in battle."

"Not all. One of the sons, your wife's cousin, is said to have survived."

The fighting over the English throne had been intense with four men laying claim to the throne. John knew that only William was the rightful heir. He had been given the claim by Edward himself. True, word of Edward's choice had been brought to Normandy by Harold Godwin who then claimed the throne for himself at Edward's death. It was always the same with bastards. Despite William's right to the throne through his father, as a bastard son, many would gainsay that right until totally false claims to the throne were recognized instead. A bastard never had a chance in this world. John knew that firsthand.

"We must catch these men in the act to prove our case."

"I have a plan, my lord."

"Speak freely."

Mark squatted and drew a crude map of John's lands in the dirt. "Here are the villages that have been attacked." The x's marked the spots and John could smell again the stink of burning bodies, the memory of the total devastation they had encountered. "This is the village that will be next. We need only wait them out there."

John saw the sense of what the man said. These attackers were not being very crafty. There was a straight line between all the villages. He was right. That would be the next village laid to waste.

"I need to get to Peter and tell him what we have learned." Standing up, John pulled his tunic on over his head. "See to my horses and gather our men. We ride out tonight."

"My lord," John turned back to the man, "perhaps we should wait until morning. If we come across the men in the night, we will have missed our opportunity to catch them in the act."

Considering this, John's glance went unbidden to the now empty window of his wife's chamber. "You are right. But you must get word to Peter this night."

"I will go myself."

"Take care, Mark."

"It will be easier to travel unobserved alone, my lord. Fear not."

John considered his own filthy condition as he made his way down the hall which led to his wife's chamber. She had not been present in the Hall and the looks her maidservant gave him would have had a lesser man fearing for his life. He knew he was in no condition to see his wife but he needed her.

The room was warm and smelled of lavender when he opened the door. Rowena lay curled up on her side across the bed and did not move when he entered. Closing the door quietly behind him, John approached his sleeping wife. The tears covering her face gave him pause. Without thinking, he stroked her cheek, wiping the tear away. Rowena did not stir. Slowly he lowered his lips to her cheek and kissed her lightly. Her smell intoxicated—cider and lavender. She moaned lightly in her sleep. He resisted the urge to nuzzle her neck and lean her onto her back with his body. He took a step back, unsure he could resist the urge to caress her to wakefulness and take her as was his desire if he stayed in the room.

John turned to leave. He had not noticed the tub before the fire. She must have intended to take a bath. It took but a moment to decide and he quickly doffed his clothes intending only to submerge himself for a moment. Standing naked in the middle of the room, he turned toward the bed and argued with himself. Rowena was his wife and he desired her. By all rights he could awaken her and see to his needs.

He approached the bed. She looked like an angel, her lips slightly parted and her breath, warm against his face, smelled of brown bread and fresh butter. Just now noticing the food set on the table beside the bed, he realized he'd only had eyes for her. He stepped away from the desirable woman. His original plan to win her over was a good one, not tempting himself with her nearness. He submerged himself in the cold water which helped quench his desire. He rested his head back and closed his eyes. Turning his thoughts towards other things, John considered what would cause men to pillage the villages of their own people. What reward could be so great that a man would turn against his own people? Red-haired man. Could it actually be Arthur? The man had sworn his fealty to William or he would not have been given charge of Rowena's holdings. If he had Rowena as well...John looked toward the sleeping woman. He knew his mind would not rest until he knew for sure that Rowena had been faithful to her vows.

What a hypocrite he was. Rowena was expected to be faithful to him but he knew he had not been so to her, not entirely. Abigail had really been a thorn in his side. She'd snuck into his room unbidden. Her smug look when he'd awoken said it all. She took great pleasure in convincing him of his desire for her.

Rowena turning over in the bed brought him out of his own thoughts. He enjoyed the view. He longed to slowly caress that bottom and hold her tightly against him. John quickly dunked his head and lathered himself deciding it best to remove himself from temptation.

He had his back to her as he quickly dried himself and began to dress. Her movements were getting harder and harder for him to ignore. Almost finished, the moan that accompanied her thrashing finally drew him to her, his boots still in his hand. It was the moan he remembered so well.

He brushed her hair out of her face. She moaned again and he put his boots down beside the bed. He took her hand in his own resting it on his chest and lay beside her on the bed. Cradling her head against him, he ran his hand along her soft curves.

"Shhh, Rowena. Calm yourself."

Despite his intent, when she turned her mouth up to him, he could not stop from responding. His kiss quickly deepened and her willing response pushed him along. When she took his hand and brought it to her breast, he realized he was losing the battle. With acute clarity, he remembered everything about her that he had discovered that first day. She was a passionate woman. It had been too long. He was a starving man, desperate to have her. His kisses traveled the sensitive area of her neck, tasting her.

"John, make me your wife now." Her throaty whisper intoxicated.

He moaned in answer to her willingness. He would have her now.

"Please. I need you," she said. "Do not go to another."

Intent on his own desire, it took John a moment to register what she'd said. His kisses stopped suddenly. He withdrew his hand and shook his head.

"Methinks I did not hear you aright."

She pulled back from him and glancing around, her eyes widened in surprise. "What is amiss?"

He lurched away from the bed. "I do not go to another."

When it is only you that I want. His breath stopped.

Rowena got off the bed, pulling her bodice back. "What?"

John's breathing returned in a rush, distracting his thoughts. "You are making accusations against me 'tis all."

She tipped her head as if he spoke gibberish. "I was abed, my lord, I did not make any accusations."

Raking his hand through his hair, he frowned. "I came in here and found you asleep, crying out for me."

She glanced away, but her flaming cheeks spoke of her belief in what he said.

"Then you told me not to go to another."

"I cannot defend what I do not remember."

"And yet you have the look of one that knows of dreams so deeply arousing that you cry out in your sleep."

She turned away. "Aye, I know those dreams."

He came up behind her, not daring to touch her again. "And in your dreams do I go to another?"

Rowena inhaled a shaky breath. "That is the way of it, methinks."

"It is not." John spun her to face him. "Why would you think so little of me? When have I given you reason to doubt me?"

§

Rowena was becoming used to her lust filled dreams. She had not realized why they suddenly felt so real. They were real. It was his hand on her breast, his lips on her mouth. The sincerity in his expression now could not be denied but Rowena knew better.

She looked askance at him. "Husband, you have not been here." She motioned to the bed.

"Do you think me an animal, rutting about, with no control? I have not been seeking pleasure elsewhere whilst you pine away for me here." He pulled his tunic over his head, shifting uncomfortably. "You are my wife. It is you that denied me."

"Until we knew each other better, yes, but there has been little evidence of you seeking to change that fact."

He pointed to the bed. "But now you would have me take you when you believe I am unfaithful to you?"

She threw her long hair over her shoulder. "I believe any man would take what I offer."

"So you believe *me* to be unfaithful *to you*?" He shook his head then realized what else she had said. "What man have you made the offer to?"

Rowena seemed stricken by the accusation. "What are you asking?"

John's hands were gentle on her shoulders as he pulled her against him. He leaned his face into her hair and spoke quietly.

"I do desire you, Rowena." A shiver worked its way down her spine. "I am bursting with desire for you." His voice was a whisper against her cheek. "I do not understand what game you are playing at."

She stilled, exhaling on a puff of air. Games were of no interest to her. Her head dipped in defeat. "Leave me."

Chapter Sixteen

The woman in his arms needed him. His wife. She wanted him for who he was. Could he let her turn him out? Should he walk away? His hesitation lasted but a moment. Determination took its place.

"I will not be leaving you alone, Rowena."

He slid his hands down her sides, feeling the curves he remembered from their fleeting encounter. She shivered. Slowly he turned her to face him, slipping his hand across her flat belly, brushing against her breast. She stiffened but her eyes remained downcast, as if to hide what she felt.

"I will not be leaving."

Torn between pulling her up against him so she could feel the power of his desire for her or insisting she admit if she'd been unfaithful with Arthur ripped at his insides. The bed loomed behind her, beckoning him to forego any conversations and just take her now and find out for himself.

John moved stiffly to the stool in front of the fire, exhaling deeply before he finally spoke. "We need to talk."

Her head shot up. "What do we have to talk about?" Rowena's clenched her jaw. "I am your wife but you have no need of me. It is a man's prerogative to cast aside his wife."

He closed his eyes and took a deep, steadying breath, before opening them. "I have not cast you aside."

"No?" Her eyes narrowed. "I have no better word for it."

"I think we need to begin anew."

"Anew? Where you accept me as your wife?"

"I am pleased with you as my wife. I am sorry I have not been here sooner to fulfill my rights."

She gasped. Her eyes widened. "Your rights? You walked away from any rights and yet I still would willingly accept you, even now, but no..." She gestured at the bed with jerky motions. "Here. Now. But you refuse. If that is not casting me aside then I verily must be daft."

"Cease this. I did not refuse. I do not wish to play with words." He stood in front of her, blocking her path. "Hear me." He cupped her cheek, her jaw tight beneath his hand. "I am *very* pleased with you but I do not share what is mine."

Her warm skin was smooth as silk and he traced her lips with his thumb. Those supple lips begged for his kisses. The memory of her passion-filled moan echoed in his mind as if he'd just heard it. He licked his lips and fought against his desires. Would it matter? If she'd been with Arthur? Damn it. Yes! But he would not let her go. He could not. She was everything he wanted.

"You must be truthful with me about what Arthur means to you."

Her face screwed up into a frown. "Arthur?"

He couldn't keep his hands off her and caressed her cheek, tracing along her jaw. "Do you have feelings for him?"

"He was my friend." She eyed him warily.

"Is that all?"

She lowered her head. "He was my protector."

"That is all?"

She nodded, still not meeting his gaze.

Something was amiss. "He has not touched you?" John dragged his finger down her neck, pausing where her blood pulsed, quickening.

Heat flushed her face.

"Has he taken you into his arms?" John forced himself to continue breathing. He did not want his suspicions to be correct. He wanted her to be his, untouched and pure.

She hesitated. "Yes."

His nostrils flared but he kept his voice steady. "Has he caressed you here?"

He brushed his hands over her breast, one and then the other. She was exquisite and he wanted to flatten his hand against her, cupping her. He couldn't give in yet. Not until he knew for sure, but his reasoning was becoming harder and harder to remember.

She opened her eyes and held his gaze. "Not like you touch me."

The words hung in the air between them. Rowena had been intimate with another. Like a dagger in the gut, John's entire body froze as he considered the implication of what she was admitting. Arthur had touched her then. He jerked his hand away from her.

"How was it different?" Hearing again the sound of her moan, his longing for his wife burst into full desire. The way she had looked with her eyes closed, her lips parted and the sound of her longing. He would surely die if he didn't have her now. "Answer me."

Her eyes did not even blink. "I did not feel this way with him. His touch meant nothing to me."

His touch meant nothing. God, he wanted her anyway. He needed to be tasting her and caressing her, bringing her passion to full bloom but he needed to hear everything. "How did he touch you?"

"He held me in his arms. He kissed me." She gripped her hands tightly. "He tried to coax me into desire. I felt nothing." She sniffled loudly. "He had told me he loved me. When you came back and did not come to me," she wiped at her nose, "I thought I could love him but I felt nothing for him. His kiss on my lips disgusted me. His touch was wrong." She picked up her head, imploring him with her eyes. "I am ashamed at my weakness. I have been alone for so long, I wished only to be loved."

I have been alone for so long.

He understood her pain.

I wished only to be loved.

He knew that longing first hand.

"You have done nothing wrong, my lady." She was his lady, his wife, and he wanted to fill her desire to be loved. The realization made him feel very vulnerable.

"You did not desire him," John's voice was steady, firm. "Your desire is for your husband, as it should be."

Satisfaction filled his chest and he pulled her in closer, working his fingers beneath her long hair, rubbing little circles against her sensitive neck. He nuzzled against her neck and he was surrounded by her scent. "I desire you as well, my love."

When he turned her face to him, she resisted slightly, but then he kissed her and she relaxed in his arms. Her lips were soft and yielding, and he teased her with his tongue. She opened her mouth to him. He slid his hand to her breast, its weight fitting so perfectly in his hand. Her nipple responded to his touch, hardening into an eager nub that he longed to suckle. He lifted her in his arms and carried her to the bed, laying her down ever so gently. He lay down beside her without taking his lips from hers.

She was absolutely perfect from the taste of her mouth to the softness of her hair. Her tongue met his and he deepened the kiss. He dragged his hands down her body finally cupping her bottom, pressing her against his firm desire. He shuddered. He wanted her like he'd never wanted anything before.

His breathing was ragged when he broke the kiss. He stared into her eyes. "You do desire this?"

She nodded and closed her eyes, wrapping her arms around his neck and leaning up for his mouth again. He kissed her back but it wasn't nearly enough. He had to touch her. What he wanted was her naked beneath him, writhing with desire, and begging him to enter her. No. He wanted to be inside her already.

He dragged his hand along her slender calf, pulling the chemise up as he went. Her bare skin his to touch, so soft and inviting. At her hips, he slid his hand along her thighs, grasping her bottom. Arching her back, he suckled her breast, slipping his hand between her legs to her heat. She was wet and warm.

The memory flooded back. He'd wanted her then and he wanted her now. His finger slipped inside and she gasped, bucking slightly.

"Do not be afeard, let me love you."

He pulled back and looked at her lovely face, her lips parted, her eyes wide and innocent. "I will make up to you all these years of waiting. That is my promise to you." He whispered the words against her mouth, plundering her with his tongue as his finger did the same.

She responded with soft moans, her hips urging him on.

"That gives you pleasure?"

She nodded, unable to speak. He sped up his movements, holding her tight against him, until she worked into a rhythm that matched his. Her breathing quickened, becoming more labored and he put his mouth near her ear.

"Yes, my love, let me know your pleasure. Let me hear your moan."

And she did as her hips pitched up one last time, held against him by her climax. Her moan was sweet to his ear and he fought for self control. He breathed, his open mouth, trying to remember how the cold water of the loch felt in winter—anything to keep his mind from letting his body find its release.

She exhaled a shaky breath, her hands still rubbing little circles into his shoulders. He worked the chemise the rest of the way over her head, nearly exploding with his desire at the sight of her nakedness once again. It was bittersweet and his agony seemed like just payment for her abandonment. He tossed her chemise but when he would stretch out beside her, she pulled back.

"This does not seem good to me."

He'd done something wrong? He couldn't think of what it was.

"Why am I naked but you are not?"

He sighed in relief and quickly doffed his own clothing then stretched alongside her, taking her into his arms again. Her mouth was eager on his, her hands sliding across his chest and lower. He grabbed her hand.

"Best not to tempt fate."

"I do not understand. I want to touch you."

"This may not be the best time."

"Why?" she glanced at his erection. "I am not afraid."

That was all he needed to hear and she was under him. His mouth on hers as his hand moved to cup her buttocks, then gripping her thighs and spreading them so that he dipped between her legs, the head of his tarse at the juncture of her wetness. She stilled suddenly.

"Perhaps I am afeared."

He looked down into her face, a crease marked her forehead and she nibbled at her bottom lip.

"There is only one first time. You do not know what to expect this time, but I tell you it will be more pleasurable than my finger was."

"But...it is so big. Will it rip me asunder?"

He leaned away so that his ready cock was easily visible. "Touch me then."

"But I thought you said—"

"Touch me so you see I am not made of wood but of flesh."

He gasped when her fingers gripped him so hard, so sweet.

His jaw clenched. "Do you see that I am flesh?"

She caressed him gently, squeezing as she pulled, and he nearly exploded in her hand. He placed his hand over hers to still her movements. "If you have enough proof I will not rip you apart, may I please continue?"

She beamed her smile and spread her legs wide. That was his undoing. So wet and ready he quickly entered her. She grabbed at his shoulder and gasped when he broke through her maidenhead. John had never been with a virgin before so he didn't know for sure how long her pain would last. Sweat broke out on his forehead. His heart seemed to burst through his chest, and his arms trembled where he held himself away from her and still.

"Umm, is there more to it than this?"

John sighed and dropped down on her. He rocked into her gently.

"Oh, that is much better," she moaned and he moved more insistently.

She arched her hips up to him, and he bit her neck. He couldn't hold back but he could feel her tight around him milking him in her climax and he let go with hard thrusts, finally spilling his seed into her until he was spent.

Rowena was a virgin no longer.

Her breathing still labored, every movement she made seemed to reverberate through his body but he knew she needed to recover from their first time. She would be sore.

He pulled her up alongside his length, and she snuggled against him, her head resting on his chest. She fit perfectly into the crook of his arm. He kissed the top of her head then grabbed the cover, tucking it securely behind her.

"Is it always like that?"

He smiled. "I take it you found pleasure in it."

"Oh, yes," she sighed. Her enthusiasm came through in her voice. It increased his desire.

"No, it's not always like that."

"Oh." Her tone dipped in her disappointment.

"Some people do not suit." He could smell her. He wanted her again.

"So, for them it is not like that?" She crossed his legs with her own, rubbing against him.

He was already hard. "I would say not."

"But...for us? It will be like this? We...suit?"

God, he could take her and fill her again and again. He never wanted a woman like he wanted her. He struggled to keep his breathing steady when he answered her. "I would say so."

She nodded against his chest, her breath warm. How long did he have to wait before taking her again?

"Rest, my love." He tightened his jaw and tried to think about something else.

After a few moments of quiet, Rowena spoke up, "John, I do not feel tired."

"No? And how do you feel then?"

She picked her head up. "Hungry."

He frowned and looked askance at her.

She smiled. "Like I've been given forbidden fruit and I want more."

His breath caught. Yes, but it wasn't forbidden.

"I'm certain we need to take some time." John shuddered with yearning when she rubbed slightly against him, his own leg dipping betweens hers and against her wetness.

"Let me feel again your body inside of mine." She stroked his face. "Make us one."

She was under him. Her firm bottom filled his hands as he raised her hips up to receive his thrust, her tightness pulling against him with each withdrawal.

He bent his head close to her ear. "I believe I've found heaven."

She shuddered. He encouraged her to move against him, showing her what was pleasing to him. She held on tightly at first then moved more willingly with his guidance. Too soon for him, it was over.

He had been a long time practicing abstinence which may explain his insatiable desire but it was more than that. It was her. She fit him like a glove. She was more than willing and her satisfaction became the center of his enjoyment.

Spent, he easily pulled her up to straddle him. With one hand behind his head, he grinned at the sight of her loveliness. Her breasts still heaving as she rolled her shoulders and stretched languorously, her hair disheveled about her. She slowly licked her lip, her eyes hooded.

"You are too enticing by half."

She reached to smooth her hair and he laughed. Clearly taken aback, she demanded. "Why do you laugh?"

"I say you're enticing and you fuss about yourself."

She frowned.

"These..." He slid her closer up his chest and held her soft globes in his calloused hands, "are beautiful breasts." Her knees were bent and rested at his shoulders. He smiled. "Quite a view I have."

She sat up straighter, uncertain what she should do. When she started to move away from him, his hand on her back stopped her. "Be still. I enjoy the sight."

He dragged his hand along her spine and leaned her toward him until his mouth enclosed her breast. Her eyes closed in pleasure, her lips separated. Lightly he nibbled her and her head dipped to her chest. He slid his hands along her bottom, grasping her hot flesh, and he was amazed at his own unbridled passion, his own response to his wife. When he leaned back, she pulled away and opened her eyes to look at him. He turned his head to the side and kissed her inner thigh just above the knee, never breaking the eye contact.

"Is there any pain?"

She shook her head slowly.

"Shall we try this again then? More slowly?"

She smiled with mischievous eyes and nodded.

He began his unhurried exploration of every part of her. With firm strokes, he touched her, encouraging her not to hide her pleasure. He sought to know what she enjoyed. She, too, joined in the exploration, boldly touching and taunting him until he couldn't hold back any longer. Each release became more satisfying because with each encounter, he knew his wife more intimately.

Every time, her throbbing pleasure resulted in moans that pulled at his manhood for sweet release. When their breathing eased and she lay still against him, he whispered in her ear. "That, my sweet, was your wedding night." He pulled her against him. "Soon, we will have our honeymoon."

"I am well pleased with you." Rowena said quietly just before she dozed off to sleep.

A deep chuckle filled his chest. She was like no woman he'd ever met. He kissed her forehead and was quickly joining her in sleep.

Chapter Seventeen

In the early dawn, Rowena awoke to her husband's mouth against her neck, nibbling and licking, sending little shivers down her body and stirring her passions again. Never could she have imagined what marriage would be like.

She rubbed against him when he pulled her close, his own arousal nudging firmly against her. Despite her fears, he had fit her perfectly.

"John?"

"Yes?" He nuzzled beneath her ear. His answer rumbled through her.

"Should we not break our fast now?"

He stilled. She waited. Had she said something wrong?

Slowly he slid his hand around to her belly to pull her onto her back, and he looked her in the eye.

"Are you saying you'd rather break your fast than be made love to by your husband? Have you tired of me so soon?"

She giggled and shook her head. "Never would I say that."

He brushed his nose against her cheek then smiled a big radiant smile. "Ah, that is very pleasing to me."

"And to me."

His smile dipped and blossomed again. "You are forthright. That also pleases me."

He took her lips with great eagerness, as if they hadn't just made love a few hours earlier. She wrapped her arms about his neck, pulling his hardened body closer to her. His hands were hot on her, his touch firm and demanding.

"Mmm." She wanted him to understand how she felt. "I do find you quite satisfying."

His hand stilled where he had been stroking her back. "Do ya now?"

Realizing how silly she sounded, she shrugged as she answered. "Yes."

His hand resumed. "Mmm."

They made love slowly, savoring each other.

"Ah, my sweet wife," John's voice was barely a whisper. "I find you quite satisfying as well."

He drifted into a heavy sleep accompanied by loud snoring. Rowena shifted closer, covering them tightly with the heavy blanket and did the same.

Rowena was awakened by the door opening and the gasp of her servant. Sitting up slightly, a finger to her lips, Rowena's sheet dipped before she could grab it back, exposing her nakedness.

"Shhh, Joan. Do not awaken him." Her voice sounded loud against the quiet of the room.

John now lay flat on his stomach, his hands spread out. One arm lay across her, holding her to him and the other lay off the side of the bed. How like a little boy he looked with his tousled hair and peaceful expression.

"Well, you do look happy, m'lady." Joan placed her tray of cheese and cider soundlessly on the table. "I am happy to see it but what of the other women?"

Rowena frowned at her maid. What of the other women? "He said there were none."

"And you believed him? You didn't settle that between you before you let him bed you?"

"Shhh, Joan." Her voice was getting a little louder with her exasperation, and Rowena didn't want to address the problem Joan was reminding her off. Smiling down at John, she was only slightly startled when his hand slid down her stomach and came up between her legs, settling between her thighs.

"I just think you should have made sure he hadn't made you a laughing stock before you bedded him is all, m'lady."

Rowena tensed at what she was saying. Her friend had no idea how she was ruining what had been a very wonderful night. In all her dreams, she could never have imagined the feelings she'd experienced. His total desire to please her was something she would never have expected. He made her want him like she had never wanted anything on this earth. She had yelled out his name more than once, and he had taken her moans of pleasure in his mouth, urging her on to a deeper and deeper satisfaction. No, no one could have told her this was what it was like to be married.

When he had whispered that this was their wedding night, tears had filled her eyes. If only she'd known how she had been made for him and him alone. No one else could make her feel like this. She could trust him with her most intimate being, and he treasured her in the way he held her, the way he sought her pleasure, the way he took his release in her, filling her. When he'd said she had her honeymoon to still look forward to, Rowena had been overjoyed. Now she was feeling uneasy.

"Leave now, Joan." John's low voice was firm although muffled by his pillow. "Forthwith."

Joan's wide-eyed expression was full of fear. When he made to sit up, she jumped to run to the door, shutting it loudly behind her.

John propped his head on his hand, his face dark with a heavy growth of beard and his forehead creased. "Well?"

Trying to adjust her leg so that his hand was not quite so intimately placed, she hesitated in her answer. What should she say? Hadn't he answered the night before? His hand refused to be dislodged.

"Is there something you'd like to ask me?" His fingers moved suggestively, grazing that special spot.

"Stop." He did not listen but then she didn't sound very forceful.

"Is there something you'd like to ask me about then?"

Her eyes closed. Catching herself, her eyes flew open and she tried to adjust her location on the bed only to find his hand kept her put.

"Is there?" His mouth was hot as he suckled her, making it hard to think.

He pulled her beneath him, cupping her bottom against him. He filled her well. Giving in to her passion, she accepted his advances as he moved in her, his powerful thrust igniting her again and again into that wave of passion, and she was once more moaning his name.

Chapter Eighteen

"My lady." The noonday sun brightened the room around Rowena, causing her to become disoriented. "My sweet lady," John's insistent voice pushed through her sleep muddled mind.

"Yes?" Rowena opened her eyes to her husband's smiling face just a few inches from her own.

"You look well bedded."

Closing her eyes, she stretched languorously. The heat beside her was subsiding and with a start she realized her husband was no longer in the bed.

She sat up quickly and he tugged the blanket away when she tried to cover herself.

"Why are you up? Where are you going?"

He was dressed for travel but his eyes slowly admired her nakedness. Her heart sank as she remembered Joan's words from the night before.

"You are done with me?"

His eyes widened in surprise. "Why would you ask such a thing?"

When he moved to fondle her exposed breasts, she pulled away from him, wrapping herself with the blanket as she stood on the opposite side of the bed.

"You appear to be ready to go somewhere." She tried to stop her voice from sounding harsh but the shift from well satiated to discarded was a quick one.

"I must continue to oversee my property. I came back to be with you." His dimples came into full bloom with his grin. "I admit I was sidetracked from my mission. Pleasantly so."

The heat on her cheeks extended down her neck as she searched for the right response. She had none. All she knew was that she fell asleep totally contented and awakened to the fact that the source of her contentment was leaving. "When will you return?" Will you see another while you are gone?

His uncertainty was apparent to her now in the way he rubbed his thumb along his lower lip. Was he uncertain because he was unsure of the answer or because he was making up a lie? "I must complete my mission. The king's orders, Rowena. You understand?"

The reminder that it was indeed his land now didn't seem intentional but it had the same effect on her. And what of the other women? Had he made her a laughing stock?

"Will you come back here when you do return?"

"Where else would I go?" He had been making his way toward her slowly and when he reached her, her body leaned into him of its volition. His lips were warm and promising but when she would have pushed more insistently against him, she learned he would not be budged.

"I cannot stay with you yet. When I return, we will spend more time together." His hand caressed her bare bottom, exposed as it was from the ill-wrapped blanket. "We will learn even more about each other." His hand worked like magic, making her desire him.

"Please, John," she spoke against his lips. While he was kissing her goodbye she was wanting much more. "What of my honeymoon?"

"Anticipation will make it even sweeter." When he pulled away from her, she struggled to find her footing. "Awww, do not disappoint me by pouting."

Her eyes flew open. "I do not pout." She could see his surprise, and she stood more firmly on her own, determined to not show how vulnerable she felt.

"I see." He was searching her face and she hoped her desire was not apparent to him. "Perhaps I will be backer sooner than I had thought."

"Perhaps you should not leave just yet." She bit her lip and looked away from him, ashamed for having said what was in her heart.

His groan as he unexpectedly pulled her firmly against him was pleasing to her ear. Pulling the blanket out from between their bodies, he leaned her back onto the bed.

"I believe you are correct. I have time to leave you with a proper memory since you are so willing," his hand worked its magic again, traveling up her thigh, "so very willing."

She waited but a second for him to make quick work of his fine clothing and he was again pressed against her, bringing her to that special place she had discovered in his arms. She knew the blessing of God was on their marriage. This was indeed the man she was supposed to be with despite the strange turn of events that had caused their marriage. He was worth waiting for and God willing, they would have many more passionate moments and even a family.

When she would have napped against his chest, he quickly left the bed and prepared to dress again. "You are a temptation I rather enjoy." He laced his breeches as he spoke, his smug look of satisfaction couldn't be missed.

"I take that as a compliment."

"As well you should."

"I rather enjoy you also, my lord." His face lit up at her comment. Self-conscious, she turned away from him.

Coming to kneel beside her as she sat up in the bed, he gently turned her face toward him. "Do not. Do not ever turn away from me when you share your feelings, Rowena. I want to learn all about you. I want to know all your feelings. I want to *know* your passion. I promise I will treasure your feelings."

She wrapped her naked arms around him, pulled him against her, and kissed him passionately. Although he seemed surprised by her reaction, he returned her kiss just as ardently.

"I look forward to your return." Her eyes were level with his as she spoke.

"I will not be over long." He strapped his broadsword to his side and kissed her again. Then he was gone. She sat on her haunches. Her heart dropped to her stomach as the door quietly closed.

Chapter Nineteen

"Mark never arrived?" John paced with agitation before the dark-haired man he'd left in charge. "No word at all?"

He knew he should have come himself. His guilt was palpable. Why hadn't he come himself to warn Philip. That is what he should have done instead of pleasuring himself with his wife. Rowena's face flashed in his mind, and he felt even guiltier at the feelings those memories caused in him.

In her arms he had found a peace he had never known. All his life, he'd felt the outcast, the bastard, always trying to measure up to standards he could never meet. In her arms he'd found complete acceptance, serenity, and peace. He hoped the cost for this peace was not the life of one of his own men.

"We need to send men out to look for him."

Philip quickly organized search parties for all possible routes Mark would have taken from the castle.

"Perhaps he is nearby and just missed us when we left camp yesterday," Philip suggested when he returned.

John ceased his pacing. "I pray you are right."

Unpacking his bag, John considered the possibilities. Mark could have followed the wrong road and missed their camp, or he could have tracked the camp from their previous night. It was true that there could be many reasons he hadn't made it to them yet.

"The information he had, my lord?"

"My suspicions were confirmed."

"Then they are verily Saxons burning their own villagers out?"

"They are." John told Philip what they had discovered at the castle.

"The red-haired man? Is he your seneschal?"

John was surprised by the accusation. "You heard something?"

"No, my lord. It was more a feeling in my gut."

John thought about his first impression and realized he had felt animosity from the start. He had later attributed that to Arthur's interest in Rowena.

"You spoke to him?" John asked.

Philip shifted uncomfortably. "My lord, our first night, do you remember? There was a problem with the horses?"

"I do remember the incident. I was told the Saxons were afraid of our horses."

"I saw Arthur during the commotion. He was standing off in the shadows just watching. I got the impression he enjoyed the ruckus."

"Mayhap he found humor in it. He is probably just a strange man." Despite his attempt to explain what he saw, John took Philip's impressions very seriously.

"That might have been it except when I saw him later he was with a small boy. He gave him what looked like a gold coin"

"Gold?"

"Yes, my lord. He tousled the boy's head and told him he'd done a good job."

"I see. Any sign of what specifically the boy had used to rile the horses?"

Philip shook his head. "He left the barn by the back presumably so he wouldn't walk in front of us. We were still preparing the horses since the remaining stable hands refused."

From the first, it seemed, Arthur was working against John not only with his wife but with his soldiers as well. Would he have noticed himself if he hadn't been so wrapped up in winning his wife?

"I appreciate you sharing this with me."

"Mayhap I should have done so earlier." Philip's own feelings of guilt were apparent.

"No mind. If we are correct in our suspicions, he will be dealt with." The proof was not conclusive against Arthur. As it was, John would have to wait and hope to catch the man in the act. That old feeling of jealousy reared its ugly head at the thought of confronting the man. It lost its venom, however, when he remembered his time with his wife. Rowena had indeed been a virgin and though obviously new to lovemaking, a very willing pupil. Shaking his head to mentally remove the memory and the longing it created, John focused on the problem at hand.

The people believed that the Normans were despoiling and laying waste their villages. There were a group of Saxon men intentionally misleading the people into believing this. Every village John had visited was full of people afraid for their lives. They didn't trust the Normans and by association, John. King William had ordered their allegiance by the spring. John's mission seemed doomed before it had even started. If it was indeed Arthur leading these Saxons, there would be hell to pay.

"When Mark gets here, we will need to head east. We believe that will be the next village attacked. Mark had come here to warn you of that. If we can get to the village by daybreak, we may be able to catch the men in the act."

Philip offered, "Drink?" John nodded, and the man poured him some mead. "Any word of the king?"

"He was spotted in Portsmouth and Peter should have arrived by now."

What would the king think when he heard of the disturbances here? He could hardly be pleased. At least John had handled the lesser of his problems. His wife was well and truly bedded. There was much relief in that. He had corrected his wrong from his previous visit and William need be none the wiser. That John felt great satisfaction was the crux. This was satisfaction he could have had from the beginning if he had just given her a chance. The guilt he experienced as her father's murderer had added to his desire to leave her untouched. She had never mentioned it but he clearly remembered her crying over his body. Mayhap it was something they never had to discuss. So be it.

One by one the men sent out in search of Mark came back with no information. John needed to move on with his plan and hoped that Mark would find them. Traveling at night would be more dangerous. Had Mark not taken proper precautions for his safety? There was no way to know, but they needed to be in Towton by first light.

The orders were given for the men to break camp. Moving cautiously by the slim light of the waxing crescent moon, the men moved like shadows into the surrounding woods. They approached the village soundlessly. Smoke from their many fires hung like a blanket over the village as the inhabitants slept safe and sound. Unknown to them, they were surrounded by a protective army of Normans ready to fight off their own kin who would lay waste to their homes.

John waited somberly for the bloodthirsty group. He was not sure how the perpetrators would react when confronted by his soldiers. His men had their orders to take them alive if possible. If a redhead was among them, they were told to bring him immediately to John to deal with. One way or another, John hoped to have his long awaited confrontation with the man that had taken too many privileges for himself. He hoped to teach him a lesson.

At dawn, when they expected to see movement within the village, the stillness gave John a strong sense of foreboding. The sun made its way into the sky. They still waited silently. No one stirred in the village. The blanket of smoke had long since dissipated. The animals moved restlessly in the few barns and the roosters repeated call went unanswered.

"Something is wrong here." John signaled for his men to hold back. Pulling himself up slightly, he ran to the closest outbuilding and waited, watching for any sign of movement. There was none. Again hunching low to the ground, he ran to the town well house and found nothing. The closer in he got, the bigger the knot in his stomach grew. At the first house, he pushed the door open and found it empty. The hearth was cold.

In each house, he found the same until he got to the manor of the overseer. The iron knocker indicated the wealth of the occupant. John knocked on the wooden door.

"Show yourself." He signaled for his men to come down with him. Busting open the locked door, they located the massacre.

"They've already been here." Philip headed in and started pulling at the dead bodies, checking to see if anyone had survived. "Damn." John was beside himself. How could they have gotten there before them? Who were these men that they traveled like a vapor and disappeared like the fog?

"My lord?" John slowly turned toward Philip, his voice sounded tight. Balling his fists at his side, the sight of Mark's body thrown among the others that had been left dead pushed him over the edge.

He clenched his jaw. "Can you tell if he was killed with the others."

"Not for sure but you should take a look." John fought down his anger as he squatted down beside the man. His shirt had been ripped open, etched across his chest like the scoring of an animal was the word "SCUM".

Chapter Twenty

"So they seem to know our moves before we make them." Philip gently pulled the ripped tunic together over Mark's chest. "They are cold-blooded bastards."

"And they lay it all at our feet," John replied

John was at his wits end trying to piece together what had gone wrong. How had they missed the men who did this? How long could it have taken them to bring about such total destruction on a village? Most importantly, when was it that they'd come across Mark? Had they followed him when he left the castle?

Remembering his time at the castle, John closed his eyes. His emotions were in turmoil. His guilt overwhelming; guilt over letting Mark go alone; guilt over the pleasure he'd found with his wife when he should have been with Mark; and guilt over choosing her company and his own desires over his duty. John needed to know for sure that his being with Mark would not have saved his life.

"We need to trace Mark's steps. Have any of the men returned?" John stepped into the light from the darkened building. Philip followed him to a clearing a short distance away.

"Henry!" Philip called. A bearded man turned at his name, and Philip waved him in. "David and Maurice are helping with the bodies."

The two watched as the men reverently carried Mark's body to the grave that was being dug for him. A burial shroud had been brought out from the church and placed on the ground. Philip adjusted the man's tunic again before wrapping him solemnly in the sacred cloth. Closing his eyes and lowering his head, Philip said a prayer over his body. John bowed in respect but inside he seethed.

This man should not be dead.

John strode to where the horses waited. He dug deep into his bag and retrieved his most treasured possession from his youth, the codex of scriptures he had copied himself. The frail book was wrapped in deer hide and tied with a leather binding. He could again see the brothers hunched over their trestles with their various bottles surrounding their vellum. That would have been his destiny if not for Duke William.

The unsmiling face of Brother James came to mind. "John, the Duke would like you to go with him."

"Why? I haven't done anything wrong."

William knelt beside him. "I would like you to be able to carry that sword. And even learn to fight with it...for me."

Full of excitement for his new adventure, John had packed his meager belongings and gone on to learn to be a knight. A position with honor and power. It was not turning out the way he had hoped, however.

John closed his eyes to rid his mind of the memory. He carefully opened to the Psalms of King David and read for himself that God would not let his enemies go unpunished.

"*O Senior, eripio mihi ex malum populus. Servo mihi ex qui es vehemens, qui consentio malum in suum pectus pectoris quod concito perturbo totus dies porro.*"

"O Lord, rescue me from evil people, protect me from those who are violent, those who plot evil in their hearts and stir up trouble all day long."

John took a moment for himself. He struggled to find peace and strengthen his own resolve. After a moment, he walked to Philip and handed him the codex. That he tried to forge an understanding with the people now under his protection was a noble act. That someone else was intentionally misleading those same people so that they would turn against him was intolerable.

Philip held his gaze. "You do not wish to read it for us, my lord?'

John shook his head, unable to speak. He needed to hear the words said out loud and find comfort from those words, a comfort he couldn't offer himself. Philip's voice was strong and clear as he read the Latin words. John translated them in his head. He prayed that Mark had indeed found peace.

When the grave was covered with dirt and covered with stones, John turned to Henry.

"Tell me exactly where you went when you looked for Mark. Where you stopped, anyone you met along the way. We need to piece together all that we can and figure out where Mark went and where he was killed."

John turned back to the house where the bodies had been left and shook his head.

"The people who did this have no sense of right. This is not about the Normans. This is about something evil and greedy and we need to put a stop to it."

"Yes, my lord," Henry tipped his head respectfully.

"Let me get the others." Philip went toward the house now being emptied of the rest of the bodies. As before, there were no survivors. Except for the one boy that they hadn't realized was alive, there were no witnesses to these attacks.

The boy. He was really their only chance.

"Where is the boy?" John asked Henry who stood beside him, watching Philip approach the rest of the group. Henry looked surprised.

"I don't know, my lord. He was much improved when I left yesterday. I have not seen him today."

The men Philip had gathered approached John, their faces showed their upset at this turn of events.

"Philip, where is the boy?"

"He rests at the camp, my lord."

"Tell me he has not been left unprotected." The men turned to each other, questioning who would have been left behind for protection. "No one was left to guard him?"

John could not believe they would leave their only witness unguarded. He rewrapped his codex and nestled it safely away. He quickly settled himself atop the big destrier and turned toward the men who had followed him.

"Philip, put together an accounting for me of where these men searched for Mark. Leave out no detail, what roads they took, who they spoke with, anyone they passed on the way. No detail is too small. We need to put together Mark's last hours so that we can avenge him. It is reprehensible that these Saxons would kill their own and lay the blame on us but when they kill the king's own men, they go too far."

The words hit home and John winced at the realization. He was putting his own above the others, above Rowena and her people. No wonder the Saxons hated them.

The fire at their camp lay dying with an ominous trail of thin, gray smoke as John approached. Aside from that, there was no movement.

"Where is the boy?" John asked in a quiet voice, jumping from his horse to look around the desolate area.

Philip led the way. The lean-to was set in the darkest part of the woods. They'd left the boy to rest.

"This way."

John followed on foot, leading his horse behind him. Snorting restlessly, the beast seemed to sense the tension.

The shadows were growing longer and the primeval forest allowed little light. They crouched at the sound of the heavy wings that preceded the hungry owl, passing close to their heads, in search of his breakfast. Philip whistled the call and they awaited the answer.

"That's it," he smiled.

Moving quickly, they found the boy sitting up in the little hut.

"How fare ye, Aldred?" Philip approached the boy first, motioning John inside.

"I am well, sir." Perhaps sensing the tension, he asked, "Should I not be?"

The resilience of the lad brought shame to John for his own selfish concerns. The young boy had witnessed a massacre but considered he was doing well because he was still alive.

"No one has troubled you then?" John squatted down beside him and handed him his water skin.

"None at all, my lord." Aldred drank his fill from the skin before returning it.

"You seem in good spirits. I wonder if mayhap we could talk."

"I can't remember any more than I told you before, me lord."

The boy was quickly throwing away childish things and speaking as a man. Who would be there to help him make the transition complete? His mother had been killed. He hadn't spoken of a father.

"No matter. How does your hand heal?"

He waved what remained of his hand, now covered with a tight leather sack. Aldred smiled sheepishly. "I was always good at ciphering but no one could read what I wrote."

John was surprised. "For whom did you keep books?"

"Oh, a lot of different people in the village. The butcher...the priest...me mum." John saw his misting eyes at the mention of his mother.

"That is quite a trade. Where did you learn it?"

"Me dad was part of King Harold, excuse me me lord, Harold Godwinson's men." His eyes became distant, as if remembering the battle. "He died in the fighting."

The reality of all he'd been through in his young life seemed to haunt him. He closed his eyes. John waited for him patiently. The boy was strong. He would survive.

When he looked at John, he snorted in resignation but continued. "When he was alive, he would take me with him to the castle, and I would help with the stores, running accounts, counting items."

John nodded understanding before he took a sip of water. "Your father had a title?"

"No."

John's surprise must have been apparent because the boy explained himself. "There are a lot of people with titles that use others to do what they cannot."

John knew that to be true. Having been taught in the monastery, he had an education that many of William's knights did not have. Many couldn't even read. John could read and write French, English, Latin and Greek, and work numbers. His education was an exception, not the rule.

"Did you enjoy the work?" He smiled with the question, trying to encourage the boy to be honest.

Aldred snorted again. "I did." He smirked and raised his eyebrow jauntily. "I was a man of importance."

They exchanged easy smiles.

A boy with his knowledge could be an asset anywhere. "I think I might be able to find a place for you at the castle if that would please you."

Aldred's expression quickly went from excitement at the proposition to disappointment. "How can I write then?"

John tipped his head up at his butchered hand. "If you were not very legible with your right hand, mayhap you will do better with your left."

Aldred considered the offer for a moment, then grinned, his eyes becoming mere slits. "Mayhap you are correct."

John left the boy to return to Philip. "He is in good spirits."

"He has recovered very well."

"Don't take chances with his life, Philip. If they are watching and know our movements, the boy's life could be in danger. They don't know that he can't remember aught."

"They may not even know who he is or why he is with us," Philip offered.

"So we will take a defensive stance anyway."

"Aye."

Chapter Twenty-One

"Any word, Joan?" Rowena smoothed her hands down her kirtle, assuring the ties at her waist were secure. She needed to stop asking about John and get about her life. When her handmaiden rolled her eyes, she was sure of it. She just didn't care.

Her days were filled with seeing to the keep and maintaining proper stores in both the pantry and the buttery, and all sundry items brought in as payment. She wanted word of her husband. He had been gone nigh on two months and although she knew he was dealing with the trouble in the villages, she had to fight down the nagging feeling that he would not return to her.

"No, my lady, there is no word of your husband's return. I would tell you if there was. Nay, I would *run* to tell you if there was. Nay, I would run screaming…"

"Yes, yes, Joan, your point is well taken. Rest assured that I do not doubt you would let me know immediately if you heard aught. Understand that I must ask."

"What good does it do you to ask me?"

Rowena pondered her answer. Did it help her feel more in control? Yes. Did it give her a way to let out her thoughts that ran around in her head morning, noon and night? Yes. Did it really do her any good to ask? No. "It just does."

Rowena turned her back to the room, and Joan sat behind, braiding her hair as she spoke. "It does you no good at all to pine away in here either."

Rowena knew exactly how Joan felt about her wayward husband. "I do not pine away."

"You spend no time outside, my lady. Look." Joan held her hand in front of Rowena. A long clump of her hair was clasped in her fingers. "Your hair is falling out, my lady. End this."

"Joan," Rowena tried for a stern voice even though she too was concerned at the sight, "you overstep yourself when you speak to me so."

Immediately contrite, Joan lowered her eyes as she came to stand beside Rowena. "Forgive me, my lady. I am only thinking of your welfare."

"I know. Mayhap some fresh air will do me good."

Joan finished her braid without another word on the subject. "Raisins with your oats this morning?" She looked so hopeful that Rowena couldn't help but smile back and nod enthusiastically. Joan was happy with her answer and closed the door behind her as she went to get the food. Rowena's smile quickly changed to a grimace at the nauseous feeling she got at the idea of raisins.

Picking up her brush, Rowena could see quite a bit of her hair had come out. What was wrong with her? Her normally thick hair felt thin and scraggly. Was she pining away? She didn't feel like she was. True, she wished her husband would come back but the time they'd spent together had left her happy. Even cherished. She just wanted him to return to her.

"My lady!" Joan's voice preceded her flinging open Rowena's bedchamber door. "My lady!"

"What is amiss?" Rowena held her breath as she stepped toward her. "You look as if you've seen a ghost!"

On a whisper, Joan found no additional information much to Rowena's irritation. "My lady!" Shaking her head in disbelief, she stepped out of the door just as a tall woman would have pushed her aside.

"So you're the wife my lover is saddled with."

Rowena was unable to exhale the gasp that had been sucked into her belly. Her eyes bulged as she tried to process what the woman had said. She couldn't possibly have heard her right. Like a tempest, the woman stormed into Rowena's private chambers as if she'd every right to be there. Her disdainful gaze did not miss a thing as she looked around the room. "I'm a little surprised he has stayed away from me this long."

Joan's mouth gaped open in disbelief as she looked from the regal woman with the black hair and green eyes and back to Rowena. The petrified look on her servant's face finally broke the spell.

"And who are you, pray tell?" Rowena stood a little taller as she addressed the woman who seemed to tower over her.

The woman blinked as if discerning whether Rowena truly had the audacity to speak directly to her.

"No. Better *you* tell *me*." She paused, no doubt for effect, assessing Rowena from head to toe, finally lifting the corner of her lip and raising one eyebrow. "Are you 'the wife'?"

"Joan, get the guards and remove this woman from my chambers." She gave the orders through clenched teeth.

Joan fled to do her bidding. Rowena's pulse quickened and her fury kicked in. Such behavior was totally unacceptable from anyone, but to have a woman claiming to be her husband's lover invade her bedchamber and speak to her as if she were of no importance at all was outrageous.

Out of nowhere, Rowena was hit with a tremendous wave of nausea. Horrified, she realized this stranger would be a witness to her illness if she remained.

"Oh, ho, ho. A temper have you?" The woman moved in closer to Rowena, looking down her long nose as she spoke. "Your temper will not match mine, little girl."

Despite the pretty hair and eyes, the woman reeked of dead fish and flowers which increased Rowena's nausea. The bile accumulating at the back of her throat made her force her hand.

"How dare you speak to me so." Swallowing as hard as she could, she continued. "You have come into my room unbidden, and you will leave immediately or the guards will be happy to escort you to the bowels of the castle for your display of disrespect."

The woman did not back down. Instead, she stared at Rowena as if she had two heads. Rowena tipped her chin up and tried to stare her down but she caught a whiff of the fish again. It was her undoing. Lurching back toward the bed, Rowena barely made it to the chamber pot before vomiting.

Rowena was at her most vulnerable while this stranger looked on. This stranger who said she was John's lover. This stranger who acted like she owned John. This stranger who acted like Rowena was something that crawled out from under a rock. This was the woman who got to watch as all her stomach contents came gushing up.

Her humiliation grew and the vomiting continued. Just when she believed she was done, she heard Joan return with the guards. Being otherwise occupied, she wished to be anywhere but retching in front of this woman.

"Well, get her out of here!" Joan sounded incredulous. "She came up here without invitation. Remove her!" The guards were clearly intimidated by the woman's demeanor, imperious as she was, and seemed reluctant to just grab her and drag her out.

The contents of her stomach emptied, Rowena leaned slightly against her table in time to see Joan roll her eyes in disgust at the guards who just stood there. Fighting for enough composure to end her embarrassment, Rowena's knees wobbled beneath her dressing gown.

"Joan speaks for me." The guards immediately made to remove the woman who backed away, pulling her arm out of their reach.

"Are you sure you aren't even a little curious about who I am?" She addressed Rowena but her eyes were on the guards.

Rowena wiped her hand across her mouth. She felt surprisingly better but needed to lie down.

"Not in the least. Remove her."

Inching her way back to her bed, Rowena was asleep as soon as her head hit the pillow.

The room was brightly lit when Rowena awoke from her nap later that morning. Lying on her stomach, she assessed how she felt. Much better. The smell of the oatmeal caused her empty stomach to growl in answer. She started to turn onto her back when she noticed the tingling in her breasts. She had noticed they seemed fuller than usual and now they were even sensitive to her touch.

"My lady?" Joan's voice was very quiet but Rowena decided to face the woman rather than to feign sleep.

"I am awake."

"Oh, good. My lady, whatever shall we do?" Joan's face was pinched with worry, her eyes red and puffy. Rowena could not remember why that would be or what they needed to decide about.

"You are so melodramatic." Sitting up in her bed, she reached toward the bowl which Joan handed to her. Her first bite of oatmeal was warm and sweet with raisins, very good. As she swallowed, a feeling of contentment filled her. That was until she was hit with the memory of the woman. Her eyes flew open.

"Oh, no! Where is she?"

"She took herself out of the castle as if she were the Queen of Sheba!" Joan didn't try to hide her disgust.

Rowena struggled to remember what the woman had said? The wife her lover was *saddled* with? In a flurry, she jumped off the bed and pulled her bed clothes off, giving orders all the while.

"My gown, Joan, quickly. Did the guards have to threaten her? When did she arrive here? There was no gossip about a strange woman in the area? Joan, what is taking you so long?" As she tied up the opening of her chemise, she turned to find Joan waiting patiently with her tunic. She dipped her head into the opening and allowed her to follow that with her outer gown. "Do you know where she went?"

"Well, I sent the lad out to follow her. He said she stopped at the inn. The same one that his lordship…"

"Yes, I know."

Rowena interrupted her story before she heard again that she should have cleared up the misunderstanding with her husband before she allowed him to have his way with her. Of course, Joan couldn't know that she had also had her way with him. It had been mutually satisfying to say the least.

Joan frowned. "Why are you turning red, my lady? You haven't done anything wrong."

Rowena turned her back to Joan so she could pull her long braid out. "Did you get a name?"

"Abigail."

Biting her lower lip, Rowena tried to remember if John had ever mentioned an Abigail. He hadn't really said much about his life at all. No, she was sure there had been no mention of an Abigail.

Rowena shook her head with conviction and turned toward the small blonde. "She was a liar. I don't know who she is, but my husband will explain it when he returns."

"When will that be?"

She had received no word from John since he'd left. With fall quickly passing, the stores were being stockpiled, the fields had been harvested and turned over, and the preparations for winter were well advanced. If her husband did not return soon, it could be he would not be able to return until the spring. That would be true especially if he had left for Normandy. Her heart sank at the very thought.

"Please," Joan took her hands as if reading her mind, "do not think the worst. It is not good for you in your condition."

"To what do you refer? What condition?"

Joan's voice was quiet in the small room. "You do not know?"

"Know what? Why are you speaking in riddles?" Rowena was quickly losing patience.

"Your queasiness?"

"I think the eel soup was bad last night. Did no one else succumb?"

Joan's eyebrows were raised in expectation but Rowena had no answer for her."Verily, my lady? Bad eel soup?"

"Something did not sit well with me."

Joan shook her head and it irritated Rowena.

"What? Pray tell then, what is my condition?"

"You are with child," Joan replied.

First disbelief then excitement gripped Rowena. Realizing she had not had her menses since right after her husband's arrival, it was very possible that she was with child. It had been two months since she'd lain with him. She touched her tender breast. Of course! That was why her breasts were filling out, in preparation for the child that would soon suckle them.

Her complete joy knew no bounds as she imagined her very own child. A child conceived by their long awaited wedding night. The realization that God had blessed their union with a child was almost too much. For so long she had thought God had abandoned her to be alone the rest of her life, and in a short few months her life had changed drastically.

Thank you, Lord, that you are ever faithful even when we lose heart.

She grasped her hands to her chest and smiled. "I think you are right. A child! I have conceived!"

Sitting on the side of the bed, she ran her hand over her abdomen and thought of the babe asleep in there. It was a girl. She knew it was a girl. She would have dark hair like her father and a dimple on her cheek.

"A child." She whispered the words to see how it sounded. Wonderful.

"We will not allow the woman in again," Joan spoke with conviction but the reminder dampened Rowena's happiness.

"That is as it should be, methinks. If John were here, he could prove her for the liar that she is. Since he is not, we do not have to deal with her lies."

"It is decided then." Joan's hands on her hips, she nodded her head with finality.

The woman was insistent. Every day for more than a month, she came to call on Rowena. Each time, Joan intercepted and told the woman she was not welcome. It was becoming tiresome. The vile woman believed she could visit the home of his lordship whenever she chose and be welcomed. Usually, Rowena accepted many visitors at the evening meal but Joan was ever diligent and would not allow the woman entrance.

Still there was no word from John.

Turning her attention from her absent husband to the child they had created gave her a much better outlook. As the winter skies grew gray and the rain came down in droves, Rowena often found herself before the warm fire just holding her needlepoint, staring into the flames imagining her future.

A husband to love. A child to care for.

The morning sickness had subsided but her hair was still ratty and thin. She knew she wasn't exactly blossoming but she was happy. She did not glow radiantly like her friend Katey had, but she still had several months yet to go, and things would be better when John returned.

The memory of his hands sliding over her belly and cupping her breast slipped through her mind. Would he still desire her? Or would he set her aside? She did not like to think there would be no more intimacy between them. He had said he would not go to another. But like so many other things about John, Rowena didn't know how he would react to the news or to the woman who hounded her incessantly.

Chapter Twenty-Two

"Soldiers are crossing the bridge!" Joan had all but run to her with the news. "I do not see your husband yet. I will go keep watch."

Rowena stood and smoothed her skirts, pushed at her hair, and finally started to pace when no one came to join her in the Great Hall. How would John take the news of their impending parenthood? Did he long to be a father as Rowena had to be a mother? Perhaps not but he would surely adjust to the idea and be glad. He would be a doting father, giving their little girl rides on his shoulders and taking her for long walks in the woods. Rowena would teach her about herbs and how to heal ailments like her own mother had taught her. After what seemed an eternity, Joan came slowly back into the room. She was alone.

"I am sorry, my lady. They had come to advise the rest of the men. There has been some trouble not far from here, and your husband wanted to see that you were well protected."

"They said that? That John wanted me protected?" Her sadness at John not coming was quickly replaced by the reality of his concern for her. He did care.

"Well, not in so many words."

Turning away to hide the tears that came so easily now, Rowena struggled with her emotions. She wanted to feel glad that she knew John was well and that he was nearby. The bubbling in her belly brought a smile to her face. She placed her hand where she'd felt the movement, but it had stopped. Still she knew that the truth was she would never be alone again.

Rowena turned back to her friend, a genuine smile across her face. "Would you send word to my husband that all is well here?"

Joan tipped her head, a quirk of an eyebrow like a salute to her lady's resilience, and said, "I will be sure to do that, my lady."

Joan quickly ran out leaving Rowena standing alone before the fire, fighting the somberness that threatened to engulf her. She knew the moment the unwanted woman had entered the room behind her.

Without turning, Rowena let Abigail hear her disgust in her voice. "So you've made it in despite our wanting to keep you out."

"I am nothing if not clever. And trust me, I am much more."

Slowly turning to face the woman, Rowena had forgotten just how beautiful she was. Her thick, dark hair swept down her sides, blanketing the cape she wore draped about her shoulders. Her bright eyes showed intelligence, missing nothing as they assessed Rowena. As if peering into her soul, Rowena was acutely uncomfortable with the woman's sudden frown. It was as if she had figured out her secret. But that couldn't be. Rowena barely showed at all.

"Abigail, is it?" Rowena did not try to hide her disdain.

Resignation was now etched on the woman's face as if she had come across an unhappy truth. Rowena waited patiently for her reply.

"I am Abigail of Moulineaux Castle in Normandy."

Her arrogance at laying claim to John's estate was galling. "Are you now?"

Abigail raised her nose. Suddenly tired again, Rowena sat next to the fire before her legs gave way beneath her. Debating whether she should order the woman to leave or finally give her a chance to say what it was she had to say, Rowena preferred the former.

"If I ask you to leave?"

"You will have to make me leave."

"It can be done."

Smiling indulgently, the woman answered her, "I believe you will not do that...not again."

"So speak your mind and be gone." Rowena tried to sound uninterested but the light in her nemesis' eyes spoke volumes about her failure.

"Yes, I would like to sit. Thank you." Sweeping her long black cape around the bench in front of Rowena, Abigail sat down as if she were royalty. How long ago was it that John had sat in that same spot causing havoc to Rowena's senses, causing her to desire him above everything else. It seemed so very long ago.

"Thinking of him, are you?" Abigail said.

Shocked that she was so transparent to this woman, Rowena sat up straighter. "What is it that you want?"

"That is simple. I have come for John. I'm sure he has missed me and our son as much as we have him."

Cut to the quick, Rowena wished that it didn't feel like she'd been punched in the gut. She knew the rumor the woman was spreading, that she was indeed John's mistress and she had come to see that he had not taken ill. Abigail claimed that he had assured her he would return to her by fall. That she and John had a son was something Rowena had not heard before.

"My husband is not here. He is seeing to his property."

"So I've heard. Weren't able to keep him with you for very long were you? I'd venture to say he had no interest in you at all." Her perfectly red lips stretched into a smile that didn't reach her eyes.

Rowena reconsidered and decided the woman was actually very ugly. For her to think she could come and arrogantly make comments regarding John's feelings showed how ugly she was inside. Her heart was probably made of stone.

Unable to hide the pain the words caused, Rowena was relieved to see Joan stomping toward them from the kitchen.

"What are you doing in here?" Joan said, her voice resonating authority. Rowena was very glad she was an ally.

"She was just leaving." Rowena held Abigail's gaze as she spoke. "She has said her peace, and now she will go without any problem. Isn't that right, Abigail?" Despite her weariness, Rowena rose when Joan came to stand beside her, her friend's presence bolstering her sagging confidence. "Thank you for your visit but you need not return. You are not welcome here."

Taking Joan's arm for support, Rowena left the woman behind her as she headed back to her room.

"My lady, you look ill," Joan whispered as they ascended the stairs.

"Is she gone yet?"

Joan glanced behind and nodded. "Young Peter is showing her out now."

"Please help me to bed. I have a tightness in my gut that does not seem right."

Rowena stretched on the bed. When Joan started to cover her with the blankets, Rowena was startled by her gasp. "My lady..." looking down at her clothing, she, too could see the spreading crimson stain.

Joan placed a wadded cloth tight against her, trying to staunch the bleeding.

"Fetch the midwife," Rowena said.

"I will bring her to you right away."

Alone in the room, the shadows fell as the time ticked by and she waited to see if her baby would live or die. The shadows looked like ugly monsters that seemed to leer at Rowena, laughing at her weakness. The wind whipping against the glass sounded like crying children and her cramping seemed to increase with every cry.

She awoke once to find Claire, the midwife, clucking and checking, rambling on but it made no sense. There was so much blood and then she was forcing something bitter into her mouth. Rowena retreated back to her sleep. When next she awoke, John was beside her. His kind brown eyes were full of concern for her, his hand gently stroking her cheek, and his lips warm against her forehead.

"Sleep, my love." His words echoed in her head. That he would call her his love made her feel safe and wanted. Yes, my love, I will sleep now.

The bright daylight shone through the window that Joan had just opened, causing Rowena to squint her eyes in pain. "Where is John?"

Joan clutched her hands to her chest, and she came to stand beside the bed. "What do you mean?"

"He was here. Where has he gone?"

Joan put her hand to Rowena's forehead but she pulled back in annoyance. "I am not fevered. Where is John? I haven't had a chance to tell him about the baby."

"My lady, he is not here."

"He left without speaking to me?" Rowena started to sit up and was shocked by the pain stabbing in her abdomen. "Get him." Tears filled her eyes as she slipped back on to the pillow.

"I cannot, my lady. He is not here. He hasn't been here."

Searching her face, Rowena could see that Joan believed she was speaking the truth. The memory of his lips on her forehead made her instinctively reach to touch the spot. "He was here with me." Her voice was quiet.

Joan shook her head, barely able to suppress the concern that revelation was having on her. "You are wrong. Your husband has not been here. You need to rest."

"The baby?"

"Claire said you may still lose the child unless you stay in bed." Tucking her blankets tightly around her as if to physically keep her from moving, Joan smiled and patted Rowena's hand before she left the room.

Rowena's initial relief at finding her baby had not been lost was quickly replaced by worry over John. She looked around, searching for any sign of what she knew had happened. John had come to her and told her to rest. She could still see the way he had looked, hair all tousled, his tunic caked with the mud of his travels. What did that mean? If it wasn't John...what was it then? His ghost? Is that why he has not returned? He is dead? Slowly shaking her head in disbelief, the tears quickly grew into a torrent and Rowena buried herself up to her chin in the blankets until she cried herself into a fitful sleep.

Chapter Twenty-Three

"Oh, my lady." Joan dropped the stack of blankets she carried onto the floor, catching Rowena's arm just as she started to stand beside the bed. "Are you sure you should be out of bed?"

Her hand pressed on her temple, her eyes closed in pain, Rowena wondered the same thing.

"I believe I am getting my strength back. I only wanted to look at the snowfall."

Joan smiled slightly at her answer.

"Foolish, yes?"

Joan helped her to settle back down without a word. Rowena slid her legs back beneath the blankets.

"It is just white. No more. Just white."

"Do not try to humor me." Rowena frowned at her maid once her dizziness subsided. "Snow is not something we see every day. Do not tell me you did not run through it this very morning!"

Joan looked away in embarrassment.

"I noticed your wet hem," Rowena explained.

"It was soft and cold!" Joan's excitement was quite apparent.

Years had gone by with not a speck of snow and now to have several inches accumulating! This was an event.

"But you should stay abed," Joan said. Her concern was evident, and Rowena felt shame at her childish desire.

"You are right." She ran her hand across her swelling abdomen. "Some things are even more important, aren't they?"

Speaking more to her unborn child, Rowena looked sheepishly up at Joan.

126

"I was just getting bored."

"My lady, I am sorry I took so long to return." Collecting the items she dropped, Joan continued, "There was news of the men."

Instantly alert, her child responded with a slight kick, bring a smile to her lips.

"Is there more movement?" Joan had her hand out to feel what could not yet be seen. The babe kicked in answer. "Strong! That is very good."

Rowena rubbed gently, soothingly. "Well? News?"

She asked more out of habit than in expectation of receiving any information. It had been so many months now without a word from her husband. In all honesty, she was convinced he had returned to Normandy and left his men to see to the troubles in the area. The only thing that didn't make sense was the continued presence of Abigail in the village. She had taken up permanent residency at the Owl and Thistle, relentlessly plaguing Rowena with her presence.

"There seems to be a settling down among the villages in the area."

"But settling of what? You never did learn what the problem was." Her irritation was hard to hide. All this time, something was going on but no one found it necessary to tell her. If Arthur had been here, he would have been sure to come and tell her. He always kept her abreast of local developments. "Is it even something we should be concerned about?" She shook her head to her own question.

"Patience, please." Joan patted the hand that rested on top of the blanket. "News will come soon."

Remembering the feel of his lips on her forehead, Rowena tried to feel contented that when she was at her worst, when the death of their unborn child had seemed imminent, John had returned and strengthened them both by his presence. Even returning the child to health, although Rowena was no longer able to get out of bed for very long, it was a small price to pay for the babe. "You are right."

"If the bleeding does not return, Claire assured me you could leave the bed safely."

"That would be a blessing to me. Sitting here is very tiring."

Joan placed one of the blankets in front of Rowena in answer. Its ragged hem prominently displayed.

"Mending?" Rowena whined childishly.

Joan settled herself on the stool close to the bed. She smiled as she started her own darning.

"It needs to be done as well you know."

Sitting up slightly, Rowena found the start of the tear and quickly had her wooden needle bringing the two sides into a neat row. The time passed and Rowena was surprised when Joan stood and stretched her back.

Glancing at the window, the bright light was no longer a subdued gray. Rowena's stomach growled in answer. She rubbed her stiff fingers.

"I am famished!"

"You were so involved that you didn't even notice the time," Joan scolded her like a child. "In your condition, you need to eat more. I can fetch you a tray from the kitchen when we are finished here."

"You're right but go now. I will finish this last one by the time you return."

Joan took longer than Rowena had expected, so she piled the blankets on the stool. She leaned back to stretch then closed her eyes. She resorted to rubbing her swollen belly and thinking about her little girl. In her mind's eye she pictured her with John's dark hair and kind, brown eyes. Certainly she would have a precocious smile and win over everyone's heart. She would have a lilting voice and learn to sing with Cedric. Rowena sighed. She missed the entertainment from the hall. There had been no visitors since her confinement. Perhaps she should ask to have some visitors. She yawned and rubbed her eyes. Mending was so tiring.

When she stretched toward the side table to put her needle down, Rowena noticed the brown leaf. Beside her candle, a brown twig was partially obscured. Retrieving it, she recognized it as a lady slipper well past its prime. Strange that it should be there. John's concerned face immediately came to mind. Tenderly she brought it to her cheek. John had been here and he'd brought her this flower.

She turned onto her side and placed the brown plant in the spot where John's head should be resting in his sleep. Her arm reached out to the cold spot where he should be lying and cried in earnest. Sleep came quickly.

§

The snowfall was a godsend. Not knowing how long it would last, the men doubled their efforts to find any sign of the murderers. They spread out through the dense forest that ran between the villages north of the last victims. This was the only way they could have retreated without being caught. John and his men had surrounded them on all sides but believing they were coming from the south, they had not adequately covered this area. John cursed himself again for not anticipating the latest massacre.

A hawk passed overhead casting its shadow across them as it flew. An omen. The bright sun would quickly melt the thin blanket of snow. They needed to cover as much ground as possible. There had to be some sign. Snorting, John closed his eyes and offered up a quick prayer for help.

The shrill whistle of an imaginary bird penetrated the dark forest. It was Peter's signal. The trees muffled the sound of the men as they quickly headed toward its source.

John stepped through the group of men to see what Peter pointed to. These tracks were half covered by the snow while others were clearly seen. They must have traveled through here just as the snow had started. They had four hours head start.

"How many men?" John asked.

"Looks like one, two…" Peter pointed as he spotted the now obvious signs, "…three…"

"Four!" Philip called from their left, pointing down as well. "Five, six."

Only six? That didn't seem right. There were at least two riders unaccounted for.

"Search more closely but do it quickly." John's irritation was rising. If the group had split up then they may realize they were being followed.

"These men are ruthless," Peter stated the obvious and shook his head in disgust. "At what will they stop?"

"My lord!" Henry called to John. He was at the forest's edge where the sun was already blurring the outline of the destrier's hoof. "It looks as if other riders are headed back east."

John's heart lurched. The castle was to the east. Rowena was to the east. Why would they go there? Looking to Peter, he saw that he was concerned as well.

"What harm could come to the castle? They are well protected there," Peter said reassuringly.

"We have taken away their only protection for this search. I left only a few loyal men behind."

"Loyalty is certainly the issue."

"We don't know who can be trusted at the castle."

Peter shook his head slowly, his mouth a thin line.

"We can't leave the castle undefended if an attack seems imminent." How many of the Saxons would follow him if there was an attack?

"This may be our only chance of catching these murderers," Peter gestured to the miraculous tracks they'd been able to find because of the snow.

"We need every man we have here."

"You need to go," Peter said.

"I need to be leading the men."

"John, you need to go back. Take Philip so that you will not walk into a trap or be caught unprepared. You two are the only ones who have a chance of getting back to the castle before these men." Peter gestured to the tracks headed due east. "If these men are as devious as we believe, they may be friends of the castle men who would let them in without a second thought. Who knows what would happen once they are inside?"

John's mind went unbidden to Rowena. Something could happen to her. If these men were after money, and they knew they were being hunted, they may very well abduct her for the costly ransom she would bring. Abducted women were not well treated. The idea of any man laying hands on his wife turned his blood cold.

"You're right. See to the men, Peter."

Without a backward glance, John and Philip urged their horses back to the castle. If they found nothing amiss, they could prepare the castle's defense.

Chapter Twenty-Four

Rowena slowly walked in the barren garden, her cloak and mantle held tightly against the frigid cold. She was exhilarated. She had spent too much time inside. The cold felt wonderful against her face and her breath puffed ahead of her as she laughed. It was good to be alive. The babe kicked in agreement. Now heavy with child, she tired quickly but was so glad to be getting up and around.

"My lady?" Joan added another blanket around her shoulders as she spoke. "Do not stay over long. Remember Claire said in small amounts."

"Nag, nag, nag," Rowena gave her an indulgent smile.

She was tired of being treated as if she were sick. The force of the baby's movements within told her the child was fine. There had been no more bleeding. She would have a healthy baby girl. And she would look like her father. The melancholy came out of nowhere, and she turned away from her observant friend before Joan could see her tears.

"I only want to keep you safe." Resting her hand on Rowena's shoulder, she squeezed comfortingly and went back inside where it was warm.

Rowena exhaled in resignation. There was no help for it. What bliss if John were to return to her. Since he had not yet done that, she needed to just keep going. Perhaps her melancholy was just natural. She felt strong in spirit most of the time. Her dreams at night were vivid. She could actually feel her husband's hand caressing her as he made love to her once again.

The cough startled her from her reminiscences. Turning toward the sound, Rowena took a moment to get over the shock of seeing the red-haired man standing in the same place she'd last seen him.

"Arthur? Arthur!" She flew into his arms and hugged him to her. "How wonderful to see you." Unexpectedly, the tears began to flow again.

Arthur cleared his throat and she pulled back. He pulled off his gloves and tucked them behind his scabbard, fingers out. His cheeks looked sunken in, his clothes were filthy.

"Are you ill?" she asked.

He tenderly wiped the tear from her cheek. His hand was rough against her skin. "Do you cry for me, my lady?" Arthur's voice was unusually raspy.

"I am happy to see you, my dear friend."

A gray cloud blocked the late winter sun and Rowena shivered involuntarily. She stepped back, suddenly awkward with him.

"How have you been?" she asked.

Rubbing his scalp, he ran his fingers through hair so dirty it was almost brown. He grimaced, seeming to ponder the proper answer. "I am well. I have been greatly concerned for you." His breathing rattled in his chest.

Her eyes filled again. She put her arm on his leather armband. "I appreciate your concern."

His eyes brightened. He took a step toward her, closing the small distance and she fought down the urge to retreat.

"I have always been concerned for you," he said.

He took the hand that rested on his arm and brought it slowly to his mouth where he kissed it tenderly, his eyes never leaving her face. "I would do aught for you."

Rowena knew it was true. He had always said as much to her. Now it appeared she was alone again and he had come to her rescue.

"Shall we sit?" She used the opportunity to put distance between them and led him to the garden bench. The baby lurched inside her and she gasped lightly.

"Are you well?" Arthur still held her hand when he sat beside her. His frown deepened. She smiled reassuringly and nodded. "How have you fared these winter months?"

"Well enough although I have been lonely," she said.

"Ah, is that why you sit out here in the garden? You are overcome with loneliness?"

"I needed fresh air." The isolation of the space suddenly made her uneasy, and she wondered how she could move their conversation inside. It seemed silly to not feel safe with Arthur. "Perhaps we should move inside."

When she started to stand, he held her hand fast, forcing her to remain seated. His grip was overly firm. Her uneasiness grew.

"Let us talk first," he said.

Relenting, Rowena settled down again. His eyes were cold, unreadable.

"Do you have news?"

"I would not have you be here alone," Arthur said.

"This is my home. Where else would I be?"

"Do you fear you have been abandoned?"

The frankness of his question surprised her. He appeared to be holding something back.

"Have you news? I know there has been unrest in the area but I have not heard what the cause was."

Arthur shook his head in disgust. "It is always the same trouble. The Normans push the Saxons around and we fight back."

He spoke as if distracted. Rowena waited for him to say more. He did not.

"It is just the same fighting then?"

"Did I not just say as much?" His voice rose in irritation. Rowena never knew Arthur to speak so to anyone and especially not to her.

"Arthur." She reached her other hand out from her cape, exposing her swollen abdomen underneath. "Tell me what you know."

Arthur seemed mesmerized by the sight of her body. Rowena resisted the urge to pull the ends of her cape back together. She was not indecent. She was just pregnant. When his eyes met hers, she would swear she saw tears.

"What is amiss?" Quickly the look was gone. "Has something happened to John? Tell me, please. I need to know."

Arthur stood suddenly, and he let her hand drop abruptly onto the bench. He walked a short distance away before turning toward her again. His face was red, his jaw clenched while he looked to be struggling with what to say. "I am afraid you are correct. John has been injured."

Rowena's body tensed in response. She stood and reached out to Arthur. Stepping away from her reach, he continued. "I have come to bring you to him right away."

"What? Why did you not tell me immediately? I must tell Joan…"

"No!" Arthur's grasp hurt where he pulled her arm unexpectedly.

"We must leave now. I told Joan when I saw her. There is no time to wait."

Rowena frowned, uncertain what to do. It did not feel right to just leave. She wanted to tell someone. "But…"

"There is no time! We must leave! Now!" His harsh voice broke through her befuddlement, and she allowed him to lead her roughly through the outer bailey.

"Please. You are hurting me." She pulled against him but he didn't seem to notice. Thoughts of John maimed and dying caused havoc to her senses. "How far must we travel?"

Arthur was pushing her up onto his horse. "It is not far. We will do better traveling together."

"Are you sure? My horse is…"

"I am sure!" The force of his command startled her. He didn't seem to notice as he settled behind her and took the reins, effectively imprisoning her where she sat. "Keep silent and we will arrive shortly."

She sat stiffly and tried not to lean against him. The fear she felt was as much for her as for John. Arthur's behavior was strange. The baby lurched in response, and she rubbed it soothingly. Arthur roughly pulled her hand away and wrapped it around his side.

"Hold on so you don't fall."

She had no choice but to lean against him. His woolen tunic stunk; its roughness chafed her cheek as she was jerked against it by the speed of the horse. "I'm concerned for my child. Do we need to travel this fast?"

"I don't want John to die before you get there."

The reality that John was near death overwhelmed her. She turned her face against Arthur's shirt and cried. No, John could not die. He had a child and didn't even know about it. He couldn't die on her. She wanted him to raise their child with her. He may not be a Saxon but he was the man she wanted. Her sobs racked her body, and she clung tighter to Arthur, trembling against him. She had always felt such comfort from him. She realized with some trepidation that his hands remained holding the reins. Then she noticed how stiffly he held himself. He wasn't offering her any comfort. He appeared angry.

"What is amiss?" She pulled back to ask the question. His face was a mask of rage.

"Shut up."

Fear cut through her like a knife and she gasped at his words. "What have I done that you would speak to me so? How have I wronged you?"

The eyes that finally met hers were dark with his fury. "You are a good for nothing whore." He pulled the reins sharply to a stop. The horse reared slightly. Quickly jumping down, Arthur grabbed her off the horse none too gently before she could dismount on the other side. "Look at you!" He yanked her cape open and pointed accusingly at her unborn child. "Just look at you!" He spit his words at her as he paced. "Why couldn't you wait for me? I would never have left you there for long."

Rowena shook her head, shivering in fear. When she opened her mouth to answer, he slapped her, hard. Her hand flew to her face in reflex. She tasted blood when her tongue ran along her numbing lip. Arthur was a madman. Fear gripped her tightly. Her heart raced in her chest. There was no way to know what he would do next.

"That Norman bastard should never have touched what was not his!" Arthur shouted the words at her. His face twisted in a snarling rage of disgust.

"I am his wife." Rowena tried to speak calmly, tried to cover the fear twisting in her gut.

"You are a Saxon. He had no right to take you!" Tears sprang to his eyes, and he added as if to himself, "They have taken enough." His mouth twisted into a pout as if he would cry. Despite her fear, Rowena felt compassion for his obvious pain. He finally looked her in the eye, his voice a mere whisper. "How could you let him have you, Rowena?" His words were spoken so tenderly. "You are mine."

She wiped the blood that slipped down her chin. He made no sense. Where was John? Glancing around, she realized she had no idea where she was.

"Where is he?"

"Who?" Fear gripped her heart. Arthur seemed incoherent.

"John." She spoke slowly, as if to a child.

His face showed only contempt as his eyes raked her body. He shook his head as if finding her lacking.

"Arthur? Is John hurt? Can you take me to him?"

He pulled the blanket off her shoulder, pulling her off balance in the effort. "Whore!" The mantle and cape came off next. She struggled to remain standing against each yank of material.

Disbelief spread through her. He was going to strip her naked.

"Please, Arthur, it is so cold." Was there any part of the compassionate man she once knew still within him? "I need to stay covered."

Rolling the heavy material into a ball before throwing it on the ground, Arthur's face was tight with anger, his nostrils flared. "You have no idea what you've done, do you?" He dug his fingers into her hair and cruelly pulled her up against him. Nose to nose, he spat his words at her through gritted teeth. "I tried to protect you."

The madness in his eyes was so apparent to her now. How could she have missed that gleam? He snickered as he continued with his taunts. "You never deserved my protection, did you? You made *me* beg. Me! A Saxon." Grabbing a fistful of her gown, his breath was hot against her face. She turned, pulling back as far as she could. "I won't beg anymore."

Already off balance, the force of his shove knocked her to the ground.

She didn't have time to catch her breath before he was pulling up her skirts, his filthy hands grabbing at her. She kicked at him, her sobs nearly choking her. His eyes bulged in his outrage. He slapped her hard. Her head jerked back with the force, to slam against the ground.

On her back, the weight of the baby was heavy. Then Arthur's face was looming over her, leering down. His hands were hot touching exposed skin. The sensitive area between her legs burned where he rubbed himself against her. Flattening himself on top of her as best he could, she closed her eyes. *Let my child survive this unharmed.* Arthur paid the child no heed until the situation became impossible for him to complete his task. On his knees between her spread legs, he roughly tried to flip her over. She resisted, grabbing his arm, desperate to stop him.

"No, Arthur!" Determinedly she pulled against his tunic, sitting up with difficulty. She implored him with her eyes, pushing against him. "Don't do this. Please."

The force of the baby's kick seemed to break Arthur from his madness. Looking at her swelling abdomen, he quickly pulled himself to standing. He acted as if he'd been burned. She tucked her legs beneath her skirts. Shivering in the cold air, her body began to shake uncontrollably. Her teeth chattered loudly in the silence. Arthur continued to stare at her belly. The hot wetness between her legs was spreading beneath her. She didn't know if she was bleeding or if it was something else. The shooting pain across her abdomen doubled her into a ball.

The movement seemed to break through his obsession with the baby. His eyes searched her face. "Please," she said. Her voice was tight with pain. "Help me."

Scooping her up into his arms, he held her against him as he walked toward the open field. With each step she bit her lip to hold back her cry of pain. If he dropped her, the child would not survive. The smell of mold and rot surrounded them as he carried her feet first between abandoned hay piles, riddled with debris and vermin, through a small opening. The pain lessened as his movements slowed. The opening could easily have gone unnoticed, overgrown with brush as it was.

Arthur kicked at the twigs along the ground revealing a much larger entrance to an underground room. A dungeon! The stone steps that led into the darkened cave were moist and the air was hot. He stood her gently against the far side of the cavern. She trembled, backing up against the damp wall. The pain shot through her again and her knees buckled beneath her. She crumbled to the ground. Her eyes tightly closed, she held her breath against the excruciating pain. All her insides seemed to tighten against the all encompassing pain.

Breathing heavily when it finally passed, she opened her eyes to Arthur coming down the same stone steps, her cape in his hands. She touched the sticky wetness on her gown. It wasn't blood. The baby was coming.

Arthur loomed over her, his face an unreadable mask. Sweat trickled down her neck as her body slowly returned to normal. She was already exhausted. "Please, Arthur. Help me." The baby was coming. She was desperate for his assistance. Her words were barely above a whisper. "I need you. I can't do this alone."

He squatted beside her. She resisted the strong urge to pull away from him when he smoothed her hair out of her face. She had spoken the truth. She was totally at his mercy.

"Oh, my lady." His voice sounded like the old Arthur, and when he smiled, her breath caught in her throat. "It should be our child you're having."

Her gasp of disbelief hung in the air between them. Could she really have ever cared for this man? What had happened to turn him into such a monster?

Afraid to anger him, she tried to keep the fear out of her voice. "I'm sorry."

Tipping his head as if a thought had just occurred to him, he smiled reassuringly at her. "Did he force himself on you then?" There was such hope in his eyes.

"Yes." She lied easily. Aught for her child.

He nodded understandingly and she found herself nodding with him.

"The Norman bastard." His voice was low and menacing. He searched her face, for what? She didn't know. Finally, he stood and straightened his tunic. "He will pay for this. Rest for now. I will return."

Panicked, she reached for him. The pain overwhelmed her again. He clucked and turned around to leave her there. She looked to the opening and the light on the stairs he had just ascended. Hope that she could make it to the steps on her own was all she had but her body tightened beyond endurance and somewhere in her mind, she saw the light go out.

Chapter Twenty-Five

As soon as John broke through the trees, he saw the guard in the tower. Relieved, he loosened his hold on the reins and allowed the horse to pick up speed as he crossed the open field. He wasn't sure what he would find when he finally made it to the castle. There had been signs along the way of one man on horseback not far ahead. He looked to be riding a Norman destrier but John knew it was no Norman. It was Arthur.

John jumped from his horse before it had completely stopped, and the stable boy grabbed the reins to still the animal.

"Has Arthur been here?" The young boy shook his head. John grimaced and quickly assessed the area. "Is the Lady Rowena about?"

His pulse quickened at the thought of seeing her again.

"In the garden, my lord."

Why would she be in the garden? The bitter cold made it a miserable day to be outside. He pulled his gloves off as he headed through the garden gate. There was no sign of Rowena. A strong sense of foreboding spread up his spine when he noticed her needlework fluttering in the breeze on the bench. Picking it up, he wondered why she would just leave her handiwork. As he headed toward the kitchen, he stopped short at the sight on the path. A well-worn riding glove lay there. Someone left in a hurry. Retrieving it, he looked more closely at the man's glove. Disbelief strangled him. He let the glove drop to the ground and headed in through the kitchen.

"My lord!" Joan's eyes widened in surprise at seeing him, and she looked behind him, expectantly. She frowned. "Where's the Lady Rowena?"

Joan strode past him, catching the door before he could close it. She

138

turned back to him after looking into the garden. "Did you not pass her?"

John brusquely handed her the needlework. "She is not out there."

"What?" Her voice trembled. She grabbed the shawl from the hook alongside the door. "My lady?" Joan called out as she headed into the garden.

John heard the fear in her voice. He was coming to his own conclusions. He was too late. Arthur had come and now Rowena was gone.

"When did you last see her?" he asked when Joan returned. Regardless of how his wife felt about his enemy, he needed to track the man down.

"It was just a short while ago. Where would she go?"

"Was anyone with her?" He cursed himself for the spark of hope that question caused him.

Joan shook her head. "She was alone."

She did not look directly at him. A lead weight settled in his chest. She was lying. The weight twisted and threatened to cut off his air. He realized he didn't want to know why she would lie. He already knew. Striding past her, John found several men sitting at a table in the Great Hall. They were Saxon soldiers. They stopped speaking as soon as they saw him. John had to make a decision. Did he treat them as his own men, which by rights they were, or did he continue to let them stay apart from him, treating him like the enemy? They looked him up and down, assessing him. Perhaps they were as unsure as he was. They visibly stiffened as he approached. He resisted the urge to do the same.

"Do you know about the trouble with the villagers?" He swallowed hard to ease the tension in his own voice.

The men exchanged questioning glances. John needed to know if he could trust these men so he waited. Finally, the tall man with the dark wavy hair and full beard nodded slowly. "We know there's been trouble about."

"What do you make of it?" John asked, calmly pouring himself a drink from the pitcher that sat on the table while inside his gut tensed.

A thin man with dirty blonde hair spoke up excitedly, almost tripping over his own words. "I know what they want us to think."

"Enough, Rolf." The dark-haired man spoke sharply but barely moved, quieting the excited man.

John drank his cider slowly.

The man's eyes were on him as he sized him up. "There are rumors." He finally added in explanation.

Placing his cup on the table, John stood tall when he turned toward the man. "What kind of rumors?"

"That the Normans are trying to kill all the Saxons." The big man sat up a little straighter, intently focused on John.

This man would be a worthy opponent. He recognized him as one of the men who had watched him in the practice yard so many months ago now.

"What do *you* think?" John met his level gaze. He held his breath. A strong winter wind whipped against the narrow windows causing the candles on the walls behind the men to sputter slightly.

"I think—why? Even if you don't like us, we are of more use to you alive than dead."

"So you don't believe the rumors?" John asked.

The man's eyes never wavered from John's face as he slowly shook his head.

"Then who is doing the killing?" John's question hung in the air. The other men shifted uncomfortably, avoiding each other's eyes.

"Someone who stands to gain from the continued unrest, I'd venture."

"Would that be a Norman or a Saxon?"

"You're the only Norman here." The man's statement sounded like a threat. John tipped his head, as if to more clearly understand the man. The man finally looked uneasy.

"Speak clear, if you would." John's words were congenial enough but the man didn't miss his icy tone.

"My lord, I do not believe you would wish us harm." Turning back to John, the man slowly and deliberately raised his hand and offered it to John. Hesitating but a second, John accepted the gesture and clasped his arm. "My name is Robert."

"Nor I, my lord," Rolf spoke up next. "Well, you know my name."

Rolf looked down sheepishly. The others around him muttered their agreement. John looked at their faces. They could be Normans or Saxons. They were men first. They had as much to lose as he did, perhaps more, if these massacres continued. John made his decision.

"The fact is the men attacking the villages are here, at least one of them. I followed his trail back from Towton."

"Towton?" Robert asked. "That's just the next village over."

"Aye. I think they are planning to attack us here."

The men muttered in surprise at this news.

"But we are a protected castle, my lord." Robert spoke for all the men. "Surely that would be foolish on their part."

"Unless they believe you will move against me," John replied.

Robert grunted, disgust written all over his face. "So they kill our kin so that we will rise up against you? How dumb do they believe we are that we can't tell a Saxon slaughter over a Norman one?"

140

John was taken aback by this statement but schooled his features. What did they know of Norman slaughters? The question disturbed him. He'd fought a battle in Normandy years ago. He'd been told they fought against marauders. William had said as much. They had slaughtered helpless villagers, mainly women and children. The carnage was much like he'd seen here. How would these Saxons have any experience with that?

"What would you have us do, my lord?" It was Rolf, his eyes intent on John.

"We need to prepare against a possible attack." John looked each man in the eye. Their sincerity was intense. "It may be that the attack will come from inside."

"Someone we already know?" Robert asked.

John nodded. It could even be one of them but no, they had all been in here. They couldn't be the man he'd been following. "Prepare yourselves and keep your eyes and ears open."

"You think there will be someone coming in that we may know?" Rolf asked, his eyes were big with uncertainty.

"Someone like Arthur," one of the men said and the group laughed as if at a private joke. John was filled with the overwhelming sense that someone was walking over his grave.

"What about Arthur?" He held his breath. Like a wolf, he had his prey in his sight.

"He's a strange one, is all." Robert seemed embarrassed by their inside humor.

"How so?"

"He never seemed to like to practice. The king wanted a fighting force ready even in your absence, my lord. Arthur was always reluctant to keep us fit and ready," Robert explained.

Rolf picked up the story. "Robert here would ride us out to the open field, up by the Roman ruins, so we could practice. We had to do it without Arthur knowing about it. We're nothing but soldiers, my lord."

"Yah, we're lousy farmers," an older man with salt and pepper hair spoke out. The rest of the men smiled and nodded their agreement.

"Hate farming," Rolf spoke under his breath. "Boring as hell."

John frowned. "How did Arthur expect you to be ready?"

They looked blankly at him. Robert finally shrugged his shoulders. "Don't know. He seemed more interested in chasing after the Lady Rowena...begging your pardon, my lord." Robert looked down as if embarrassed by his loose tongue.

John had thought the same thing. So Arthur didn't want these men ready if William called them into service. Was it to make John look bad or William? "Then, Robert, I suggest you take your men out into the yard for a long overdue practice."

"What about Arthur?" Rolf asked.

"Have you seen him?" John's jaw tensed.

"Just a short while before you came, my lord. I saw him headed toward the garden," the older man said.

"But then he left the garden with the Lady Rowena," Rolf added, looking at the older man.

Damn. Feeling like he'd been punched in the gut, John struggled to breathe normally. His suspicions were confirmed. He had been right not to trust Rowena. She had gone off with Arthur as soon as he came for her. Was she in on the plotting against him as well?

"Practicing may need to become real sooner than you think, Robert," John took the man's hand in a firm grip, "I am glad you have been so diligent."

"My lord, when you were wed to our little Rowena and left her alone, we doubted your intentions were honorable. When we see you with her now and how happy she is, we admit we've had second thoughts about you. The area has been in sore need of a fair man for a long while now. Let us know whatever we can do for you." Robert led his men out of the hall to prepare for battle.

John didn't show the surprise he felt at the man's candid words. Rowena was happy? She had seemed so to him as well but the fact that she was gone said it all.

Heading up the stairs to her room, John had no idea what to expect. He paused before the wooden door. Why was he here? He pushed the door open and burst into the empty room. The fire was banked and the curtains were drawn. The darkened space was hushed like a sick room. With no forethought, he picked up the nightgown that lay across the bed and held it to his face. It smelled of lavender and Rowena. A tightness he hadn't experienced for a very long time spread slowly across his chest. His breathing seemed to just stop. He sat by the stool in front of the glowing embers.

He rubbed the material against his face, and he could feel her body against him, hear her moan of pleasure. The tears came silently, sliding down his cheeks. He was not worthy of love. He could have sworn he'd finally found that elusive gift in Rowena's arms. At least for a little while, the aching in his heart had subsided. He'd filled it with hopes for a future, a family, a loving wife—none of these things were intended for him.

So be it. He tossed the nightgown into the fireplace and strode out of the room without looking back.

Chapter Twenty-Six

John strode past Joan as he headed out to the practice area. She was waving her arms around with her story as she spoke with a somber faced Perceval. John felt the man's eyes on him as he walked past.

"It wouldn't be like her." Joan's voice trembled with emotion.

John shook his head in disgust. His lady was quite good at disguising her intentions even to the ones closest to her. She had probably only stayed in the castle this long to wait for Arthur. He came and she left with him.

"My lord," Perceval's deep voice rumbled toward John as the man came up behind him. Hesitating but a moment, John continued toward the barn.

"What is it now?" John called over his shoulder without breaking his stride. The older man was forced to trot up to him if he wanted to be heard.

"Decided have you?" The man was elderly but didn't appear winded as he kept up John's quick pace.

"What are you talking about?" John didn't hide his impatience. Why didn't the man just leave him alone?

"You've decided you should never have trusted her."

John stopped in his tracks. How could this man know that was how John felt?

"I don't know what you're going on about. I've a horse to saddle. There is trouble brewing."

"There's been trouble for awhile, my lord. I tried to tell you that."

John squinted as he looked the man up and down. "So you did. You just weren't very forthcoming in what you knew."

143

"I was interrupted."

"Out with it then. I've matters of my own to see to."

"These are matters of yours as well." Perceval's face was set in a stubborn grimace, his hands on his hips.

John crossed his arms about his chest and waited. This man had had many opportunities to broach whatever concerns he had before now. What had held him back? John was tired of the uncertainty game. He needed action. Coming to the end of his patience, John raised his eyebrows, waiting for compliance with his command.

"She didn't leave of her own will."

The crease between John's eyes deepened. Was that possible?

"What do you know?" John stepped close to the man, intimidating him with his size. "You tell me now or I will have the information beaten out of you."

Perceval seemed unimpressed. "My lord, your lady wife was taken against her will."

"How do you know that?" John bellowed the question. The blood rushed in John's ears. Could Rowena be in trouble at this very moment? There had been no sign of a struggle.

"Arthur came and took her."

John spit on the ground in disgust. "Would Arthur need to take her? Or would she just go willingly?"

"She would go willingly..." John pushed past the man as his words hit home "...if she believed you were grievously injured."

John stopped again, turning back. "Arthur told her I was hurt?"

Perceval dipped his head, acknowledging the statement as fact. "That is what I believe."

John shook his head. Uncertainty churned in the pit of his stomach. It was so easy for him to believe Rowena didn't really care for him. It was easy for him to believe she would just walk away and go off with someone else at the first opportunity.

The memories of their parting assaulted him, weakening his resolve to believe the worst of her. She had pretended to be strong in saying goodbye to him. He could see she didn't want him to leave but she had kept her head up and wished him well. She had said she was pleased with him for a husband. Surely that wouldn't be necessary to say if she had plans to be away with Arthur.

"I see you struggle with what I'm telling you. Let me assure, my lord, it is the truth."

The memories persisted. Rowena grabbing him against her to kiss him goodbye, the feel of her sweet lips on his. His eyes closed in defeat. He wanted her to be the woman he believed she was. He wanted her to care about him and only him.

John opened his eyes and shifted uncomfortably. Finally searching the older man's weathered face and clear eyes, he decided to take a chance. "If I believe what you say, I must rescue her."

"It is not just her you must rescue." Perceval's eyes pierced into his own. "It is also your child that you must rescue."

"What?" Unsure of what the man had just said, John fought to keep his emotions in check until he was sure of his meaning.

"She was happily carrying your child, my lord."

John's breathing quickened. She had conceived? So soon? He was to be a father? A grin broke across his face. "There is no doubt?"

Perceval tipped his head to one side, a look of deep thought on his face. "She was fairly large."

"We must find her." His joy was quickly overtaken by fear for her and their unborn child.

"Wait!" Perceval grabbed John's arm before he could put action to his words. "You need to know where they are."

"Do you know?"

"I know Arthur's story. His family lands were located near the Roman ruins of a stone fort, north of Crowhurst."

"Would he take her there?" Why go to such a desolate place?

"It was his family home."

"But would he take her there? So far?"

"I do not believe there would be anywhere else he would rather take her." The older man shook his head slowly, his eyes rounding in sympathy as he spoke. "He wanted her to wife. That was his plan before…before William brought you here."

All the pieces finally clicked into place. To have it said aloud made it so much clearer. Arthur couldn't have Rowena so he took her.

"Do you think he would mistreat her?" Fear for his wife became a tangible thing, working its way into the darkest recesses of his heart.

Perceval avoided looking directly at him as he answered. "I believe Arthur is stricken with grief at having lost his last chance to regain all his father had lost. He is desperate."

"Then show me where you believe he has taken her. Quick man!"

They headed to the barn and prepared two strong horses. Traveling at a steady pace, Perceval led the way to Arthur's family home. John was struck with a feeling of familiarity about the place. He finally realized it was where he had been based with William after they'd first come ashore from Normandy so many years ago. The entire location was beyond desolate. The woods were burned to the ground. Even after all this time had passed. It was as if nothing dare grow there ever again.

"Here." Perceval quickened his horse to the edge of the small crofter's garden, the remnants of the building a crumbling shell. A stone wall pushed out of the ground where it had settled steadily over the hundreds of years since its original use. He jumped to the hard packed ground and pulled the branches away from the small opening.

"How did you know about this place?" John was amazed, joining him to look down the darkened stairs that led below ground.

Perceval seemed insulted by the question. "I have lived here my entire life."

John drew his dagger at the sound of the moaning from within the darkened area. He cautiously led the way down the steps. The little bit of light coming in from the opening cast strange slats of light on the stairs ahead of them. The enclosed area smelled of rotted timbers, sickness...and lavender.

"Rowena?" John's call was a raspy whisper. "Are you here?"

The moan that came back to him was from someone in deep pain.

"I can't find you." He moved toward the sound, stubbing his toe as he tripped over something on the ground. "Rowena?"

The moaning ceased abruptly. John moved more quickly toward where he'd heard the last sound. His foot slipped in something but then his eyes became adjusted to the darkness. He squatted down beside her where she lay on the ground, against the far wall. She was shivering but no longer moaning.

He propped her slightly against his leg, rubbing her arm as he spoke."Rowena?"

John brushed the hair away from her face, her eyes were tightly closed, her body stiff with pain. Perceval had stopped halfway down the steps.

"Where is Arthur?" Perceval whispered the question, his own dagger at his side. "He can't have gone far."

Rowena's eyes fluttered open and she struggled to sit up.

"Are you hurt?" John felt her body tense then and she fell back against his thigh, pulling her legs up tight as she moaned. She was in great pain. "What has Arthur done to you?"

Perceval came to squat beside the two of them. "I don't think it was Arthur."

She shook her head with her moan, deepening until its sound reverberated against the cold stone walls.

"What then?" John was totally helpless at his wife's distress.

Perceval turned toward John, gripping his arm firmly. "The baby's coming."

"What? No! That can't be. It is too early."

146

Rowena's head rolled back in exhaustion when the pain ceased. She finally saw John. "Are you really here this time?" Her voice was hoarse, barely above a whisper. "Or are you just a dream?"

"I am here," John answered and helped her to a sitting position, his arm firm under her own. The movement caused her to again tense and moan in pain. "What can I do?"

"You can't do anything, man. We need to stop the baby from coming. Cramp bark would do the trick." Perceval headed out the small opening, quickly returning with a branch with shiny red berries.

John grimaced. "She can't eat those. They'll make her sicker."

Perceval was using his dagger to strip the bark from the plant. "It's not the berries. It's the bark. Here." He handed John a small wad of bark. "Try to get her to chew on this."

John sniffed it, suspicious about something he had no firsthand experience of. Cocking his eye at the older man, and Perceval gave a stiff nod and headed back up the stairs.

Rowena was in so much pain, her face was contorted.

"My love, this may help." John slipped it between her teeth. "Bite down on it."

She gagged when it went into her mouth. "This would do better as tea."

"We're doing the best we can." He rubbed her back.

She sniffled then put it back into her mouth. Her face still filled with disgust.

Perceval came bounding down the stairs, twigs and leaves fell from his armload of wood, a dented pot sloshed water on the ground where it hung from his wrist. In no time, he had managed to build a small fire, setting the iron pot close by.

"I've dropped some bark in the water. It works best when drunk."

"So I've heard," John answered.

Perceval stood silhouetted against the dimming light drifting down the stairs. "I will go and get help."

"Do you know of anyone here abouts?"

"I will do what I can as quickly as possible." The man went up the stairs two at a time.

Rowena's face was pinched in pain. She seemed to be holding her breath, the cramp bark clamped tightly between her teeth. John had never seen a woman in labor before. She still had ahold of his arm and pulled against him. He was surprised by her strength. Her face turned dark with the effort. Pushing herself against the wall, a low growling noise came from deep inside her.

"What can I do?" She seemed focused on something behind him but he saw nothing there. Where was Arthur? Was she waiting for him to come back?

"I am here now. I will help you." He hid his own self-doubt.

Suddenly exhaling, her efforts ceased and she sucked in the air with her exertion, coughing the bark out. "John. You have come back at a most inopportune time." He smiled at her attempt at humor. "I wanted to tell you I was pregnant when you came home before, but everyone said you had not really been there."

The last time he'd seen her was when this child had been created. Perhaps she was fevered. Her brow was cool to his touch. He quickly counted how long it had been since then and realized the baby could not live if it was born now. She did not seem to recognize that fact as she continued.

"I believe we will have a girl. She will have dark..."

Gripping his arm, she bent her head to her chest as the pain assaulted her again. Her body tensed and she pulled her knees up tight. It was apparent even to John that this child was coming. He tried to prepare her and saw the top of the babe's tiny head pushing its way out. His breath held when he saw the size. It was barely bigger than the palm of his hand. His eyes misted.

He gently caressed her leg as her hand continued its death grip. "Shhhh, Rowena. Try not to push."

Rowena growled an answer that sounded like a word he would not have expected from her.

"The need to push does not come from me. I cannot stop." She finally answered. Leaning against the wall in exhaustion, the baby's head retreated. Her pain gone, she tried to ease her breathing.

"The child will not survive if it is born now." He spoke quietly to her, his eyes again full of tears.

When she finally looked at him, her expression said it all. She already knew. Still she shook her head in firm denial, her face wet with tears.

"Please, John, save our baby." Her anguished request made his tears fall heavier.

He kissed her forehead and went to the small fire for the pot. "We can try this."

She nodded, accepting the warmed pot of cramp bark tea. "It may work."

After a few sips, John was relieved when she slumped against his side. Thinking her asleep, he gently rubbed her side. Her swell bulged against his hand. He jumped at the sudden kick.

"That is a good sign." Rowena's voice was quiet but she started to rub the baby gently in her womb. "She has not moved in quite awhile."

"Strong. Like her mother, I'd say." John was assaulted with how little he actually knew about this woman. But strong, yes, he knew she was that. She had stood up to him. She had kept her home and tolerated treatment he could never have imagined.

"I am from strong stock." The weak sound of her voice contradicted the statement.

"And so is our daughter."

"My father had wanted sons. I was a great disappointment."

"I don't know who my father was." Surprised at the admission, John's breath became unexpectedly shallow. Why would he tell her that? He waited for her reply. She snuggled closer to him. The tea was doing its work. The cramps had subsided.

"I am sorry for you then. Even though I was not what my father had wanted, I know that he loved me. His love ended too soon."

John saw again the blood dripping from her father's mouth, his eyes glazing over. What a thing to have to live with.

"I'm sorry." It just didn't seem enough. He waited again for her response. Her gentle snoring soothed his anxiety. He held her tighter to his side.

It was the ungodly moan that ripped him from his sleep. The smell of death was in his nostrils, and he realized it was coming from Rowena. His own leg was stiff from the cold and dampness around him. Her body stiffened beside him again. John closed his eyes, his heart heavy with regret. Her labor had returned.

Gently pushing her back against the wall when the pain gripped her again, he prepared himself to accept the baby. Rowena fought against the urge to push. It was all for naught. The perfect little body slipped into his hand with little effort. She gasped. Her wide-eyed look of horror seemed frozen on her face, afraid to look down. "Is it a girl?"

He lifted the baby up for her to see. It fit in one hand. Ten fingers. Ten toes. A beautiful face with little bow lips. His tears dropped onto the still body of his daughter. Rowena sat forward and finally looked at her child. She shook her head as she carefully took the baby. Holding it to her breast, long sobs racked her body. "No. No." She resisted the truth as she gently held the lifeless body.

John wrapped his arm around his two girls. Rowena leaned heavily against him. Her body shook with her heart-wrenching sobs. As if in a nightmare he couldn't wake up from, John looked into his daughter's beautiful face, memorizing every detail. His first fatherly instinct ripped through his body when he realized with absolute clarity that he would lay down his life without the slightest hesitation if his daughter could just have lived.

He would have gladly saved Rowena yet more pain. She had been through enough. Alas, this he could not do. He could not bring his daughter back to life. He could, however, avenge their pain and loss and hunt down that bastard Arthur, treating him to a slow, painful death. For now and with great restraint, he would try to comfort Rowena over the loss.

Rowena's sobbing finally subsided. Her voice was dead when she finally spoke. "I knew it would be a girl."

"She is beautiful."

Rowena stroked the little cheek with the tip of her finger. The baby's lips were tinged with blue. "I think she had your dimples."

John didn't realize he had dimples. "My lady love, she is as beautiful as you." Kissing her cheek softly, they leaned their heads together and mourned together the loss of their first child.

It was midday when Perceval finally arrived with Claire and Joan in tow. Stiff from sitting on the cold, hard floor, John knew that Rowena was much worse off. Claire gently took the child from Rowena's arms and Joan came to replace John at her side.

Suddenly feeling awkward and helpless, John stood a few feet from the scene. It sickened him to think that Arthur had somehow brought all of this about. Ah, revenge gave him a purpose. Something to do. He didn't want to bother his wife with the details, but he needed to know.

"How did you get here?" His voice sounded loud in the small cavern against the quieter reassuring womanly words being exchanged.

Rowena's eyes bore into him but there were no tears when she answered. "Arthur." Joan was seeing to her needs, and John knew he should desist. There was so much blood everywhere. He had gone through the whole night without asking what was most on his mind. How had she come to be with Arthur...here? When she spoke again, he was surprised by the loathing in her voice. "He called me a whore."

Joan's gasp reflected what all present felt. "Did he take you from the garden, my lady?"

Rowena nodded slowly. The anger closed in on Rowena, and John's rage only deepened. "What did he say?" He forced his voice to sound calm. He did not need to upset her any further. He didn't dare breathe as he waited for her answer.

"He told me you were near death." Perceval had been correct. Arthur had coerced her into leaving willingly with him. "He lied. He called me a whore and hit me. I fell to the ground from the blow." Her voice was dead. "I fell too hard for the baby to stay inside."

Many woman survived childbirth by sheer determination. He prayed she had that.

Perceval came down the stairs again with a litter to lay Rowena on. Claire packed her up to staunch the bleeding. Joan tucked Rowena in with her cape once she was laid out on the makeshift bed. Tousled around as they moved her, Rowena did not open her eyes once.

"Will you see to her safety?" John's voice was low so the women could not hear.

"What are you going to do?" Perceval was clearly concerned for John.

"I will take care of Arthur."

Understanding, Perceval nodded. Each took an end and brought Rowena, no longer with child, up into the sunlight.

Chapter Twenty-Seven

Rowena awoke from a deep sleep to an intense burning sensation between her legs. She settled deeper into her bed, rocking gently. She watched the eerie shadows cast on the walls about her room while the wood crackled in the fire. Joan was the first to notice she was awake. She stooped close and talked softly to Rowena.

"How fare ye?" Her wide eyes were full of concern.

Rowena gently cupped her blurring friend's cheek. "Will I survive?"

Joan nodded slowly. "But your beautiful daughter…she did not. I am so sorry, my lady."

Tears slipped down her face and into Rowena's hair but she tried to smile. "I know. She was beautiful, wasn't she?"

"Oh, yes. I have never seen such a perfect little baby." Joan sniffled loudly and Rowena took her into her arms.

"Shhh." Rowena's body shook with her sobbing as they clung to each other in their sadness. "I am overcome with my grief, Joan."

"I know. I know." Joan's voice was muffled in her hair.

Having spent her tears for the moment, Rowena's exhaustion quickly took hold. Her entire body ached.

Claire interrupted them.

"How do you feel? Is there any pain?" the midwife asked as she poured freshly warmed water into the basin on the table.

"Yes. Here." Rowena indicated the afflicted area then slid her hand along her stomach. The flatness felt strange, the precious swell no longer there. The gentle pressure no longer pushed against her hand. Her heart ached at the emptiness. "My belly has pain. Is it the loss of the child?"

Claire pulled down the covers to inspect Rowena. "Does this hurt?"

Claire pressed gently against her womb. Rowena winced in answer. "That may not be good."

Standing behind the older woman, Joan wrung her hands helplessly. "Is there anything I can do?"

"That green bottle..." Claire pointed to her basket, "...yes, mix it with some warm water for her to drink." She turned back to her patient. "It doesn't taste overly bad but it will help with your pain."

Rowena moved as if in a dream. She watched Joan glide across the room and wondered why they both spoke so slowly. Claire's voice sounded as if she were very far away. "I feel dizzy." Rowena couldn't remember speaking yet she heard her own thoughts coming back to her. The world spun violently just before it ceased to exist.

§

The leaves on the trees hung heavy, soaked from the constant drizzle. John stared straight ahead as he rode back along the path to their camp. At least he knew the men he'd left in charge would protect the castle if he wasn't able to stop Arthur himself. They were good Saxon men and there was certainly some satisfaction in that knowledge. Rowena had loyal people around her but they were afraid to show any sign of it, afraid there would be repercussions.

The horse jerked suddenly, nearly unseating John. He shook his head to clear his mind and was relieved to see his men coming toward him. How could he not have heard them coming? They were not very quiet.

"Hail, my lord." Philip spoke first. "We have brought news."

The young boy came up on the smallest of the palfreys, pushing his way ahead to stop beside John. He smiled at the boy before turning back to Philip.

"What news?"

"The enemy camp has been located. We have seen five men present. They seem to be waiting for something or someone."

John's lips curled with contempt. Arthur. So he hasn't made it back to them. "Anything else?"

Philip looked to the young boy, who seemed suddenly shy, unable to look John in the face. "Speak plain. Don't be afraid."

"It's the red-haired man, me lord. He'd said he'd get his family land back, one way or another. I didn't understand what he meant until I heard your men talking."

"What is it he meant then?"

"He must have been Arthur the Red's son. The Normans slaughtered him and burned his lands. It was worse than anywhere else. He had fought against the Normans. He wouldn't pay homage."

John's mind went unbidden to the early days of their landing when William had looked for supporters among the villagers against King Harold. Those who went against William were treated cruelly. None survived those early days. William slaughtered them all. Surprised by his own contempt for the behavior, John wondered why he had just gone along with such horrendous acts.

Philip interrupted his thoughts. "Arthur had every reason to want to keep the fight against us going. He wanted his land back."

Every man there knew William's code for surrender—swear fealty to him and survive—fight against him and lose everything.

"It must not have been enough for our greedy friend."

John tried to piece together the events that would have led to William giving Arthur the demesne. It didn't make sense. Why would William trust someone who had every reason to hate him?

"My lord, we believe we know where Arthur and his men have gone."

Philip and John looked at each other. "Their family lands," John stated.

§

It didn't take long to pick up Arthur's trail when they knew where he would be heading. The Roman ruins had been at the very farthest corner of his family lands. They had been extremely wealthy with many men at their disposal. John learned from Aldred that Arthur had sided with Tostig Godwinson over his more powerful brother. Arthur the elder and his son had traveled to the north to fight with him. Backed by the Danish Canute, they were sure that they would win. Instead, they were quickly beaten back. It was a setback for Arthur's future hopes for himself and his son. The news that William of Normandy was making his way across the channel had set them all at a run back to protect their homes.

Passing by the burned out shell of what was once Arthur's family home, John saw the proof of Arthur's loss. The once well-maintained lands were overrun with tall, wild grass, brown from the miserable drought. The castle's only source of water, the stone well, had been smashed to pieces, the strewn rocks now interspersed with tall clumps of weeds. The wooden bucket hung forlornly from the winch, its wooden support nearly rotted in two.

John could imagine why Arthur would choose this place to finally face him. Here, Arthur had been someone of importance. Here, Arthur could finally stop running, surrounded by all that he had lost. Perhaps even putting an end to the guilt that probably plagued him ever since his father's death. Today Arthur would be present to defend his family home against the Norman usurpers, John, and take back what was his or die in the battle.

The unnatural silence sent a cold shiver of anticipation through John's body. Arthur was close by. He sensed it. Slowly approaching the fallow fields, little tufts of tall grass had taken over the once well-maintained path. The lingering death and destruction after all this time gave John a glimpse of what Arthur had lost when William had laid claim to the area.

John's horse snorted but kept its head low. No imminent danger. His hands ached where they clenched the reins, the persistent cold drizzle saturating his leather gloves. The branches from the surrounding woods creaked sharply in the breeze. John scanned the distant tree line. He heard their horses before he saw their approach through the fog.

Arthur had four men with him, so this would be an easy fight. No, this was just a necessary fight. The memory of Rowena's ashen face flashed in John's mind. She would be avenged. Arthur had to die. John's two men followed directly behind him, closing the distance across the uneven fields. The horses' approach was muffled by the damp earth. Each side stopped. Their breathing vaporized in the mist. At the sight of Arthur's smirking face, John's jaw clenched. He squared his shoulders. "Ready to end this?"

"You arrogant bastard!" Arthur shook his head, his nose crinkled in disgust. "She never had any use for you."

Refusing to take the bait, John waited. His horse shifted impatiently beneath him. John released his tight hold of the reins. The weight of his mace rested comfortably against his thigh. He caressed the worn handle of the formidable weapon. He would enjoy smashing this man's brains in. He smiled at Arthur.

Arthur sneered back, struggling to control his skittish mount. "I have to say though..." He lifted his chin in defiance. "She wasn't really worth waiting for. Disappointing even."

John reached for the heavy mace at the same time his knees squeezed his battle-ready horse beneath him. It reared slightly in anticipation of its target. Arthur did not hesitate as he, too, advanced his horse, closing the distance between them. As if on cue, Peter and Philip cut Arthur's men away from their leader. Their horses unequal to the task of warfare quickly turned tail and ran. They were easily chased into the dense forest.

Arthur continued toward John at full speed. He leaned forward, his spear at the ready. John's eagerness increased as the distance closed between them. Arthur's horse unexpectedly broke the advance and made a wide arc around him. John snorted in frustration. With satisfaction, he heard his opponent's muffled curses at the animal's lack of training.

John laughed, bringing his horse around with ease to face his opponent. "You can pretend to be Norman but you...and your mount...

verily fall short!"

Arthur pulled up sharply on the reins, his animal reared in distress. His face was a mask of fury. He pushed his horse forward. John smirked. He remained motionless. The horse would not come close. He was right. Arthur nearly unseated himself, his raised spear unable to make contact.

Turning his horse back around, Arthur faced him, huffing in his outrage. John crossed his arms, leaned against the mace in front of him, and gave him a menacing smile. "Would you like to see how it is actually done?"

Arthur's nostrils flared in anger. John spurred his horse forward, hunched low for speed. His body protected by his shield; his other arm honed into the rhythmic arc of his mace. He focused on Arthur's skull. Jerked at the reckless pace, Arthur's horse whinnied in distress. With a firm pull on the reins, John cut off their retreat. The weighted mace swung in a downward arc. His heels pushed into the stirrups. He prepared for the impact.

Arthur's skull was cracked under the impact. Unseated, he dropped to the ground. The shaft of his spear snapped loudly beneath him. Arthur lay motionless, face down in the mud.

John dismounted. The jolt of the ground ran up his body. The weight of the mace pulled at his arm. Exhaustion. Blood matted Arthur's hair to his head. John approached cautiously. Moaning, Arthur shifted his arms. Thrashing would begin soon if it had indeed been a death blow. John waited. Thick drops of rain started. It pounded against his helmet, against his throbbing head. His mace rested head down against the ground. He leaned slightly against its shaft. Arthur moaned again. There was little movement. Wiping the rain that dripped down his nose, John was caught off guard by the sudden movement. The mace flew away from his grasp. He struggled to remain standing. In one movement, Arthur swung the spear handle as he planted himself before John.

Unarmed, John was pressed backward by Arthur's quick advance. His broken spear shaft whipped by, hissing near John's ear. Arthur's speed and accuracy surprised John, and he stumbled, unable to move fast enough. The ground beneath his feet turned to muck and oozed around him. He staggered back with one foot sucked into the mud, costing him precious seconds and Arthur was on him. He swung the shaft again. Contact.

The pain shot across John's upper body. Arthur's smug smile spurred John to react. His foot now free, he charged at his body, just missing Arthur's swinging shaft, grabbing his chest. The rain pelted down on them. They fell to the ground. Arthur's soaked hauberk slipped easily through John's frozen fingers.

Air whooshed from John's lungs, Arthur's knees squeezing as he straddled his body. Arthur steadily pushed the shaft across John's chest, closer and closer to his neck. The slivers pierced John's hand where he strained against the downward motion. Arthur's strength was far superior. John's injured arm dipped first. Fear shot through him like a hot iron. If he died here, Rowena would be forced into marrying this man. If he died here, this devil's spawn would rally the Saxons against the Normans. If he died here, the rest of Rowena's people would be caught up in a bloodbath not of their doing. No. That is not the way of it.

A sudden surge burst through his arm and the shaft came up unexpectedly cracking against Arthur's face. Blood dripped from his nose as he pulled back in pain. John pushed and tumbled Arthur onto his back, John's elbow against his neck. Arthur's eyes were wide with fear. With his free hand, John grabbed the spear head and jabbed it into the unprotected inner thigh of his nemesis. His life's blood gushed onto the ground. John pushed the spear in deeper until the man struggled no more.

Arthur's heavy body relaxed against John's hand. Dead. The cold ground numbed John's body when he pulled away from the corpse. The rain puddled around him. As if in a dream, John's friends emerged from the mist, his own horse in tow. Hanging back, they gave him time. John knew they had taken care of the other men. He didn't need to ask how. They had been Arthur's lackeys. What now? There was no satisfaction. A threat had been dealt with. No more. No less.

John shook off his heavy helmet, the rain cool against his sweaty head. His deep breath was cut off by the shot of pain across his throbbing chest. It would take time to recover, in body and spirit. His arms were dead weights, and he peeled the bloodied glove from his hand. Arthur's blood. The rain washed it clean. John sighed in resignation. Returning to the present, he stood to face his friends. He silently mounted. They headed back across the barren land.

Chapter Twenty-Eight

Rowena could smell the dampness, the blood... her blood, and feel the cold floor beneath her uncovered legs.

"No, Arthur. Do not slake your anger on me." Her plea made no impression on the contorted face of her former confidant. "Why?" The whisper penetrated into her ear when she spoke the word aloud, forcing her to awaken from the nightmare. Sweat dripped down her neck as she propped herself to sit in the bed.

The room was empty. All had left her to sleep or perhaps die? Rowena placed her hand on her empty womb. Many women died at childbirth. Some before the baby was even born. Many after. Some during the birthing, killing the child as well.

Closing her eyes, she again saw her husband's haggard expression, his tears slipping down his face to fall on little Beatrice's cold face.

Where was John now?

He had told her he was a bastard and didn't know who his father was. It pained him to share that. She remembered his face, almost a look of surprise at his own admission. Why would he bare that inner shame, holding her all night long and rubbing her arms to keep the chill away, and sobbing with her at their shared grief?

Rowena opened her eyes. She brought her hand to her mouth, a slow smile spreading across her face. She was loved by him.

He had said he would not go to another. It was her choice to believe him and even trust him. He could be the very man she had always wanted as a husband. Most importantly, his love could help her through this loss. She no longer had to suffer alone. She was not alone.

Turning to her side, Rowena stroked the pillow beside her. He would return to her. She wanted him now, beside her. She needed his arms around her. If she died now, he would never know that she had loved him. The very idea felt like a stab to her heart. She pressed her lips in a determined line. She best not die now.

§

The heavy black material of mourning was draped across the gate as John approached the castle. Peter followed not far behind but passed on to stop abreast of him.

"Your people share your loss, my lord," Peter said.

There had been other signs along the way; boughs of dried flowers and thistle, a cairn already as high as his horse's flank, and the deafening stillness. In their own way the villagers mourned their lord and lady's loss.

"Out of love for their lady no doubt," John answered.

The sight of Rowena huddled with the women sewing flashed in his mind. A smile on her lips.

"Ah, you underestimate your own worth."

John had seen the villagers, their heads dipped with downcast eyes in solemn respect as he'd traveled the well-worn path to the castle door.

"And you have rid them of an omnipresent evil when you killed Arthur. They will not forget that." Peter continued on into the stable.

Their return trip had been one of silence. All appeared as if through a fog to John's mind. Perhaps now that the death of his child and the abuse of his wife had been avenged, the pain of the loss was making itself known. He was tired. His hands stiff where he gripped the reins.

"Lord John!" It took several more steps for his numbed mind to register the voice and a few more after that before he pulled back on the reins and stopped his horse. Peter continued on ahead to the castle on foot. The saddle was hard beneath John and when he turned to look behind, pain shot through his side.

"Damn," he cursed beneath his breath, his irritation growing. "What is it?"

Perceval took a step away. John's deadened senses stirred. He was being cruel to one who had been his helper.

"Forgive me, Perceval. Please." John gestured for him to continue.

John felt removed from his own surroundings, as if watching his own movements. Fatigue was setting it. Suddenly filled with an urge to laugh, John coughed into his hand, trying to focus. The man's mouth tightened into a grimace and his eyes were cold. More bad news.

John held his hand up to stop Perceval's story. "I cannot hear you now, man."

He impatiently gestured the man aside and proceeded on his horse into the stable yard. Why would the man think he should approach John now? Exhausted. He needed sleep. Tilting forward in his saddle, he was able to catch himself before he tumbled out. A stable boy quickly grabbed the reins.

"Good man," John mumbled as he came down off the horse, jarring his tired body. A twinge shot up his back, and he bit back a groan. He exhaled slowly.

"Is Lady Rowena within?" he asked.

The young lad shook his mop of hair, stroking the horse's snout. "My lord?"

John wanted to scream to leave him alone but the boy's face was grave.

"Yes?" he patiently asked the boy.

"I am sorry for your loss, yours and Lady Rowena. I hope you will have many healthy children still." Such hopeful words. The boy gave a small smile. John nodded in response but his thoughts were of his wife.

Rowena knew the truth now. His stomach lurched at the realization. He had talked far too much in the wee hours while their child's death had been imminent, baring his very soul to her.

What madness drove him to tell her of his own childhood? Open himself up to any woman's scrutiny? John shook his head.

John questioned why he had been allowed to live many times. In a different land, unwanted infants were left out in the elements to die alone. So why was he allowed to live? There was no answer.

During those hours in the cave, Rowena's eyes had been closed for much of the time. He had been trying to distract her, ease her burden. In the process, he probably lost the only good thing he'd ever found.

"Damn fool," John muttered to himself and headed away from the stairs and Rowena, toward the darkened room off the Great Hall. The dank smell of wet wood and parchment was heavy in the air and he shut the door, entombing himself within. The quiet of the room was interrupted by the scurrying of the unseen varmints scattering away at his approach.

Plopping heavily into a chair, John was amazed at how comfortable a simple cushion felt. Wine and cup sat like sentinels on the trestle, and John did not hesitate to pour himself a liberal amount. How could he face her after his revelations?

John tossed back the bitter wine and poured himself more. Even the lees of the cask for the bastard lord. The room shifted around him. John closed his eyes. The floor dropped from beneath him. He draped his arms across the heavy wooden table and laid his forehead flat against the cold wood.

Nothing ever went well for him. He'd learned that early enough. Most of his childhood had been spent on his arse looking up into the nasty grimace of Bruce the stone cutter. Bruce had been a moose of a man. Working stone had made him an extremely strong bully who liked nothing better than to beat his mouse-like wife and the unwanted lad left under his control.

The door opened. His lids were heavy, and his body refused to move. It didn't seem to matter if he roused himself enough to see who stood on either side of him. The room shifted again. The overpowering scent of flowers assaulted his nostrils, stirring a memory just out of reach. Its cloying smell caused his mouth to water. A surge of warning wormed its way up his chest. His mind was unable to grasp it...but surely whatever it was would wait until after he rested.

Chapter Twenty-Nine

"My lady?" Joan's concerned voice seeped into Rowena's dream until it made sense that the horse she shared with John as she snuggled against him would suddenly find a voice.

Waiting for the pain to start behind her eyes, Rowena was relieved to find it gone. "Joan?"

"Yes, my lady?"

"The pain seems to have subsided." Rowena slowly opened her eyes to the dawn pouring into her chamber. "Yes..." questioningly Rowena rubbed her face,"...I do believe the pain may really be gone."

Relief surged through her and the bright light of day was like honey dripping from the comb. With great care, Rowena pulled herself to sitting. It was going to be a good day. Although her heart was still heavy from her loss, her future with John assured her there would be many more births.

Rowena turned to her friend. "I can see your deep frown, my dear. What concerns you so on such a beautiful morning as this?"

"My lady...Lord John cannot be found."

"I don't get your meaning? How can he not be found?" Who was looking for him and where exactly had they looked that he was not found?

"My lady," Joan's urgent tone cut into Rowena like a knife. "Your husband has left."

"What are you prattling about?"

How quickly the unease grew despite the earlier self-assurances of how John felt. Where had he gone to? Why did Joan need to make it sound as if he'd abandoned her?

The naysayer slowly shook her head. Rowena felt the twist of the knife in her heart. The blonde's eyes were wide with the fear. Or was it dread?

"He has left the castle," Joan said.

"When had he returned to the castle?" Her tone was hard but she didn't care.

"I was told he had returned last night. It was very late."

Rowena searched for some memory of his presence. He had been in the castle and hadn't come to see her? Wouldn't he be interested in how she fared?

"Mayhap they were wrong. Who was it that saw him?"

"Sean."

Her sense of urgency grew. Like a physical thing, it seemed to push her to slide her legs to the edge of the bed.

"We must find him then."

"No, please, my lady. You are still too weak to stand." Joan was at her side the instant her feet touched the cold, stone floor.

"Rest assured, Joan, I will be getting up and now."

Rowena was startled at the sound of her own strong convictions. But she did indeed have something to fight for...her marriage...her husband...her people, even. They should not live in constant fear of these Norman invaders. *She* should not live in fear of these invaders.

"Call my guards, please," Rowena said. The cold from the floor seeped into her limbs. "Help me to cover myself."

Joan turned abruptly to the chest at the foot of the bed. She pulled a thick, woolen robe from the chest. "Allow me to assist you."

She helped Rowena guide her tired arms in through the sleeve. Rowena took a deep breath to steady her trembling muscles. "I fear it has been a long time since I have been out of this bed."

"It has been two weeks since you lost the babe." Joan pulled the thick material together in front to hide Rowena's nightgown. "Sit back down and I will fetch the guards."

Having spent her small reserve on her initial surge, Rowena felt suddenly tired and overwhelmed. "My thanks."

Joan helped her to slide her legs back under the heavy bed coverings.

"I will return." Joan dashed through the door, leaving Rowena.

How could John just be gone? Perhaps she slept right through his visit. Without forethought, she turned to the undisturbed film of ash covering the table beside. No lady slippers or dying flowers, no sign at all of a missed encounter.

He wouldn't have left without seeing her. The time in the cave had changed everything for her—for them. The dread he had been unable to hide was too real. He had admitted his deepest fears to her—abandonment. He'd never belonged anywhere.

"I have no one to call my own. When I was born, I was quickly discarded, of little importance. Do you see why marriage is…was…not for me?"

The heavy weight of his head leaning against her own in his sadness tugged at Rowena's heart. She realized he did not know his own true worth. He was not just a knight or a conqueror; he was a good man, a decent man.

"You are a good man, John of Normandy." The words echoed back to her from the chamber walls. "I will believe in you even when no one else does."

The door was thrown against the wall as Joan entered with three soldiers.

"Sean, come quickly," Rowena demanded, leaning forward in her determination. She refused to acknowledge the look of pity that passed over her servant's face. "Tell me when it was that you saw John."

"It was very late, m'lady. He was well worn, near exhaustion. I had seen the stable boy catch him when he all but fell off his horse."

John was exhausted. Pride and gratitude swelled within her breast when she realized he must have gone to avenge her.

"Arthur is dead." Rowena's voice was a whisper but she knew that it was true.

"M'lady?" Sean's brow creased in question.

Rowena pushed on with new orders. "Sean, see if his horse is in the stable. If it is, you must search the castle and beyond. Some terrible fate has befallen my husband."

He averted her gaze and shifted uneasily before her. His voice was quiet when he finally spoke. "M'lady, many of the soldiers believe he has returned to Normandy."

Pain tightened her heart and all sound seemed to stop. Joan's expectant face showed concern. The similar look of pity on the other men's faces caused Rowena to pause but only for one small second. No! She would not be taken in by this. John would not abandon her. He had gone and avenged her mistreatment. Rowena held her head high.

"You overstep your ground, sir. You will do as I bid." Just beyond him, the other soldiers straightened at her tone. "You two, help him search. Perhaps in his exhaustion, he has had an accident." She turned back to Sean who had stepped away. With a stern tone Rowena spoke her mind knowing the message would be carried to the other soldiers. "My husband would not abandon me." Pausing for emphasis she searched their faces for any contradiction. Seeing none, she continued. "My husband loves me. Since he is not here beside me, clearly something terrible has befallen him. Go…find him!"

The soldiers moved quickly to do her bidding.

Joan, her rounded shoulders speaking volumes, stepped closer to the Rowena. "Are you cert—"

"Enough, Joan!" Rowena's tone brooked no further discussion. "You are of no help to me if I must convince you of what I already know in my heart. I spoke the truth to my men. Either you are with me and believe John loves me, or you are against me and of no further use. Please send Evelyn to assist me." Rowena sat up straighter in the bed. The pain in her friend's eyes needed to be ignored. Her loyalties shifted. She loved him, and she chose to believe all that he'd said. "Now."

§

The pungent odor assaulted John's senses, creating a terrible taste at the back of his throat. He lay flat on his stomach with his arms trussed up behind him. Pulling at the bindings on his wrists, John's eyes flew open when he recognized the odor.

"Abigail."

"Oh, my love, you have awakened." Her bright green eyes came into full view as she kneeled beside him. "You look so surprised."

"You expected a different response? Then why am I tied up? Except that you knew I would wring your pretty neck if my hands had been free!" His voice had gotten louder with every word and she backed away at his display of anger. Closing his eyes, John took a steadying breath. He had no idea what was going on but he needed to stay calm. He needed to get his hands free.

Searching the small area he saw from his location, he spotted her a few feet away. Aw, her smugness. How could he have forgotten her true reaction to his constant irritation with her?

"Well?" His voice now under control, he waited for her to show her true intention. If he had acquired nothing else of value to his character, he did have great patience.

He shifted his legs slightly to find they were not tied down. Knowing now that he did indeed have a means in which to acquire the upper hand and stand over a cowering Abigail rather than be the mouse which she chose to play with, his patience increased.

"My love, I thought you would be happy to see me again. I have missed you." Her syrupy voice grated his nerves. As she returned to squatting by the bed, John took in her full attire. The laces at the bodice of her gown were loosened enough to reveal a good amount of bosom and her real purpose for being there. When she dropped her hand to his face and traced her finger down his arm, he did not lurch in revulsion.

"Why would I be happy to see you again? You have again disobeyed my orders."

Her eyes widened in mock innocence. "Orders? What orders would you give me?" She dragged her fingers down his side, drawing circles along his back.

Raising his eyebrows as he compressed his lips, he paused before he answered. "Abigail? What did I say to you when last we parted?"

She tipped her head coyly and avoided looking at him. "You were not yourself. I knew you didn't mean it." She leaned in closer to his face. Her breath hot against his cheek, a mere whisper meant to entice him. "You can't have meant to never see me again."

"My intent was not for you to reason." His voice did not reveal his boiling anger at the situation. He rolled onto his side. "My orders were to be followed. I am not moved by disobedience."

"My lord, forgive my disobedience. It was my desire for your company that has brought me to you."

John closed his eyes."Will you untie me?"

She paused, then moved in closer. "Do you forgive me?" Her voice was low and sultry. Her hands roamed over his body.

"Do you deserve to be forgiven?" He opened his eyes and watched her struggle to hide her fear at the anger she must have seen there.

"I have missed you immensely." Her hands were moving more boldly along his body."I have been very lonely."

"You were lonely long before I sailed for England."

"I have missed you so." She tucked herself in close at his neck. "Do you not desire my presence at all?"

"How would I ever desire you when you tie me up like a spring hen?" His voice remained steady. "Untie me and I will see to your loneliness." He turned to her, pressing his lips against hers. "Do it now, Abigail."

His words spoken against her lips were getting the desired results. Her body melted against him. She reached behind him and pulled on the rope at his hands when he heard a loud bang, as the door was thrown open behind him.

Abigail drew back, her eyes round in fear at the sight behind him.

"Yah are such a whore!" A man's voice boomed in the small room. John was kicked from behind to fall flat on his stomach again. "He was not left here merely for your pleasure."

The man who finally came into John's view was no one he'd ever seen before. The hairy man grabbed at Abigail and shoved her past the bed, out of sight. The door slammed shut. John waited but there was no one left in the room.

His initial reaction was that Abigail was playing some sort of cat and mouse game with him although he did wonder how she'd gotten him here. The fear on her face had been real. Perhaps the only real emotion he'd ever seen her have. So who was the man that she was so afraid of? What was this all about?

John rolled back onto his bound hands and worked at the rope with his fingers. The binding was not so tight that he was unable to shift the rope up and down, loosening the knots. The hammers against his skull were causing havoc to his thinking. The wine had tasted bad. John should have realized it was poisoned. Only the best wine was served to the lord of the manor. He had always been treated with respect there. How Abigail treated him was another story.

The woman cared little for others, and thought only of her own welfare. She would not have left his manor in Normandy unless a better offer presented itself. In Normandy, no one would gainsay her authority, and she would have been left to her own pleasure. The gain by coming here must have been great indeed.

Who was the man she'd been so frightened of? He'd called her a whore and the feel of his foot pushing John down spoke of a large, powerful man. Perhaps even a trained soldier. A Saxon then? John dismissed that notion despite the strange accent. He was safe here among Rowena's people. They were his people now. And he would do whatever he needed to see them protected from harm.

It must be a stranger. If John had been here these past few months, news of a stranger would have come to him and he'd have been prepared. As it was, he had no such warning.

The ropes slipped over his hands just as the door burst open. John stayed his hands.

Let him believe I am still trussed up.

A blonde man with a grimace distorting his face stood in the doorway.

"What do you want with me?" John spoke in forceful, demanding tones.

The man's long white scar stretched down his face and tugged at the smile the man wore making him look like a man with only half a face.

"Who tah hell do yah think yah are asking *me* questions? Yah're not lord of the manor here."

John rested against his hands and tensed his legs, ready to push himself up but kept his face blank. "So you do know who I am?"

The man stepped closer to John, stopping just short of his face to spit out, "Aye, and I don't care."

John sprang from the bed, gripped the man's chin, and pushed it up as he backed him against the wall. He grabbed the pathetic little dagger from the man's belt. "Speak quick. Tell me what you are about before I break your neck."

His would be abductor's eyes bulged and gurgling came from his mouth as he tried to speak. John squeezed his throat.

"Quick now or I may find no mercy for one such as you."

"Not me, m'lord."

John released the pressure. "What are you saying?"

"It's not me. I was hired tah grab yah."

"Who hired you?"

"Leofrid."

John shoved the man away from him. He landed flat on his arse and smacked his head against the wall.

"Explain yourself."

The man's wide-eyed expression convinced John he'd been telling the truth. "Leofrid wanted yah taken. He was going tah offer you as ransom tah the king."

John searched his memory. The name was familiar, a Godwinson. Surely they were all dead. All but Rowena's cousin.

"When were you to hand me over to him?"

A noise behind alerted John to someone else in the room but it was the odor of flowers that gave Abigail away. He stepped and grabbed her in a single motion, the dagger tight against her throat but she offered no resistance. "What have you to do with this?"

She shook her head.

The blonde tightened his cheeks with disgust. "Yah frecking whore. Tell him yahr part. Yah're the worst part of the whole damn plan."

John put the point of the dagger against her cheek. "I suggest you listen to him."

"No, John. He is a liar. I came only for you."

He shoved her toward the other man, who propelled her away when she would have fallen against him.

"So tell me. When does Leofrid arrive?"

His adversary pressed himself against the wall, standing as he spoke. "No, we're tah bring yah tah him."

"And?"

"That is all I know."

"When?"

"By eventide."

John glanced at Abigail's drawn face.

"What was her part?"

Scar face grunted his dislike. "Her? She hired me." Abigail did not look up. "She's the one with all the gold."

"And yet you call her a whore? And manhandle her? Methinks something is amiss."

The man shook his head, his disdain for her evident. "She had all the answers. Finding me. Hiring me."

"Well, Abigail?" John was near the end of his patience. Either she spoke or he got his answers another way.

Abigail took a deep breath. "I need you to return with me." She finally picked up her head, tears glistened in her eyes.

John's eye s widened. "Do you believe you can move me by your tears?"

Scar face canted a grin toward her before facing John. "I'll tell yah what I can do for yah. It was a red-haired man I saw her with—"

Abigail's movement was small but the ghastly sound the man made urged John to lurch toward them. Crimson color spread across the other man's belly. John grabbed the woman's hand to find the blood-stained dagger in her grip.

"Drop it." He pushed her hand above her head while the man slid to the ground.

John squeezed her wrist. Abigail tried to yank away but he held her fast. "Release it. Now!"

She opened her hand and the weapon dropped to the floor. She breathed heavily, her eyes now wary as she looked at him.

"I thought you were working with this man."

"He was a whoreson. Raped me last night while we waited for your return."

John took a closer look and found the man was no longer breathing.

"So now you're a murderer, too?"

She spat on the corpse and turned her face away. John took her chin in his hand and forced her to look at him. "A red-haired man? Would that be Arthur?"

Abigail pressed her lips into a thin line.

"You didn't come here on your own. Arthur somehow found out about you and brought you here." The black of her eye widened. "Ah, yes, I could always read you like a book. Will you give me your defense?"

She shook her head.

"As you wish." Using the rope still on the bed, John tied her hands behind her. She gave little resistance. "I'll oblige your request to be with me by placing you in a cell and under watch so that no more mischief can come from you."

He was beside himself as he ushered her out the door, his head banging miserably as they made their way through the town. Her disheveled state had many villagers stopping and staring as they made their way toward the castle.

Damn.

The door at the Owl and Thistle burst open as they passed. Almost as if they'd been spotted through the tavern window. The jingle of bells made John's jaw clench.

"My lord." The high pitched call was from Mort, William's spy.

John stopped and took a deep breath before facing the man. "Yes?"

Mort's surprised look said it all. He gestured to the woman, his hand dropping and raising to bring it all to the forefront. "What is amiss, my lord? It is unseemly for you to be traipsing through the town with this woman in tow." Shaking his head, Mort guided them back to the door he'd just exited. "Please, my lord, come inside, away from prying eyes."

The absurdity of the situation did not pass by unnoticed by John. Felicity stopped in the hall and glanced at the commotion as the three stood just inside the closed door. She approached slowly, a frown on her face.

"What is this?" she asked, absently drying her hands on a towel as she spoke.

Mort glanced toward her, his nostrils flared, "I asked the same."

As one they turned toward John. He tightened his jaw. "This woman is a murderer."

He opted not to mention the abduction knowing all would be reported to the king.

"Who has she murdered?"

John hesitated before answering, deciding to bluff his play. "A good for nothing seeking to gain power from the king, and she was his accomplice until she sliced his gut open."

Abigail's eyes widened in surprise. He had hit the mark. What other use would Leofrid have for abducting him and demanding the king's attention. He must have been seeking some sort of recompense, probably land, for John's return.

Felicity blanched. "My lord, this is the same woman that has been harassing your lady for months now."

John jerked Abigail to face him. "What have you done to Lady Rowena?"

Abigail smiled. "Nothing, John."

"Do not address our lord with such little respect." Felicity was in her face as she barked the orders at her.

Abigail pulled back slightly, turning her head away.

John's heart beat faster with anger at the possibility of anyone hurting

Rowena. "What have you done?"

Mort settled his hand on John's where he clenched Abigail's arm. "My lord, we can see to this here rather than bring it to the castle. The soldiers there have been on high alert searching for you these past hours."

John turned on the man. "They know I have returned?"

Mort nodded. "And they know that you are missing."

"'Twas the Lady Rowena," Felicity piped in, a slight smile on her face. "She insisted you would not leave on your own and that something must be wrong or you would have come to her."

His sweet Rowena. He wanted to find her and tell her Arthur would trouble her no more. He turned again to the woman held in his grip. "You sought to cause trouble? Methinks you were unsuccessful at that as well."

Her eyes rounded at the pain his words caused her. "Out of love."

"Then out of love tell me where you were to meet Leofrid?"

She glanced away, seeming to measure her options. Finally, she squared her shoulders and faced him. "He expects us to bring you to him at moonrise by the Clouden ruins."

Relief flooded through him. "I thank you for that."

When he started to turn away, she grabbed at his arm. "But I do love you, 'tis true."

"You wouldn't know love if it slapped you in the face," John replied.

Mort pulled away with a look of utter disbelief, shaking his head.

"Well, my lord, clearly she needs to be punished for what she attempted as well."

That's right. Mort had the king's ear. It would not be long before John would be called to answer for the way he botched up his orders.

They must swear their fealty to me by spring next.

His deadline was upon him. The clock was ticking but perhaps with Rowena's help, he could win the villagers over and fulfill his duty.

Chapter Thirty

Rowena stilled her fidgety hands. John would be found. She had to believe it was true. Glancing across the Great Hall, she averted her gaze when she caught sight of Joan. The woman's stubbornness would try a saint.

John did not abandon me.

Would screaming it in her face prove it to be true? No. John being located with a good explanation for his absence is the only thing that could do that.

"My lady." Young Sean dipped his head and handed the folded parchment to Rowena. Her heart stopped beating.

"From where did you get this?"

The boy shrugged. "It was lying on the trestle by the door." He pointed to the symbol visible on the outside. The seal. "It is marked for you, my lady."

Rowena breathed in relief. "I appreciate you delivering it to me." She smiled and ruffled his hair. "Now, why don't you see if the cook has any sweets for you? Tell her I sent you so you don't get your ears boxed for showing up at such a busy time."

He grinned from ear to ear and skipped off toward the kitchen.

Rowena looked down at the seal of the House of Godwin. It had to be from her cousin. How brazen he was to use the family crest on a missive that anyone might have found. She glanced toward the door and around the room. No one seemed unfamiliar. She was happy to find Abigail was not among the guests this evening. The meal would be served soon and she was not up for a battle at this time.

Peter entered and looked around, his eyes finally settling on Rowena.

Peter veered toward her with purpose in every step. He had news. She swallowed the lump in her throat.

Standing beside the bench she'd occupied, she took in a slow, deep breath, preparing herself for the worst.

"Peter."

He moved toward her and accepted her hand, bowing low in respect over it. "My lady. Is there any word of our lord?"

Her shoulders slumped. "There is not. I had hoped you brought news."

"The only news I have is that when we parted at the gate, he continued on to the stables while I continued on with your men to their village."

"My men?" It had been a long time since a Norman referred to them that way. They had once been her men, her parent's men, ready to rise and do battle at a word but not for many years now.

"My lady, they are your men. Yours and Lord John's. They have stood by your husband as their lord. It is only a matter of time before they will swear fealty to the king."

That was an important step toward peace and Rowena knew it. It was also the only reason John had come here in the first place if what his soldiers spoke of was true.

"That is good news indeed."

"News that will make your husband a very happy man." Peter scratched at his head revealing his own distress. "I am beside myself. I do not know what has befallen him. I needs be off to look for him although I have nowhere else to search."

His response sent a chill through her body. "I fear the worst has befallen him."

John's dear friend searched her face with great intensity. "My lady, I did not wish to worry you. Forgive my glib words. He will be found. Rest assured."

Tears welled and she dipped her head, not wanting him to see her weakness. "I pray you are correct."

Peter took her hand again. "If you would sit with me for a moment?"

She sat at the edge of the bench, her knees turned away from Peter. She tried to catch the tear before it fell down her cheek.

"Oh, you are under great duress."

"I'm sorry for my lack of control."

Peter smiled, tipped her chin up and looked into her eyes. "I'm sure it is an endearing quality to your husband."

Her eyes widened. He spoke of John as if feelings were involved. "Perhaps not so endearing."

"Aw, I believe he finds all about you endearing."

She narrowed her eyes. "Speak of me often do you?"

"I listen only. I believe the man values you above all else."

Her breath caught. Perhaps it would not be long before John did realize he could and did love her. "Above all else?"

Peter's face hardened. "The love of a woman has been the downfall of many men."

"And you think it will be so with John?"

He shook his head slowly. "No, I do not believe it is so with you." He measured each word carefully. "You are of noble blood and hold honor above rewards. That is what John needs now. He needs to know that he can be counted as deserving by the one who holds his heart in her hands."

Rowena's family had been destroyed by these Normans. To hear this knight speak of them as they deserve to be spoken of filled her with joy. The Godwins were a noble line. To be defeated by a stronger force did not take that away from them. Peter's respectful manner warmed her heart. She wanted to show her intent with the Normans was sincere as well.

She tilted her head, the last tear sliding off her chin. "Peter, I find nothing lacking in my husband. I wish only to have a peaceful life for us all, Norman and Saxon."

He stood and brushed his lips across her knuckle before releasing her hand. "Then Lady Rowena, I will bring your lord back to you."

She stood as well, tipping her head in agreement. He strode to the door without looking back. The room filled in anticipation of the evening repast but neither Saxon nor Norman soldiers were present. They searched for John.

Suddenly exhausted, Rowena's first instinct was to look for her handmaiden but stopped herself. She would make her way to her room alone. A rest was what she needed now so that when John returned, she could greet him as he deserved.

§

John came in through the garden beside the cooking area to avoid detection. The smells reminded him that he hadn't eaten for more than a day.

"Oh! 'Tis you!" Ada gasped, dropping the armful of bread on the table and ran to him.

He held his finger to his lips causing her to look around. She took his arm, pulled him close to her face, and whispered. "Are you hurt anywhere?"

John wanted to laugh at the motherly concern. "No, well, yes, but I will be fine."

"Nay!" She declared and pulled back, not releasing the firm grip she had of his arm. Grabbing a pitcher from the table, she poured a good amount of mead. "You look ready to collapse."

John knew if he chose this moment to collapse, this woman would keep him standing upright by her determined hold. "I am fine."

He started to protest but quickly downed the mead that had been brought. It soothed his parched throat, easing the tension in his head. He smiled. "My thanks."

"My lord, is your return to be kept secret?"

He quickly swallowed the second cup and accepted the bread she offered. "Yes. Can you do that for me?"

"I will, my lord, and you—Tsk. Tsk. You need to look like you've not lived through hell when you see my lady. She'd pass out at the sight of you."

The image of Rowena, wide-eyed with fright caught him by surprise. He choked on the bread and followed it with a third cup of mead.

"My thanks again." He disengaged her hand from his arm. "I need to find Lady Rowena."

"She's just gone to her room," a young lass offered. It was the serving girl Sarah.

They hadn't heard her come up to them. John hunkered down in front of her. "Thank you, Sarah."

"She's missed you something awful, my lord." The girl reddened at her own outburst. "Forgive me, my lord."

If only Rowena had missed him as he'd missed her. He'd rushed home as quickly as his tired mount would allow once Arthur was dead. Damn Leofrid for delaying his return even more.

He smiled at the little girl. "No need. You spoke your mind in a respectful manner but I need to ask a boon?" She nodded. "Don't let anyone know that I am here."

The girl screwed her face up in apparent confusion. "No? But you will see Lady Rowena?"

John tussled her hair. "Aye, I'm off to see her just now."

"Then I'll be sure to tell no one I've seen you."

He headed to the stairs, keeping to the shadows, and took the steps two at a time. At her chamber door, he paused, his hand poised above the handle. Should he knock or just walk in?

He chided himself for the mistrust he'd shown her. Convincing her of his trust now may be a tough battle. Perhaps persuading her to give him a chance to be her husband in all things would be an even bigger obstacle since she knew the truth about him. He tapped on the door.

"I will be down anon. I require rest now." Rowena's voice was faint, laced with irritation. He opened the door to find her lying across her bed, her arm covering her eyes. "I said anon." She sat up, her eyes widened with surprise.

"My lady, I have returned."

John fought down the many fears that crowded his mind of what she could be thinking. She slowly stood beside the bed as if afraid any sudden movement would cause him to disappear into thin air. A smile blossomed across her face that rivaled the most beautiful sunset. "I see that you have, my lord." She dipped into a curtsy. And went to him, taking him by the hand, leading him to the stool.

He'd have none of it and took her into his arms. Her warmth radiated through the length of him, and he sighed. "Ah, this is where you belong."

She pressed tightly against him before meeting his eyes. "You look near to exhaustion."

He sat down heavily pulling her onto his lap. The exhaustion she mentioned became overwhelming. "Methinks you are right."

Scrambling off his lap, she knelt beside him with a smile and began to remove his boots. "I will order you a bath." The smile left her face. "Not that you stink, my lord. No. Just so you will be more comfortable."

She dropped the second boot and went to the door to call for a bath to be brought up. The smell of lavender jerked John awake and he realize he must have dozed off. The mead was having a strong effect on him. He opened his eyes to find Rowena's concerned face before him. "Are you not well?"

"I have been better." He tried to smile. She did seem happy to see him. He sighed in relief. "I have missed you sorely."

John took her hand in his, stilling her from the busy work of stoking the fire. She looked down at him, her eyes still wide. "And I have missed you."

When he would have pulled her onto his lap again, a knock at the door announced the arrival of the tub. John was surprised to see it carried by a woman whose name he did not know. It was quickly filled with hot steamy water and every ache in John's body suddenly throbbed.

Rowena stood beside him, helping him to remove his tunic. At the sight of his wound, she gasped. "John, what has happened?"

He snorted. "Your friend did not go quietly."

Too late he'd wished he hadn't mentioned Arthur. A shadow passed over her face. "He was no friend."

"That is true enough. Do you know what all he was about? Besides trying to turn you against me and win you for himself?"

"I have heard. I was taken in by him." She turned away, the pain of her loss still visible.

"Oh my sweet lady," John turned her face toward him, "You have had much to contend with whilst I have been gone."

She stood taller. "I have seen to my duties when I was able to leave my bed."

"How long were you abed?"

She shook her head. "It was not long. I had a fever." She shrugged as if to make light of it but wouldn't meet his gaze. "I was afeared for my life."

He stroked her cheek with his fingertip. "Forgive me for not being here for you."

Rowena smiled. "It was all for naught. I would not die now—not when I have what I have wanted."

She took her position as lady of the manor very seriously. In the short walk through to her chambers, the tremendous improvements in the smells and cleanliness were apparent. There also seemed to be an orderliness in the kitchen.

"You have done your duties well with all that I've seen."

"And now I must care for your wound." She picked up his arm and prodded at the skin.

"Methinks it is a little late to do aught else with it. I cleansed it as best I could." John peaked under his arm as well. "How fares it?"

"It is healing well." She tugged at the sleeve of his tunic, his arm dropping out, and smiled at him. She carefully peeled the crusted material away from his chest and removed his soiled shirt. When he stood, she hesitated.

"Would you allow me to attend you? Or should I get another?"

John swayed slightly where he stood. The smell of Rowena drifted to him. "Oh, no my lady, would that you could attend me, wife."

She eased off his chausses and hesitated only slightly at his braies, then helped him climb into the tub. He settled into the warm water and sighed.

Her glance slid down his chest to take in every inch of him. Despite his tiredness, blood rushed to his manhood. He took a deep breath, exhaling it slowly, and leaned back against the side of the tub.

Rowena took the soapy cloth and dragged it down his arms, working the lather between his fingers. He watched her intently, refusing to take his eyes off her. Assisting in a bath was not unheard off. It was a common courtesy offered to guests but as a high ranking lady, she would oversee the duty not administer it herself. Her breathing grew quicker.

The wound was below the water, red and puffy, but clearly visible.

She was careful to not damage the healing skin. He gasped under her ministrations anyway.

She pulled away, her eyes meeting his. "I'm sorry. I did not mean to cause you more pain."

He closed his eyes and exhaled, taking her hand and holding it to his chest. "Here, you will not cause me pain."

Her hand was hot on his chest, and she worked the circles as she washed him. The water was soon clouded, hiding all that lay beneath the surface. She jumped when he took the cloth from her hand and placed it in the water.

"You have taken great care of me, my lady. I believe you have worked my body to a sparkling cleanliness." A smile played on his lips as he spoke. "Now, I would have a taste..."

His finger under her chin stilled her head when she began to turn and reach for the bread behind her. He urged her closer, her lips parting to receive his kiss. Her lips were firm and demanding, parting slightly as she leaned into him.

"Mmm, I have missed you," she said, her dark gray eyes sparked with desire.

"Do you speak the truth or wish to flatter me that a woman so lovely as you could even notice my absence?"

"I did more than notice your absence. I had dreams of you every night."

"Ah, dreaming about me."

She blushed prettily. "Yes. You know what they can be like."

He placed a gentle kiss on her cheek. "I do. I find them much to my liking, as is everything about you."

He kissed her again then leaned back in the tub with closed eyes.

"Dear husband, you are verily spent." Scooping the water, she began to rinse his body. "Can you rest before you see to your duty."

He opened one eye. "But that I could do more. Mayhap just a little reprieve with my wife in my arms?"

"I will be most obliging." She took the cloth and stood beside him as he stepped outside the tub.

There was a loud commotion in the hall and a rapid knock on the door.

John frowned at the intrusion, quickly wrapping the cloth around his waist. "Who is there?" he called.

"John? Is that you?"

"Yes." John rolled his eyes. Rowena smiled. "Enter if you must."

Peter burst in with a rush, his gaze intently perusing John up and down.

"Well?" John asked. "Is it me?"

"Damn it, John. We thought you were dead," Peter snarled. "If I hadn't found our little spy, I would still be looking for you now."

John motioned for him to close the door. "My apologies. I was in no way wanting to spend more time separated from my wife."

Rowena seemed to stand a little taller.

"I would like to know what transpired."

"As would I." Her concern quite visible.

When his stomach growled, she stomped to the door, jerked it open, and ordered that food and drink be brought immediately.

Peter raised an eyebrow at her commanding tone. John felt a surge of pride at her desire to see to his needs. She came to stand between them, coming only up to his chest.

John studied her a moment and then began his story. "I was drugged upon my return and abducted."

Both dropped their jaws.

"From within the castle?" Rowena asked.

"I was in the room off the hall, the wine was on the table and I drank it. I awoke to the stench of flowers."

Peter and Rowena spoke as one. "Abigail."

Peter added."But she couldn't have abducted you alone."

A knock at the door took Rowena away.

"You are correct. She had help. One man with a scar down the side of his face—"

Rowena gasped where she stood carrying a heavy tray covered with an assortment of foods.

"Do you know the man?" John asked her.

She placed the tray on the table, poured the wine into a glass and brought it to him. He took the cup and studied her face.

"I have seen him near the chapel. There have been many here whom I no longer recognize. He appeared quite menacing."

Peter snorted. "It seems your assessment was correct."

Settling herself on the stool, Rowena placed her hands demurely on her lap, her eyes averting his. Something was amiss.

"Did the man approach you?"

"No. He did not." She still refused to look at him and a growing uneasiness spread through him.

"Is there more you can offer, Rowena?"

Peter glanced at her and frowned.

"Would you be so kind as to give me time with my wife alone?"

"As you wish, my lord."

Peter closed the door behind him. Rowena darted a look toward John.

"You appear to have much on your mind."

"You have no idea." She rounded her eyes as she spoke, with another cloth she began to dab at his shoulders, patting him dry.

"I would like to have an idea." He glanced at her over his shoulder. Her ministrations were getting a bit rough. "Methinks I would fare better if you tell me."

The cloth splashed when she dropped it and stood beside the tub. "My lord, I am unsure what to do with something."

She went to the table beside her bed and returned a rolled parchment. Holding it so he could see the seal, John frowned. "The House of Godwin?"

"I was given this by a young lad this very evening. I do not know what it is about."

It was unopened. "Have you any idea who would send this to you."

"I do have one idea."

She searched his expression he knew not for what. Nibbling at her lip, John waited patiently. When no further details were forthcoming, he asked. "Do you have something to tell me?"

"My lord, I was approached by my cousin Leofrid."

John felt like he'd been punched in the gut. "And you didn't feel you should share that with me? That your cousin was alive?"

"It was earlier. In the fall. You had only just arrived."

"Rowena, he is the enemy."

"Am I as well?"

John frowned at her obtuseness. "You tell me."

"No." Her annoyance was apparent in her slanted brows. "But he is my cousin. I was glad my family was not all dead."

He'd jumped to the wrong conclusion before and did not want to do that again. More information was what he needed. He took her hand in his.

"What did he want from you?"

"He said he wanted me to know he was alive." She shrugged her small shoulders. "And I verily was glad to know I was not the lone survivor."

Her sudden blush made him question her answer. "Clearly he said something that upset you. I think you should tell me."

She closed her eyes as if for fortitude before answering. "He asked if I'd been bedding a Norman." Her blush deepened, her teeth sinking into her bottom lip.

"And what did you say?"

"I said of course not."

It must have been before their marriage was consummated. That would be embarrassing no doubt.

He nodded slowly. "And yet you were married to me. My apologies for putting you in that situation."

"Not for lack of trying on your part, my lord."

He took her hand to his mouth, kissing it lightly. "And yet you left me wanting but no more."

Still holding her hand in his, he filled his empty glass one handed and led her to the bed. He sat down then pushed himself back to lean against the wall, bringing her to settle upon his lap.

Offering her the cup, he nuzzled his nose into her hair. Shifting it to the side, he kissed her neck and was rewarded by a shiver she couldn't hide.

"So tell me, my lady. What do you think your cousin was doing here?"

She tipped her head to one side, giving him better access. He didn't need to be asked twice. Putting his wine on the table, he pulled the edge of her gown down for better access and nibbled at the back of her neck.

"Umm, I don't know why he was here. Perhaps he felt safe here?" She shook her head as if to clear her mind. "No, he knew he wasn't safe."

John pulled back. "Why do you say that?"

"He said he had to make alliances wherever he could find them. That's where I saw the man with the scar."

"With Leofrid?"

"Yes. He told me not to trust that man and to stay away from him." She shifted to face him better. "I was just so glad he was still alive. I didn't see him as a threat. I am sorry."

John put his hand to the back of her neck, pulling her closer, pressing her lips to his. They were soft and warm. "Hmm, I have missed you so."

Rowena wrapped her arm around his bare back. "And I you."

"We will have time for this soon."

She tipped her head. "Yes. Soon."

"But for now we must see what message your cousin has sent."

She handed him the scroll without hesitation. "I don't even know if the message is for me. Young Sean found it and brought it to me."

John broke the seal and unrolled the short parchment.

"Dearest Ro." He frowned at her. "Ro?"

"Yes. That is what he calls me. And he was always Leo."

He returned to the letter. "I am very glad yours was not a marriage for love. We are ready to move against the king. Stay closed up in the castle. I will return for you."

Not a marriage for love. The words stung and yet he knew they were true.

Had Rowena told Leofrid that it was not a marriage for love? How did she feel now?

"I am sorry to have your feelings so blatantly discussed." John didn't know what else to say. He did love her but clearly she did not feel the same.

He got up from the bed and began dressing. "We need to move quickly to catch him unawares. If he hears I have escaped his bonds, he will not be found again."

Rowena reached for his arm but he evaded her touch. "John, wait."

He needed to locate Peter and make plans. Why was he wasting his time in here with baths? And his wife?

"Please, John." Rowena placed her hand over his where he held the grip of his sword.

Lifting his eyes to her, he could see she was confused. She would have to learn to adjust. "Rowena, I must see to my duty."

"But, John, his words are not true."

He stopped at the door and turned to face her. "What does it matter?"

"It matters to me."

"It shouldn't. We were never meant to be as one. This would never work. Someone has to be in control. It needs to be the Normans."

"And with us?"

"I need to do what is best for all."

The pain in her eyes could not be acknowledged. "Then I will abide by your wishes."

Peter waited in the hall and John bid him to enter. "How would you have me proceed?"

John needed to catch Leofrid and knowing where he was to meet Abigail for the exchange gave him the upper hand.

"I was short-sighted...on many fronts... not realizing the consequences of returning here and being seen." John shifted.

"Who else knows that you are here?"

"I came through the kitchen—"

"Everyone. They have all seen him. The boys that came in with the tub, the maid that came to the door with the food..." Rowena stood, her voice raised higher with her concern. "Does it mean you are not safe here?"

John and Peter exchanged glances. "My lord?"

John shook his head. He saw his friend's considering gaze. "Rowena?"

"Yes, my lord?"

"Would your people keep my whereabouts secret to protect me?"

"I believe that they will."

"Then much has changed in my absence?"

"Yes, my lord, much has indeed changed."

Peter raised his eyebrows in question."Then I will secure the castle, bring in the men who are still searching for you, but give no details."

"We leave anon to confront the bastard."

Rowena's head shot up, her eyes wide. Peter nodded and left, closing the door behind him.

"You must leave so soon?"

"Aye. My abductor thinks he will be taking charge of me tonight. I do not wish to disappoint."

"But you have just returned. Surely another can go in your stead?" She worried her hands. "Forgive me, my lord. It is not for me to say how you complete your duties. I trust you to do what is best for us all but I would have you know one thing. Ours was not a marriage for love."

His body stiffened. The words were true enough but not what he now felt in his heart. He had wanted her to love him back.

"Had I known you as the man that you verily are, not the Norman soldier that others see, I would have willingly come to you in the chapel and spoken my vows to you. I would have willingly taken you as my husband. I will be here when you return."

John searched her face and saw the longing there. She longed for his company. He was torn between his duty and his own desires. He wanted her as his wife as well. He leaned forward, taking her hand to his lips and kissing it lightly. "I do not wish to leave again. If I could stay now, I would. You may trust in that."

He kissed the palm of her hand then placed it against his cheek. She held his gaze and nodded. "I will trust in that."

Chapter Thirty-One

The dark enveloped John and his soldiers as they moved soundlessly, spreading out around the remains of the former abbey. The flapping of an owl's wings rushed past them as John hunkered down beside a crumbling wall to await moonrise and the encounter with the last Godwinson who remained his enemy. Unbidden, Leofwine's silver eyes flashed through his mind. Would his nephew have those same eyes?

The night sounds continued, echoing through the trees around them. Peter waited to his left, unseen. The rest of the soldiers hid a short distance away, but not close enough to be spotted by Leofrid. John had time to think. Time to remember.

Will you yield?

His own words came to him from some unknown place where dark fears hide.

I will trust in that.

Rowena had offered her acceptance of him. How would she feel if she knew the truth about her father? Happiness was not something John had looked for in his life. Rowena had been an unexpected treasure, but one he knew he wouldn't be able to hold.

I will be here when you return.

That was the real reason he had believed she would leave with Arthur. John feared he could not hold onto her. He didn't deserve her. It was better to believe she would leave him if given a chance. But he had been wrong about her. She'd all but professed her love to him. How could he tell her the truth? How could he keep the truth from her?

The darkness beneath the trees shifted ever so slightly when the moon began its ascent.

I would have willingly taken you as my husband.

Rowena, forgive me. I tried to save him but he would not listen.

A twig snapped to his left, near the road to the village. All sounds ceased.

The light filtered through the trees and the dark silhouette of a tall man paced along the tree line. *Leofrid.* As planned, the soldiers would be shifting in closer, cutting off his escape path. John awaited the signal.

Can you love me, Rowena? When I have your father's blood on my hands?

One low whistle pierced the darkness. John stood and closed the distance between him and Leofrid. Coming upon him unawares, it was the sound of John's sword being unsheathed that Leofrid finally heard.

"What?" The man stumbled away, grabbing at his own sword but John was quicker, grabbing his hand before it found the hilt.

"Stay your hand, Leofrid."

The man shook his head, clearly confused. Ten well armed soldiers closed in around him. The fool had come alone.

"What goes on here? Who are you? Who is Leofrid?" The man stumbled over his words, his hands raised in a defensive stance. "Do you mean to rob me? I have nothing of value."

Peter reached out and took his sword, then felt around his waist for the gold that was promised. His hand stilled.

"Then what have we here?" Peter asked.

With one firm tug, the sack of gold dropped to the ground.

Leofrid stiffened. "Take it, but leave me with my life."

John moved in closer and saw the man did indeed have the same silver eyes as his wife. His heart lurched at her loss if this man died as well.

"What have you come here for in the dark of night?"

The moonlight twinkled in his eyes, making them dark one minute and bright with fear the next. He refused to answer.

"Leofrid, let us talk as men."

"Why would we talk at all? You have my gold, now leave me."

"You come here alone to take me as your prisoner?"

Leofrid's shoulders dropped. He ran his hands through his hair, feigning submission but John was ready when he ducked to make a break for it beneath the soldiers' arms. John tackled him to the ground before he'd moved five feet.

John forced him to his back, his arms held above him as he struggled for release. "Enough, Leofrid."

"No. It will never be enough. You take what is rightfully ours. You cannot be allowed to stay in power."

Leofrid spat in his face. Peter stilled any further movements with the tip of his sword to his neck.

"Cease your struggles or I will gladly run you through."

John got up and brushed the dirt from his clothes. "The exchange you had planned will not take place. Peter, secure him in the dungeon until I have decided what to do with him."

The other soldiers moved in to help Peter tie him up. John walked back to his horse, sheathing his sword. Rowena's cousin still lived but how could he remain so if he refused to back down? He would be a constant threat to all that King William had accomplished. How could John again be the source of more pain to his wife?

Chapter Thirty-Two

The ride to Westminster had taken longer than usual. The spring rains had made even the most traveled roads nearly impassable. Though Rowena had protested the conveyance, she was happy to not be on a horse in this weather. She'd not seen much of John since he led the party, Peter at his right. And each night they stayed at inns along the way, the men and women separated.

Rowena was not looking forward to this encounter. The king had asked specifically if she would be attending William FitzOsbern's daughter's nuptials. It was no one she knew but John had assured her she had always treated him well and he didn't want to miss the celebration since her own father had now passed.

The vaulted ceilings of the building were a marvel to Rowena and she had to consciously close her mouth with every new sight she found. She'd been here as a child but much had changed with the Norman invasion, the expansion being just one of the things she noticed were different.

"My lady, Lady Emma has sent me to see if I can be of assistance to you. My name is Bridget."

Rowena's face heated. "Yes, I could use the help, Bridget."

After adjusting the girdle of the simple blue gown, the woman took great care with Rowena's hair creating braided loops that adorned either side of her head and dipping so low they nearly touched her shoulders.

"You look lovely, my lady."

"My thanks to your capable hands."

She dipped her head in appreciation. "If you are ready now, Lady Emma is verily anxious to meet you."

187

"Please." Rowena motioned the woman to lead the way.

Butterflies fluttered in her stomach at the idea of meeting another of the king's wards. This one however, was the daughter of his best friend and sure to be treated better than Rowena had been.

An elegantly dressed woman greeted her with a big smile and open arms. "Lady Rowena. I am so happy to meet the woman who has stolen Sir John's heart."

Enveloped in her arms, Rowena was glad Emma could not see the shock she felt was surely on her face. Peter had implied something similar.

"Come." Emma took Rowena by the hand and led her to the window seat beside the huge four poster bed. "Tell me everything. The king claims responsibility for John's happiness for it was him that put the two of you together."

Rowena's jaw dropped. "Does the king verily speak of us thus?"

Her dark eyes widened, and she moved in closer as if in secret alliance. "Well, not in so many words but he does accept praise when things go well, not so much the responsibility when things turn sour."

Rowena could not hold back the laugh and Emma joined right in.

"You are so brave to say such things."

John took that moment to enter the chamber through the open door. "Ah, the two of you whispering and laughing in conspiratorial tones bodes well for no one...especially me."

"Oh. John." Emma waved her hand in dismissal. "You cannot believe you would be the topic of our conversation."

He raised one brow at Emma and then Rowena. Heat flooded her face and she bit her cheek to keep from smiling.

"Unlike you, dear Emma, my lady wife does not hide her emotions well. I can see that I have interrupted your discourse just in the nick of time."

Emma gasped. "Ah, dear John, she does show every emotion! How easy could it have been for her to hide her true feelings of love from you?"

Rowena's breath caught. Her shoulders pulsed from the lack of oxygen and time stopped. She held the lady's gaze and was graced by the look of sudden understanding that passed over her face.

"My apologies." Emma grabbed her cold hands. "My sincerest apologies. He doesn't know?"

John came to stand beside Rowena, concern etched in his forehead. "Are you not well, Rowena? You look pale."

Rowena glanced toward John. "I am a bit overwhelmed."

"Maria." Emma strode toward the open door, calling out. "Maria? Ah, please bring refreshments for my guests...and a good strong whisky from the king's private stock."

John held Rowena's gaze, dropping to his knee beside her. "Do you wish to leave? Perhaps you need some time to rest?"

His hand was comforting were it rested on her thigh. "I am fine, John. Thank you for your concern."

He lightly brushed his lips against her forehead. "You will let me know if you wish to leave?"

She nodded. Emma came to stand behind him. "You two certainly are adorable."

John rolled his eyes and stood to face the bride to be.

"You missed your chance at me."

Rowena sat up straighter.

"Aye, I believe I did." Emma's voice sounded wistful, Rowena felt her ire begin to rise.

"I tried hard enough to win you over."

"And failed." The sudden flatness of her voice and the comical tilt of her lips made Rowena realize they were teasing. The woman's wink gave her confirmation.

"That was long ago." John took Rowena's hand and kissed it lightly. "I am happy to say the loss was a blessing in disguise."

Emma scrunched her face in mock distress."What say you then? You have no depth of feeling still lingering for me?"

John bent to kiss his wife full on the lips. He pulled back and smiled at her. Rowena's heart lightened considerably at his look of love.

"Aye. Not a bit," John answered, still facing her.

"Well, is that not always the way of it?"

Refreshments were brought and Emma quickly dispensed some whisky and gave it to Rowena. "It will help you relax before you meet the king."

Rowena's stomach tightened. "So soon?"

John pulled a bench up beside her. "He does not have much patience."

"But we've just arrived. Are you sure it is me he wants to meet? Now?"

"He has said as much." John's eyes darkened. "I will make excuses if you are not ready." His eyes took in all of her. "But you do look lovely."

"My thanks."

"No married couple can really be this sweet on each other."

Emma's voice sliced through the comfort John's closeness and kind words were building within her.

John turned to face the other woman. "Have a care, Emma. Rowena does not know the king. Your joking manner is new to her as well."

Emma's eyes rounded in sympathy. "My apologies, Lady Rowena. I did not consider your fear. Please, try the whisky."

Rowena took a small sip, then another. The peaty scent floated about her and she took another sip. "Aye. 'Tis very good. I thank you."

Emma's smile broadened and with a smug look she turned on John. "See? I can do something right."

"Aye. That you can." John's smile slipped. "And who is this man the king has given you to?"

She tipped her hand, palm up. "Someone he has decided will be beneficial to his plans for me. Ralph de Gael. He is an older man."

Rowena suddenly saw through the sarcastic facade when tears sprang to Emma's eyes, balancing on her lashes.

John took the woman into a comforting embrace. "Fear not, Emma. He would not marry you to one that would not have been acceptable to his dearest friend."

"I know but William FitzOsbern did not always make the best decisions."

"You have the right of it." John patted her back, glancing at Rowena. "You are strong like your father. Do not forget that."

Emma pulled out of his arms and sniffled. "I will be strong. How were you able to be wed to one so sweet and lovely and I am wed off to some old lord with land the king covets?"

Rowena looked down, wishing the heat in her face would lessen.

"I was blessed. I know not why."

His words echoed in her heart. He considered her a blessing. She glanced up to find them both looking at her. She took another sip but the heat seemed to makes its way into her belly with the whisky.

"I've never been called a blessing before except perhaps by my father and that was a very long time ago." The kind smile of her father could lighten any situation. She missed him so much.

§

Her words pierced his heart. John would never be able to win Rowena over fully once she knew he'd killed her father. He glanced toward Emma. They had spoken earlier and she knew his dilemma. Emma glanced away unable to hold his gaze, confirming what he now knew.

"Come, my lady, let me present you to the king. It will not become easier with waiting." And John knew the truth of his words.

Rowena glanced at the hand he stretched toward her then to his face. With a small smile, she accepted the gesture hand, demonstrating her trust in him. But John knew it would not last.

"Remember what we discussed, Rowena. Do not be intimidated by his bluster. He avoids responsibility like every man." Emma reminded her.

John dropped his jaw in mocked outrage.

"Well, maybe not every man," she continued.

John smiled. This woman could cut out a heart with her tongue or bring comfort to a dying man with her smile. She was someone he held in the very highest esteem. He had once fancied himself in love with her, even asking for her hand from the king. The man had been fit to be tied. Although he had been kind to him, the king did not consider him family as he did Emma. Her kind words regarding him and Rowena, however, had moved him deeply.

When the two of them reached the Great Hall, Rowena's hands turned cold. The look on her face spoke of her inward struggle to face this man.

"I will be at your side, my love. Do not fret."

Her sudden look sent chills down his spine. He had no idea what he'd said but he was reminded of the way she'd looked when they were wed. They joined the long line awaiting the king's attention. It would be awhile before she would have to meet him. He feared she'd be sick on the floor before then. She nibbled at her lip, her eyes taking in all about her.

"Look at me." He tried to coax her. "You look verily lovely, Rowena." He touched the braids that surrounded her face. "And your dark hair is like a halo around your sweet face."

Perhaps his words of endearment would help her to calm herself. He was shocked to see her eyes fill with tears.

"What have I said that brings you to tears?"

"I cannot believe that you would speak such tender words to me here, in front of at least fifty other people."

"Why not?"

"How can I respond to you the way that I want to? How can I pull you close and return those tender words, whispering them in your ear as your heart beats close to mine?"

John swallowed the lump in his throat. "I would have you do just that anyway, no matter where we are. Your tender words to me would be a boon to my spirit."

She pulled him close, closing her eyes perhaps to shut out those that turned toward them. No doubt she could still hear their gasps and mumbled words of censure as he did.

"I love you, John, more than you will ever know." Her whispered words were spoken with conviction. Her scent surrounded him and he wanted nothing more than to crush her to him but he could not.

"Oh, my sweet lady, I love you more every day that I am with you." His whisper turned hoarse with his emotion. "Let me love you for the rest of my days, let me show the intensity of my love in everything that I do."

"Everything." She echoed his words then found his lips, pulling him to her as she had promised. Lost in the embrace it was the sudden burst of applause by one set of hands, followed by the roar of the people around them following suit that broke them apart and brought John back to the reality of the situation.

He smiled, stretched his neck slightly, and turned his bride to face the king that had come to stand beside them. He was still clapping.

"Bravo, my dear ones. What a display of emotion."

John bowed at the waist and Rowena curtsied in a deep fashion but the king pulled at her arm. "Come my lovely lady, let us speak in private."

Rowena's eyes were wide with shock when she met John's gaze. She could not refuse the king and followed him, or rather was led by him, through the doors to the left that John knew led to the king's private chambers.

Chapter Thirty-Three

Beside himself with angst, John paced Emma's chamber.

"Be calm. The king would certainly not abuse your wife."

John stopped to glare at his friend. "Think you he cares whose wife she is?"

"Ah!" Emma slapped at his arm, a small smile playing on her lips. "John, you are being ridiculous. William would never be so cruel."

"She is a Saxon." Finally voicing his concerns aloud, John was hit with an overwhelming wave of fear for Rowena. William did not value the Saxons. "I have to go to her."

The woman rounded her eyes. She pulled at his arm. "Do not take leave of your senses! The king will have you flogged if you burst in there like this."

John wrenched his arm away, turning toward her. "Do you think I do not realize what the king will do?" His voice boomed but he couldn't help himself. "That is my greatest fear."

He jerked the door open and came up against two of Williams' own guards about to knock on the wooden door.

"Oh, Sir John, we have come to take you to the king."

John glanced beyond them. "Where is my wife?"

"John." Emma's warning tone cut through John's fear.

Taking a steadying breath, he dipped his head in acquiescence. "Then lead the way."

With every step John's body tensed but he fought his panic. He could do nothing to protect Rowena if he was thrown into William's dungeon. How could he have been so foolish? He had to obey the king's summons but he should have come up with a plan to avoid being separated from her. He prayed she was safe.

"Ah, John." The king stood just inside the empty room, the door open as he apparently awaited John's arrival.

"My lord." John bowed respectively and clenched his jaw shut. He needed to be careful with what he said.

The king motioned for the guards to close the door, but one remained stationed inside. His hand not far from his sword. Did the king anticipate trouble?

"Please, sit." William indicated a chair to the right of the one he'd taken. "It has been a long time since last we've seen each other. How fare you? Or more specifically, how fares your lovely wife?"

John breathed slowly through his nose and carefully unclenched his teeth. "I am well as was my wife the last time I saw her."

Damn. The king raised a quizzical brow.

Answer only what is asked.

"Then I would say you fare very well. She is a lovely Saxon."

The title bristled him. He dare not speak of it.

"Have you won her over as she claims?"

Rowena said that?

"We have come to an understanding."

"Aye, as I knew you would." William poured him a drink from the gold pitcher on the table at his elbow. He offered it to John. "And what does she know of her cousin?"

Accepting the cup, John fought to give no indication of what he was thinking. "My lord?"

"Come, John," William threw back his drink in one swallow. "Surely, you've heard the rumors?"

John frowned in feigned concentration.

"Her cousin Leofrid?"

"Ah, yes. Her cousin. She had many cousins."

Damn, William's eyes narrowed slightly. John's heart beat faster.

"Yes, John, but only one of them is still rumored to be alive." William raised one eyebrow in clear indication of his irritation.

"There have always been rumors. I do not believe there is any truth in them." He swallowed his drink and took a chance. "Did you not wish to hear about Arthur?"

William tipped his head up, then nodded. "Yes, Arthur. Quite a disappointment, that one."

"How so?" A sinking feeling made its way into his gut. Could the king have had something to do with the brutality Arthur inflicted?

"He swore his loyalty but fell short of his duty." The king's eyes pierced John's. "I would not like to say the same of you, my son."

"I have been right alongside you, fighting every battle as my own. How could you compare me with that man?"

"Have you been accepted by your wife's people?"

They are my people. John dare not voice the thought. "Yes."

The big man breathed a sigh of relief and slumped in his seat. "Good. I knew I could trust you. Your loyalty comes from good stock."

All sound ceased.

"I do not understand."

William's eyes rounded slightly, then he glanced away. "Oh just the ramblings of an old man."

John searched his face. Did this man know who his sire was? Who his mother was?

Sitting forward suddenly, William cleared his throat. "So John, I need you to stay ready in case the rumors are correct. If Leofrid is still alive, he needs to be killed. Do you understand?"

"You want me to kill my wife's cousin?"

The king seemed taken aback by the question. "Of course, John. They're only Saxons. Their family loyalty does not run as deep as yours and mine."

He inclined his head.

William stood and John followed him to the door.

"Fare thee well, John. Enjoy your little wife."

John stood outside the closed door, facing the still crowded Great Hall. The king had taken time away from his duty to question him and Rowena. He must know that Leofrid was indeed alive. It would kill Rowena to lose her cousin. John could not kill the man in cold blood. He headed back to Emma's chamber, going up the stairs two at a time.

"John." Rowena turned to him as he was bade entry. She came into his arms, her body shaking slightly.

"Are you not well? Were you hurt?" John's need to defend his lady cut to the core of his being.

"Oh, no, John. I am fine." She turned back toward Emma who stood beside the window seat she'd just vacated. "We have been discussing the king and perhaps why he wanted our attendance at this wedding."

"Please, John, do not feel you must stay." Emma stepped closer, her hand on his arm. "It has been a most trying time for the both of you. The king will not notice your absence. I assure you."

"Then we shall leave as soon as Rowena is ready."

"I am ready now." Rowena's enthusiasm for the long trip surprised John.

"Are you certain?"

"I wish to be home. All this pomp and circumstance makes me sad for old times. I do not wish to dwell on the past. I wish to start anew with you."

Emma beamed her agreement in the smile she bestowed. "Yes, John, take your lady wife home and care for her."

"Aye. We will leave anon."

§

The roads were dark when they came to the first inn along the road. Creatures of the night offered their greeting as John helped Rowena dismount.

"We will not be kept apart this night."

Rowena shivered at his whispered words.

There had been no time for them to be together in such a long time. She just wished to be held and cherished by this man she loved.

The only room available was gladly passed up by the rest of the group. They willingly chose other accommodations as if sensing the need for their lord and lady to have some time alone.

"John, did the king speak ill of me?"

The courage required to ask the question vanished as soon as the words were spoken. Why did she need to hear the answer? Better not to know for certain.

John took her in his arms, holding her head against his shoulder. "My love, any ill spoken of you would be answered at the end of my sword."

Rowena pulled back to look up at him. His eyes twinkled with the mischief of his words. "My lord, I prefer you alive. No words can touch me if you do not lose faith in me."

A dark cloud seemed to pass over his features and he released his hold. He stood by the small window overlooking the woods surrounding the small inn. He looked to have the weight of the world on his shoulders. Rowena suddenly feared what he might say.

"John, I—"

"No, Rowena, you must let me speak." John interrupted her, but did not turn toward her.

Her heart sank. After his words of love in the Hall, there had been no time for questions. She had been swept away for a private audience. Did he wish to take back his words?

"I have something I must tell you that may change your feelings toward me."

Nothing could stop her from loving this man. He was everything to her and with him by her side, she would be able to move forward in this land they now called England.

"I was at the battle where your uncle and father were killed."

John faced her. There was a darkness in his eyes she'd never seen before. As if he was revisiting the carnage again. She looked away. She did not want to relive that day. Her nightmares had been made up of those memories for so long. She just wanted happy memories now.

"Please, John—"

"I would not speak of it if it did not need to be said."

Rowena took a deep, fortifying breath. "As you wish."

"No, it is not my wish. It was never my wish. I had seen enough death in those days to haunt me for the rest of my life." He looked off into the distance.

A shiver of fear ran down Rowena's spine and she knew she did not want to hear his words.

"I had ordered my men to take as many of the Saxons alive as they could. I saw no reason to murder when they had clearly lost the day. Most of the soldiers continued to fight, pressing forward into crowds of my soldiers even though they knew they could not survive. They came willingly to die."

Tears filled Rowena's eyes at the picture his words created in her mind.

"Your father was just as proud."

Her breath caught. He had seen her father killed?

"I begged him to yield."

He had spoken to him before he died.

"I repeated myself." John's voice got louder. "I begged him to put down his sword, Rowena."

No, no, don't continue. She covered her ears and looked away.

John's hands were warm on her arms as he gently pulled her hands away from her head.

"My love, I wanted to give him leniency, have William work out...something so that the man could survive. He had fought so hard. He was an amazing soldier as was your entire family. I have never been up against anyone that I had feared as much as them. I wanted him to live."

The tears coursed down her cheeks, her face pinched with the pain of his memories.

"He refused to yield." His brown eyes were wide. "He advanced on me and tripped, and his body fell." A tear slipped down John's cheek. "My love, I couldn't move my sword in time. He died on my sword."

John gripped her arms, a look of imploring forgiveness on his face. She couldn't breathe. His pain was so acute that she felt it in her own heart. He had held this inside all this time, knowing that he had been the cause of her father's death—no, it was his unrelenting stubbornness that had caused his death.

Rowena looked down, closing her eyes. Would forgiving this man for his part in the loss of her people cause anyone else pain? Was there anyone that could profit from her withholding absolution when all she wanted to do was ease his guilt? Was she a terrible daughter to know that war kills people, makes them throw away all that they have, disregarding all that they value, just to win the battle?

Lifting her head, she wiped the tears from her face, and faced her husband. Slowly, she wiped the tear off his cheek and moved in to kiss him where it had been.

"My love, my father is dead. I have mourned that loss for too long. I wish only to move on with you. You are my life now. You are what I treasure more than anything. If it is forgiveness you seek, you have it. Let us never talk of this again."

John's arm tightened around her, near to crushing her with the intensity of his emotions. She rubbed her lips against his neck.

"My love, I have missed you immensely."

He moaned into her ear and lifted her into his arms. The small bed groaned under their weight as he put her down and covered her body with his own.

He caressed her cheek and neck, sending ripples of anticipation where he touched. "My love, you are more than I could ever desire as a wife."

His lips were warm against her, becoming more insistent, and she opened her mouth to him. His tongue dipped inside, teasing her. His warm hands slid down her side, stopping to cup her breast that ached for his mouth.

"Make love to me," she said.

In the close quarters there was no room for secrets. Each breath was shared, each touch uniting, in every way he made love to her with not just his body but with the way he worshipped her.

When he brought her to the pinnacle, he placed his hands on either side of her body. She opened her eyes.

"Let me see your pleasure."

She wet her lips, fighting to keep her eyes on him as he drove her further and harder than he had ever done before. Pleasure quivered through her in waves. With purpose he thrust into her, prolonging her ecstasy, his eyes still on her face.

"You are my life, Rowena. I will love you until there are no more days left for me on this earth."

Tears of happiness slipped down her cheeks at his words.

"I love you," Rowena whispered.

John dipped his head and she crested with him as he drove home, surely touching her womb. He shuddered and dropped beside her.

She settled against his chest and sighed.

"May a child be conceived this night."

A child for them to share. The loss of their daughter was still heavy but the hope for a new life gave her strength.

"Aye." She covered her abdomen with her hand. "It must be so."

He kissed the top of her head, caressing her back, and she snuggled into his chest.

Thoughts crowded in her mind, demanding her attention, and she tried to dismiss them to focus on the feel of his hand as he caressed her arms. It was all for naught.

"My love, let me ask you one thing."

"Only one?" Her voice was contented and sleepy. "Are your thoughts racing as well?"

"Well, I wondered what it was William actually talked to you about."

"He could only go on and on about what a great catch you are, and how lucky I am to be married to good Norman stock."

John paused mid-stroke but remained silent. So, she continued, "He spoke of the pride of the Normans and how you come from a long line of good fighters and fertile men." She sensed the tension in him but knew she had to ask. "Do you have other children?"

"No. Why would you ask that?"

"Abigail had said as much."

John sighed loudly with his frustration. "That woman knows naught but to serve her own purposes." He kissed Rowena's forehead with great reverence. "I am sorry that she bothered you in my absence."

Rowena's relief was complete. "So you have no ties to her or great love for her?"

"*No.* I thought to never see her again when I left Normandy."

"Was she your mistress?"

"Not the word I would choose and not for lack of trying on her part, even sneaking into my bed to get what she wanted." He ducked his head. "I'm sorry to admit she was occasionally successful. No, I barely knew her but allowed her to stay at my home because I had pity for her. She had nowhere else to go."

"Then the king's comments perplex me. Does he not know your situation?"

"Aye, he knows it well enough."

"Do you think he knows more than he has said?"

"It would not be the first time."

"Oh." She tipped her head back to better see his face. "He asked me about Leofrid."

"He asked me about him as well."

"Forgive me, John, but I did not tell him what had transpired."

She nibbled on her lip when he didn't answer immediately. Would he be mad that she did not tell the king everything she knew?

"I am glad you did not tell him. I've come to a decision."

There was a sudden tightness in her gut. She loved her cousin but he could not be allowed to hurt John. Perhaps if she talked to Leofrid directly, he would see that. No. He was a Godwinson. There would be no talking to him.

"I've decided it would be best to ship Leofrid to Ireland."

She gasped, sitting up more, the bed creaking with her movement. "My thanks, John, for sparing his life."

"But he must agree to leave willingly, although under guard, and never to return. That is the price for his freedom. Oh, and he must take Abigail with him."

She narrowed her eyes. "You would saddle him with a woman like that?"

"I believe it is a just punishment. That way she can cause no further problems here."

Rowena frowned as if deep in thought, smiled down at him before kissing him, and said, "That is a sound decision. I will look to you to make these decisions...and then I will let you know what I think of them."

His eyebrows shot up, and she struggled not to laugh at the comical look of surprise. "Oh, is that the way of it then?"

"That is the way of it."

THE END

ABOUT THE AUTHOR

Thank you for taking your valuable time to read my latest novel. Below, you will find links to my website as well as my email address. I look forward to hearing your thoughts on this and other novels. I love interacting with my readers!

I have wanted to be a writer since the sixth grade. My first story was a mystery and I discovered that my classmates loved it and kept them guessing. I was a voracious reader, even at a young age, and loved the history in the novels I picked up. I was so enthralled with that history that I decided to get my MA in History. The early medieval period is my favorite, as you can tell from the novels I write.

Although all my works are fiction, I often like to incorporate authentic places, events, and people to increase the reader's enjoyment. One of the more valuable lessons I have learned as a writer is the importance of using real history with the flair of artistic license. You'll discover a world of fiction wrapped around historical people and events! I hope you enjoy reading these stories as much as I delight in writing them.

I live in New England with my husband, two cats and a yellow Labrador named Caledonia.

You can connect with me online:

Website: www.ashleyyorkauthor.com
Email: ashleyyorkauthor@gmail.com

Please enjoy these sample chapters from The Bruised Thistle, *the first book in* The Order of the Scottish Thistle Series.
Ashley

CHAPTER ONE

Dalmally, Scotland 1149

"Where have you been?" Iseabail bristled with irritation at having waited nigh an hour for her brothers' arrival. Trying to look busy alone in an open field was a challenge, especially with the cool autumn wind stinging her exposed skin.

"Getting supplies," Iain answered readily enough, but he didn't sound himself.

Their little brother Calum stood at his elbow, nodding his red head a touch too eagerly.

She glanced between them as her suspicions rose. They were hiding something. "What is wrong?" Iain usually took great care with his appearance, but today he was ill-kempt. His thick dark hair hung limp around his face, and his brown eyes were bloodshot and red-rimmed. Her irritation shifted to concern. "Are you not well?"

"Well enough. See what we've brought?" Iain's tone brooked no discussion.

Iseabail allowed him to distract her with the large basket Calum was carrying. He placed it on the ground and lifted the lid. All manner of cloths, containers, and herbing accoutrements greeted them. Iain pushed this aside to reach beneath and lift the false bottom, showing a good array of cheese, breads, and dried meat for their trip.

A shiver ran down her spine, but she smiled up at him. "Good. We are ready then."

Ready to leave the only home they had ever known, the overwhelming sadness caught her off-guard. She forced herself to remember the abuses they had suffered at the hands of their powerful uncle, the new laird of *their* lands. What he had subjected her to as a female was the most horrendous of all.

She clenched her jaw in determination. "Shall we go?"

"Iseabail." Iain's face was unreadable, but she sensed his hesitation. "I cannot go."

His words knocked the wind out of her. The thought of having to return to the hell she had been enduring left her lightheaded.

She shook her head in denial. "No, Iain, I cannot..." She corrected herself, "*we* cannot go back." Her brothers did not know about their uncle's abuse. There were no visible signs. "We cannot. We must make our escape now, while he is away from the castle."

Iain's eyes rounded with sadness and fine lines creased his forehead.

Iseabail had a terrible sense of foreboding, and the whisper of hope she had been nurturing began to dissipate. The idea of escape had come up so suddenly, yet they had all agreed straight away. Their uncle's plans to be gone for a few days gave them the perfect opportunity, and it was one they could not afford to waste. They needed help ousting Uncle Henry from their lands. Not only was he ignoring their father's last will and testament, his brutal treatment of the local clansmen had weakened them until their fear would not allow them to stand against him. Assistance from those outside the powerful Englishman's control was their only hope.

Iain firmed his shoulders, a determined set to his handsome face. "*We* will not return. You and Calum will travel on without me."

Fear slammed into her chest, and it became hard to breathe. "What do you mean? We cannot go alone. It is not safe."

Iain held her gaze and spoke clearly. "This may be our only chance to go for help. I will stay behind to see that no one follows, and then I will join you."

The look that passed between Iain and Calum made her throat tighten. Something did not seem right. "When will you come?"

"When I know it is safe and you are not followed." Iain's answer came a bit too quickly.

Calum shifted and avoided her gaze.

"How will we know that *you* are safe if you return to the castle?"

"Trust me, sister. I can take care of myself." His smile did not reach his eyes. "Do not worry so."

A thousand scenarios played out in her mind as desperation seeped into her thoughts. "And in the woods? How will we stay safe? Calum is only nine years old." She smiled an apology at her little brother for such a frank statement.

"I have protection. See?" Calum withdrew a dangerous-looking knife from its hiding place in his boot.

"You fight very well, Calum, I know, but..." She turned beseeching eyes on Iain. He had to come with them.

203

"You must remain vigilant. I know you can do this, Iseabail. Here." Iain held out a dagger. "Take this. Keep it near you at all times."

Iseabail accepted the *sgian dubh* Iain offered. She slid the knife out of the scabbard. Their father had given it to Iain when he turned ten, and she found comfort in its weight and the cold metal of its blade.

This would never work, but there was no other choice. Was it not better to die trying than to live playing dead?

"If you think this is best." She slipped it into the basket.

"Go on, and do not worry about me. I will protect what is ours. Understand?"

"It will be dangerous for you." She wrapped her arms around him and drew him close to keep him from seeing her tears, but he stiffened and stifled a gasp. She drew back. "What is wrong?"

He smiled at her with misty eyes. "I love you, Iseabail. I pray you will be safe. And you," he grasped Calum's shoulder as men do, "you must look out for her. Aye?"

Calum wiped his nose. "Aye."

"We will stay together." She straightened her shoulders and held her head high, feigning a strength she did not truly feel. "And we will get help."

Iain tipped his head, a small smile playing on his lips as his features softened with relief. He glanced around, searching the far-off woods. He pressed his mouth into a thin line, and his eyes almost looked black as he surreptitiously slipped a small leather-wrapped parchment from beneath his tunic. Their father's will.

"This is the only support we have for our claim." With his eye on the document, Iain continued, "You must protect it if we want to take back what is rightfully ours."

She nodded, solemnly accepting his edict. She shifted the silver cross that hung against her bosom then tucked the treatise down the front of her gown. The worn leather was comforting where it rested, snug between her breasts.

"When you get to the Campbell's land, look for the shepherd boy, Inus, in the lower fields. He shall get you to Hugh, who knows of our dear uncle's treacherous way firsthand. Trust no one else. Do you understand? No one."

Her brother's closest friend had always been a thorn under her skin with his constant teasing. That he was her savior now made her want to laugh, but the dire look in her brother's eyes stopped her. He held her at arm's length as if memorizing everything about her. A lump grew in her throat as she fought back tears. She wanted to be strong for him. Make him proud. Despite her concerns, despite the strangeness of his behavior, she trusted him, and she would respect his decision.

"You must promise me, Iseabail. Trust no one else."

"I promise." Despite her best intentions, tears coursed down her face. "I look forward to being with you again, dear brother." She kissed his cheek and hugged him. She did not want to let go, but when Iain made a strangled sound, she released him at once. His breathing was heavy and his forehead glistened with sweat. "Iain?"

He stepped back, his jaw clenched. He shook his head at her to stay away. "Go, both of you."

CHAPTER TWO

Seumas looked up as the two newcomers entered the hall. Frigid air swept across the room with their arrival, but it was not the cold that caught his attention—the large, wooden door opposite the great hearth had opened numerous times since dusk as peasants sought shelter from the suddenly plummeting temperatures. Something about them tugged at him. Their lack of grumbling, perhaps? Or the timid way they moved amongst the rabble? Either way, he seemed to be the only one who took an interest. Glancing at the other soldiers he sat with, he was not surprised they had noticed nothing.

"Ta hell ye did, Miguel! Dere were only five av dem!" The Irishman's indignant retort echoed across the hall. Patrick, always ready to argue, was instigating yet another fight. The bench Seumas shared with the burly man tipped unsteadily as he stood.

"'Tis the truth," Miguel responded to the insult with as much heat. Though he remained seated, he moved his hand to the dagger at his waist. "You had already turned tail and run."

Seumas shook his head and lifted his gaze heavenward. His patience with these men was gone. "Do ye need to get on like this every night?"

"Ye don't care for our company?" Patrick's bloodshot eyes did not appear to focus as he turned his anger on Seumas, his face a little too close. "Bugger off, den!"

As the leader of these men, Seumas knew what power he wielded over them. They knew it, too, but that did not change how they acted. "Methinks not." Seumas lifted the mug to his mouth, his eyebrows raised in expectation as he held the man's glare.

Patrick stumbled backward onto the bench. Seumas caught him before he fell against the wall. "Why are ye such an arse, Seumas? Have ye not got anywhere else to do yer carousing?"

The man was a son of a bitch to be sure. "Nae, Patrick, I have nowhere else to go. Now settle yerself down."

It was true enough. He had believed he would eventually get over what he had been through in Edessa and stop hating himself. Then he would go home. But he had played the wait-and-see game too long. Now his father was dead, and Seumas had even more reason to hate himself.

Needing a diversion from his troubled mind, Seumas searched the crowd again for the two. The hard frost had come too soon, finding many unprepared, and the Great Hall was cramped with villagers and peasants. Nevertheless, he soon spotted them. Covered with grime, from the hoods obscuring their faces to their cloth-wrapped feet, they blended well enough with the others in the hall, but they had a certain bearing that did not match their outward appearance. They did not shy away or shuffle their feet. The one who led the way, the smaller of the two, had a surprisingly noble posture but hesitated the slightest bit before joining the ever-increasing crowd by the fire. Interesting.

He was intrigued by their presence, but, for their sakes, he hoped he was the only one. The people at this castle were as cruel as their overlord, Lord Bryon. Any who did not belong, no matter the circumstances, would be cast out without a moment's hesitation. There would be no mercy, even in freezing weather.

Patrick slammed his cup on the table emphatically as he told his next story, the earlier argument already forgotten. The other men at the table were enraptured by the tale, but Seumas ignored it, intent on his study. The bitter mead dribbled down his chin as he took a deep swallow, and he traced his lower lip with his tongue.

They had their heads down and turned away from the room now, but were not cowering at all. Sitting up straighter, Seumas realized they were trying to avoid being noticed.

"Right, Seumas?" Patrick slapped him on the back as spittle came out with his words. "Damn beauty that one, right?"

Seumas exhaled in irritation. He had not been listening, but he nodded to keep from being drawn into the conversation.

"Not that ye could do anything about it." The man burst into laughter at his own joke. "But do not worry yerself, Seumas. I took care of her. I gave her what she wanted, since ye could not."

Seumas tensed at the insult, giving the Irishman his full attention as he turned toward him, jaw clenched. Patrick was clearly too drunk to notice that the others had grown ominously quiet. Seumas slammed his fist against the thick wooden table. The Irishman locked eyes with him, and his laughter stopped abruptly. The tin cup rolling along the edge of the table was the only sound. It landed with a dull thud on the rushes covering the floor, and perspiration broke out on Patrick's brow. He was very unwise indeed to let his tongue loose every time he drank, and he had the crooked nose and missing teeth to show for it.

The blond man across the table took up the retelling. "You might have taken care of her, Patrick, but was she pleased with what you gave her?"

The rest of the men laughed nervously. Uncertain glances came Seumas's way as he struggled to accept the intervention and let the insult pass.

"I would say ye have the right of it, David." Seumas's voice was tight. He appreciated the man stepping in, but he should not have let it get this far in the first place. He had to control himself. He was their leader not because he had earned their respect, but because Lord Bryon thought it humorous to put "God's soldier" in charge of his pack of mercenaries, and because Seumas had no other prospects. From being a man with integrity and beliefs to a man with no self-respect was a mighty fall. He had to consciously release his clenched fist.

Seumas returned his gaze to the others milling in front of the fire— some sitting, some lying down, all trying to keep warm. The dark-haired woman who had grabbed his crotch last night smiled at him, but he looked right through her. She had been hoping to share his bed, but she had been sorely disappointed, and would be again. Carnal pleasure did not interest him. He had received a wound in the siege of Damascus, and his body no longer became aroused. As such, he neither needed nor wanted female companionship. There was some relief in having his mind in agreement with his body.

A disturbance by the fire startled him back to the present.

"Get your damn dog out of here, Robbie, and do not come back to the heat of the fire until you do." A squat, gray-haired woman smacked the boy's ear as she yelled at him.

"It's too cold, Mum. He keeps slipping back in." Robbie dragged the mangy canine to the wooden door that led outside.

The leader of the newcomers—a young boy, Seumas thought— seemed to freeze in place as he too witnessed the encounter. The lad stiffened, appearing affronted by the treatment of the stable boy. Like a chivalrous knight, he reacted as if he might actually come to Robbie's defense. The person behind the lad gave him a none-too-gentle shove. When the little knight glanced back, Seumas caught a glimpse of his filthy, childish face. It was indeed a boy and not anyone he recognized. As he suspected, these two were not from the area.

The second person remained a mystery of uncertain sex and age. Though there was something about the way he moved and the protective hold the little knight had on his arm. Seumas stroked his beard. It could be a female, but the big cloak effectively hid any sign.

They were pushing through the mob to get closer to the fire when the little knight dropped out of sight. He had tripped over Perceval, the mute who lived beneath the bridge leading to the castle. He was a mean one, and the jab he gave the boy was intended to do harm. The little knight grimaced.

Seumas moved in quickly before a brawl broke out.

Without a word, he pulled the little knight out of harm's way. He kept his eye on Perceval. "Now that is no way to act."

The frantic hand gestures said it all. His mouth flapped of complaints and mistreatment without a sound while the little knight looked on, darting fearful looks between them. Perceval's eyes had dark circles and his cheeks were sunken from lack of food.

"Methinks there is something for ye somewhere else," Seumas said. When he moved closer to whisper to him, the smell of urine and feces was overpowering. "Go see Fran. Ye know Fran?"

Perceval's eyes brightened and he bobbed his head, recognizing the cook's name. He leaned in to hear Seumas.

"She is holding some sweet cakes for me, and I want ye to get them."

The boy's face fell—he no doubt thought he would have to give the morsels up to Seumas.

"But I do not want them. Ye eat them."

Perceval did not hesitate. He bolted toward the kitchen door.

"Now then," Seumas turned toward the little knight, still in his grasp. The mystery companion held back, well hidden. "What have we here?"

"I did not do anything to him." The boy's eyes were wide and round. "I got tripped up and fell. That is all."

"Aye. And yet...I see that ye do not belong here." Better to let the boy know up front he had been found out.

The little knight caught himself as he started turning to his mysterious companion. "I do, m'lord." He tipped his head emphatically, a convincing liar.

Impressed by the act, Seumas smiled at him and included his companion when he spoke. "Stay to the right side of the fire. That is where the young'uns sleep. Ye will be safe there unless they realize ye do not belong...then out ye go. Hear me?"

The little knight nodded.

Seumas glanced at the boy's companion, but the shadowed face turned away. The dirt-encrusted cloak covered him—or her—from head to toe, but the long fingers gripping the edges of the cloak together were just visible. They were also decidedly feminine.

Seumas smiled and returned to his men.

CHAPTER THREE

Someone was watching her. Iseabail woke instantly. Wedged between Calum and the wall, she feigned sleep, keeping her breathing steady though her body tensed. Through half-closed eyes, she scanned the hall. The crackling fire silhouetted Calum's slumped form. He had turned away in his sleep. The overpowering stench of unwashed bodies gave her a strange sense of belonging after being alone in the woods for so long—she probably stank as much as they. The sounds of snoring and breathing surrounded her.

The men carousing earlier could no longer be heard. They had been well in their cups, so no doubt they were either passed out or had staggered to their beds. Female laughter and low, muffled voices drifted to her from the stairs. Or had they found female companionship? She shuddered. They were mercenaries—hard men who did as they pleased and answered to no one. When she passed the group earlier, she had averted her eyes, hoping to avoid their notice. If Calum had not tripped, they would have been ignored. Now she had unwanted attention.

The draft on her leg was her only warning.

Someone clamped a hand onto her bare ankle. She opened her mouth but no sound came out; her gasp froze in her throat. She had been discovered. If Calum were older she could have called for his help, but she did not want him to get hurt trying to defend her. As usual, she was left unprotected.

Her attacker slid a calloused hand up her leg. Fear quickened her breath. He caressed her calf before grabbing on to pull her away from Calum. She bit into her lip and clawed at the ground as she fought against being dragged further. Her assailant's throaty chuckle reminded her of her uncle's, and panic overwhelmed her senses.

I will not be used again.

Determined, she thrashed and rolled, trying to turn onto her back. He bent to grab her legs at the knees, grunting with the effort. The noise made her sick. Her gown slid further up her thighs, and his low sound of carnal appreciation echoed in her head. On her stomach with her ankles held against either side of her attacker, she could not have felt more vulnerable. Or angry. She twisted and pulled, finally wresting one leg free. She tucked her knee to her chest and kicked as hard as she could, connecting with the man's tender area. Hope blazed through her. He groaned and dropped her legs abruptly. Her knees hit the ground with a painful thud, and she pressed her lips tightly together to muffle the hiss